𝕽𝖔𝖔𝖒 209

JAMES C. HENSON & ANNITA L. HENSON

DEDICATION

For James Dollar
We miss you.

CONTENTS

PROLOGUE

PART 1—HERITAGE DISCOVERED

INTERMEZZO

The Fall of the Bear

PART 2—EFFECTS OF HERITAGE

Descendants of Sebastian Schneider

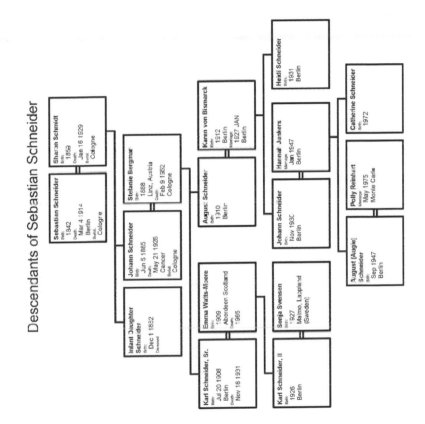

Sebastian Schneider
Birth: 1842
Death: Mar 4 1914 Berlin
Burial: Cologne

Sharon Schmidt
Birth: 1859
Death: Jan 16 1929
Burial: Cologne

Johann Schneider
Birth: Jun 5 1865
Death: May 21 1926 Cancer
Burial: Cologne

Stefanie Bergman
Birth: 1888 Linz, Austria
Death: Feb 9 1962 Cologne

Infant Daughter Schneider
Birth: Dec 1 1852
Deceased

August Schneider
Birth: 1910 Berlin

Karen von Bismarck
Birth: 1912 Berlin
Marriage: 1927 JAN Berlin

Emma Watts-Moore
Birth: 1909 Aberdeen, Scotland
Death: 1965

Karl Schneider, Sr.
Birth: Jul 20 1908 Berlin
Death: Nov 18 1931

Sonja Svensen
Birth: 1927 Malmo, Lappland (Sweden)

Karl Schneider, II
Birth: 1926 Berlin

Heidi Schneider
Birth: 1931 Berlin

Hannah Junkers
Birth: Jan 1947 Berlin

Johann Schneider
Birth: Nov 1930 Berlin

Catherine Schneider
Birth: 1972

Polly Reinhart
Marriage: May 1975 Monte Carlo

August (Augie) Schneider
Birth: Sep 1947 Berlin

PROLOGUE

LINZ, AUSTRIA, 1907—

"Bless me Father for I have sinned. My last confession was in July."

"May the Blessing of God the Father, God the Son, and God the Holy Ghost be upon you now and forever, Amen. Tell me your sins, Stefanie."

"Father, you know that I am not married but I have been with a man and now I find that I am pregnant."

"Is this man one you love, and is he willing to marry you?"

"I hardly know him, Father. He lives in Vienna and does not know of my situation. I cannot believe that I did what I did, but he was so charming and it seemed so right. It certainly was not rape or anything. I am sorry and scared."

"Do you remember the story of the adulterous woman in the Gospel of John? The Pharisees wanted to stone her but Our Lord said 'He who is without sin may cast the first stone.' When they all left He said, 'Woman, where are thine accusers?' She said, 'No one accuses me now, Lord' and Our Lord said, 'Neither do I.'"

"Your penance is to attend all fourteen days of the Litany of the Holy Name starting tonight. Go in Peace, your sins are forgiven."

"Thanks be to God."

Stefanie was comforted but still afraid.

1. A SOUVENIR FROM THE WALL

COLOGNE, February 1990—

A strong martini, and sometimes two, used to do it for him, but Public Relations guru Andrew Becker was burdened with too many worries to even think of getting a decent night's sleep. God, why now? How did a routine campaign become such a nightmare? A famous and popular guy from the majority party against an unknown professor? It sounded like a shoo-in.

Two packs of smashed cigarette butts, stagnant coffee and his sweaty shirt made the bedroom smell like a flophouse. Andy had never been in a flophouse but this surely must be what it would smell like. The caked cream ring on the inside of the cup might never scrub clean but he couldn't worry about that now. He would just add it to the collection already soaking in the sink. The bedroom, aka home office, really did smell disgusting though.

The trashcan was heaped over with crushed paper from fits and starts of ideas he had during the night. He tried to think of every angle for the press releases, but which road would it take and did he have all the answers? Should he be apologetic or defensive or just bluntly honest and let the chips fall? Could he save Karl's career? If he tried would he ruin his own? He stumbled to the loo and caught a glimpse of himself in the mirror. Jesus, what dark circles, the likes of which he had not seen on his own face before.

The slightly opened shutters revealed the sun coming up. Andy walked over to the window to check the temperature gauge and the early morning glare pierced painfully through his left eye. He felt a migraine coming on.

Heavy headed, he called his answering service. He had taken his receiver off the hook for the night and there were two messages. Larissa was upset because he had not returned her call and "who was he to think he was so friggin important as to not return her call?" Larissa knew the magnitude of his problems but she wanted to be the shoulder he could cry on. Andy was a rather independent soul but Larissa knew that this was going to balloon into something bigger than he could handle alone.

Message number two was a distorted screaming voice over the speakerphone. It was Helmut Grainger. He was volcanic about something he had heard from Carrie, his counterpart in the Social Democratic party. "Is it true or is it bullshit?" He insisted he had to see Andy immediately. He "didn't give a crap" what time it was. The call came in at 6:00 AM and it was just a little after 7:00.

****

WEST BERLIN, November, 1989—

"Holy shit! What was that?"

Alan sat bolt upright with a startled look of sudden awakening. Ka-Whoom! There it was again! He searched around the covers for his glasses that he thought were on the table. He was confused as to where he was, and the noise was ear-splitting loud.

Mary lovingly looked at her American friend... "Good Morning, Mr. Silverman...you're in Berlin." She motioned for him to hurry to the window. "Can you believe they are tearing down the Wall?"

Alan realized he had slept on the Petersen's living room sofa last evening. Alan also realized that if he didn't pee immediately, he might just die. Mary knew the pained look and pointed to the direction of the bathroom. The dust from the demolition, only about 300 meters away, had permeated the outside air and when Alan emerged, Mary grabbed his hand and said, "C'mon, let's go up to dad's office. We'll see a lot more from there." She had pulled him halfway up the stair before they noticed he was only in his briefs. He ran back to the sofa and grabbed his robe. They had to keep up the show for the folks.

The Petersen household had been totally unaware that the "Wall" was no longer enforced and travel restrictions between East and

West Berlin had been lifted the night before at around 7:00 P.M. There was a lot of commotion, but Elsie Petersen had been too preoccupied with the arrival of her daughter Mary and Mary's serious other. She, her husband Werther, and Wolfie, their younger son, were meeting Alan Silverman for the first time. The kids had arrived the evening before from New York City and Elsie and Wolfie had gone to the airport to pick them up. Werther was due in three hours later from his business trip to Tehran, but they did not wait as he always had a limo take him straight home.

****

It was Friday, November 10, 1989. Alan Silverman and pretty, wide-eyed Mary Petersen had taken advantage of a field trip from Cooper Union, the architecture school in New York City, to visit Mary's family in West Berlin. John Hejduk, the dean of architecture at the school, designed some of the new buildings in Berlin and was offering a week excused away from school for students who wished to travel to Germany to see them. Mary was beginning to think Alan was 'the one' and she had better show her choice to the family before things got any more serious. When Alan suggested the trip, she was elated.

Alan had applied for a passport the previous Spring for a trip to Israel that did not materialize, but Alan's dad had umpteen million sky-miles from his business trips and was willing to share them. A single week was not much time for travel and meeting potential in-laws, but with free fare, free lodging and course credit, how could they go wrong? Alan had never been to Europe.

Like many students in the technical fields, Alan and Mary were pretty much non-political and President Reagan's famous "Mr. Gorbachev, tear down this Wall!" speech delivered in June of 1987 didn't really mean that much to them. The student activists in New York, and there were quite a few, were not amongst their friends and Alan and Mary were just not interested in any of the rallies or protests. The architectural school, in general, was somewhat insulated and stayed to itself and the students were more interested in being in competition with each other than changing the political world.

Alan's parents lived in Larchmont, New York. When Alan applied to the Cooper Union School of Architecture, they knew very little about the place. When he was accepted and they learned that it was one of the premier architecture schools in the world and all students had full scholarships from the Endowment, they were amazed. His college fund would provide a comfortable apartment in New York and he would be pretty close to home. They liked that because Alan was an only child and Janet still had a Jewish mother attachment to him. She couldn't let him go completely, at least, not yet, especially to "that German girl."

Mary had moved in with Alan in October much to her parents' objections. The Petersens were just too provincial for that, but what could they do several thousand miles away? And, Alan's mother had relatives who had endured the Holocaust and she was not particularly thrilled that Alan had latched on to a non-Jewish German girl. She didn't like Germans, in general, but saying anything to Alan was like pouring acid on his wound. He would not speak to her for a week. Mary, nevertheless, was quite a likable young lady and Alan Sr. thought she was bright and pretty and had so much more going for her than the local girls Alan had flirted with. Mary had warmed up to the Silvermans and tried to tell Janet she had nothing to do with persecuting the Jews and neither did her family. Eventually, it became obvious that Alan had no intention of giving her up, whether anyone liked it or not.

Alan, a tall, thin young man with olive skin like his father looked a lot like Mozart or at least Mary thought he looked like Mozart with his mop of curly hair, rosy cheeks and wire-rimmed glasses. He couldn't believe that a girl as beautiful as Mary really liked him, or loved him, but she did. A lot, in fact. And he adored her. And Mary, indeed, was a charming young woman with big brown eyes and a long chestnut pony tail, 5'7" in sneakers, slender, and neat. Wearing only the slightest hint of makeup, she was not at all self-conscious about the faint freckles on her high cheekbones. She was at Cooper Union as an exchange student from Berlin where she attended Berlin University of the Arts, a sister school. Her charming German accent that she tried hard to Americanize but, unsuccessfully, was the first thing that attracted Alan to her.

Before they left for Berlin, they discussed that they would behave while staying with her parents and sleep separately. It was out of respect and both agreed that it was the right thing to do.

The rest of the family was already upstairs watching the destruction. As the noise that had awakened Alan became more intrusive, the five of them watched cranes with wrecking balls and bulldozers demolishing the Wall in a rather disorganized manner. Checkpoint Charlie was opened at about 7:15 the previous night and by 10:00 P.M. the crossing points were mobbed. Now, apparently, the citizens of both East and West started hacking away at the barrier on their own without official sanction. The Berlin Wall was really coming down. The huge iron balls hitting the stone and concrete slabs created deafening sounds and the vibration felt from the crumbling barricades was unnerving. Elsie was worried that it could damage the foundation of the house. Alan tried to allay her fears. He certainly did not expect to witness this though while in Berlin, and boy, was it a story to take back that he had seen history in the making.

The wall sections looked like molten lava tumbling down, and what appeared to be ruins of an old church were visible in the distance. Alan pointed them out to Mary but she noticed them too. The large blackened stones of the standing church structure appeared to be identical to some of the remains of the Wall. Is it only architects who notice similarities in building materials? Most of the huge wall sections were made of reinforced concrete, but why was there rubble mixed in? It was probably left over from one of the three previous attempts to keep the two sections of Berlin separate but why was it used? They guessed 'because it was there', but it looked out of place. It seemed strange that they would use part of a church.

Although they had a ringside seat from the window of Herr Petersen's office, Alan pushed Mary to get dressed so they could go down and get a first hand look and maybe take a souvenir from the wreckage. Mary had her doubts they could get that close.

The smell of Elsie's freshly brewed coffee beckoned them back down to the kitchen, but only for a brief moment. Elsie had gone out of her way to set out a luxurious German breakfast that included just about everything—eggs, sausages, rolls, ham, fruit, you name it—and was annoyed when the kids grabbed a sweet roll, choked it down, thanked her profusely and left. She knew they were preoccupied with getting involved in the action down the street, but nonetheless, it was disappointing. Werther told her not to worry, that he would eat it all.

Mary darted upstairs again, threw on warm clothes and a pair of hiking boots she had forgotten about while Alan fished his clothes out of the bag Elsie placed in the downstairs closet. They hurriedly said "good bye" to the folks and assured them they would eat more later.

Alan and Mary pushed through the onlookers who had gathered to watch the wall come down. Some were apprehensive but most seemed jubilant that the long isolation from friends and loved ones was ending.

The East German Police were "guarding" the demolition, but obviously with less than enthusiastic concentration. They waved Alan and Mary away from the wreckage and admonished them to leave the forbidden zone. Alan tried to argue that it was no longer a forbidden zone, Mary chimed in German, but their insistence fell on deaf ears and they were shoved away. There was no way to grab even the smallest pebble. The work area was being cordoned off and the curious were forced to move on. At about noon, however, the police contingent crossed the "forbidden zone" and crowded into a West Berlin Beergarten. It appeared that everyone had taken time out for lunch including the workers. Alan and Mary watched. Alan motioned to Mary that this was their chance.

As they limboed under the rope, Alan carefully headed for the large black stones that had intrigued him. It was hard to walk on the piles of demolished wall and twisted steel without losing footing and the last thing they wanted to do was call attention to themselves. Alan made sure each step he took was secure before moving forward and Mary followed right behind him. They both spotted a particularly large, rectangular block that was lying on an angle and was much too heavy to move. It had cracked in two, either when it hit the ground or from the impact. Mary pointed to the small chambers carved into it. The stone was covered with layers of soot and mold but Alan could see that the clean stone in the crack revealed a fine white marble. Barely visible above the chambers was chiseled "Grabnische." Mary translated it to mean 'a wall of burial niches for cremated remains'.

Alan noticed the neck of a bottle protruding from one of the chambers. Being careful not to break it or cut his hand on the shards of rock, he carefully worked it out. He couldn't remember if his last Tetanus shot was still in effect. Holding the bottle by its neck, he carefully knocked the years of dirt off to reveal a handwritten label "Palwin nr.10" and some less decipherable markings. The name was vaguely familiar as Hebrew. Could it be a bottle of old wine from a church or Synagogue? "Mom would really like this as a souvenir," he told Mary. "Good plan," she replied.

The particular bottle chamber was apparently deeper than the rest as the bottle was about a foot long. Although it was sealed with wax over what appeared to be an original a cork, shaking the bottle revealed no liquid. The glass was black and opaque and it was hard to tell if anything had dried up inside.

Walking a few steps further, Alan stooped to pick up a small, almost perfectly cubical stone of the same blackened marble. Before Mary could collect anything, she heard a ruckus.... "Sie dort! Gehen Sie hinaus!" The two miscreants turned around. The East German policemen were rushing towards them. "Oh My God, they are yelling at us!" Nervously, Mary grabbed Alan's arm and said that they were being told to 'Get out!'

"Oh shit! Nothing like being caught red-handed by the Communist Police." Mary sighed heavily, looked at Alan and mumbled that this would be another mess for dad to have to fix. Werther Petersen had considerable diplomatic influence that came in handy at times like this.

Realizing they might be Americans, the taller policeman spoke a little English. "Lucky for you, today you get summons. Trespassing. Yesterday, you get shot! No questions asked." That was enough to make them shudder. "Let me see some identification, please."

Mary spoke German to the policeman and explained that her companion was an American. German, American, what did it matter? They were where they shouldn't be. They both fumbled for their passports. While the policeman wrote down information, Alan saw that a press crew had gathered at the Western Zone Border. Apparently, their escapade had all been caught on tape.

After signing the necessary papers handed to them, the two policemen escorted Alan and Mary to the Western Side and admonished them to stay out of the Eastern Zone. They were warned that the next time would not be so easy. To Alan's amazement, no mention of the souvenirs was made.

Calling out in German, a member of the news crew approached Mary and asked if she could have her name and that of her American friend. "Could we get a statement?" she eventually asked in English. Mary hesitated but Alan blurted out, "Sure."

A microphone was shoved in Alan's face and the interview began with:

Reporter: "Why did you go into the Eastern Zone?"

Alan: "Because it is there and we want a souvenir of this important event."

Reporter: "You are American, are you not? Did the GDR police alarm you?"

Alan: "Well, maybe a little. American police are more courteous and restrained. The American cops would probably have taken our souvenirs away though. These guys didn't seem to care."

Reporter: "So what did you take as souvenirs?"

Alan: "A bottle and a rock. Nothing that would be missed."

The camera panned down to the sooty souvenirs and back to Alan, then opened up to include Mary and the church in the background.

Reporter: "Thank you, Alan Silverman. This is Roseann Rosensach for Channel 2 News at the Remains of the Wall."

That night, Alan Silverman and Mary Petersen had a moment of fame on the Berlin nightly news.

2. THE LONG-LOST LETTER

LATER THAT MONTH IN A POST OFFICE IN A
SUBURB OF COLOGNE—

"This new generation has just no reverence for the way things have
always been done." Old Hans, the construction manager, was a
constant complainer and set in his ways. "This desk and the sorting
cabinet. Just look at the work. No one does this kind of
cabinetmaking any more. And they're tearing it all out and replacing
it with modular metal garbage. Just what will that look like under
these beautiful windows and intricate detail trim?" "Schiesse!"

"It will look new and modern and business-like." Junior Hans,
who was no relation to Old Hans, tried to appease him. To keep
them both from answering when the name 'Hans' was called, the
postal workers named them Junior and Old Hans. Old Hans was
only about fifty. Junior noticed that on the floor behind the cabinetry
being removed was a yellowed envelope.

"What's this? An ancient letter?" Junior picked it up and handed it
to Old Hans.

"Not all that old." Old Hans looked at the envelope. "The stamp
is from the Reich. Old mustachio's picture. Good Lord, it's
addressed to Himmler himself. Like some sort of personal letter from
a friend."

"Let me see that." Junior snatched the letter back and remarked
that the University had a collection of Himmler's stuff and maybe
they would pay something for it. They could share the spoils.

The door opened and a paunchy bureaucrat guy strode briskly in "Let's keep after it, you two. You're behind schedule a couple of days already." It was Rom Burgher, the postmaster for the area who always smelled like butt and stale cigars. His gaze fell on the letter. "Give me that!" Here was a guy who took his responsibility very seriously. Letters were to be delivered, no matter how late.

"Come on, Rom. Who are you going to deliver it to? Himmler is so long dead and no one but no one will own up to being his relative. We were going to try to sell it to the university for their collection." Old Hans saw his windfall fading.

Rom, always alert for some political advantage, looked closely at the envelope. After a few moments of consideration, he thought of a plan to get a little press coverage. He had a penchant for self-promotion so a little free publicity never hurt. He called the local media and announced that a long-lost letter to the infamous Nazi would be delivered, albeit almost 50 years late, to the university's Himmler collection.

The collection's administrator was Walter Raudebusch. Walter Raudebusch was a balding man of slight build and medium height and was Berlin's example of Walter Mitty. People remembered Raudebusch as the strange little man who wore both suspenders and a belt and two pair of glasses on his head. He imagined the Himmler archives as a major block in the world's historic records as well as crucial to the German government. He was excited to find another letter to add to the collection and liked the idea of having some publicity for the school and reminding the city that he was the expert on Himmler. He accepted the letter from Rom Burgher in a quickly organized ceremony and passed it on to Eric, his son, who was a part-time employee cataloging the Himmler papers. The son recognized the name of the sender, August Schneider, as the owner of Cologne Wool Goods.

August Schneider and Cologne Wool Goods made a fortune clothing the German Army during the Third Reich. His family and factory miraculously escaped all of the bombing of Cologne toward the end of the War.

Eric, who resembled his father, had jumped on the personal computer bandwagon early on and was creating a database of the Himmler works. The database and technology were his interests and Himmler's works just a vehicle. He was also interested in photography, the Enigma cryptographic thing and espionage in general as The Cold War was still going on. Eric had more confidence in his own ability, however, and had no desire to be associated with the Himmler files. He opened the letter:

11 June, 1941

Herr Doktor Himmler,

I hope this letter finds you and yours well. Karen and the children are fine. Johann is anxious to be old enough to enlist in our cause.

I am in receipt of your order for the goods for the next year. I sincerely appreciate your confidence in Cologne Wool Goods and assure you that the high quality of our uniforms will add to the pride and polish of our brave soldiers.

Please let me know if you need further information about our operation.

Heil Hitler,

August Schneider

Blah. Blah, Blah. Why would anybody write such a trite letter to such an important person at such a time in history? Most letters in the Himmler Collection concerned logistics and strategies and political planning or intrigue. He tossed the letter down on his desk. Then a small flash caught his eye. The dot on the "i" in Himmler was reflective. The rest of the ink on the page was dull and oxidized from years on the post office floor. Suddenly the letter became fascinating.

He went to the archive and located five other letters to Himmler from Schneider dating from 1933 and one to Schneider from Himmler still sealed in the envelope and apparently never posted. Each letter from Schneider was as innocuous as the one he had just found, and in each letter from Schneider, upon close inspection, the dot on the "i" in Himmler was slightly discolored. Were there once shiny dots on these letters too? Was the discoloration caused by removing the dots or by the adhesive used to affix them?

He opened the unposted letter to Schneider. "What's this?" On the unposted letter, he thought that the dot on the "i" in Schneider was a little brighter than the rest of the writing. It, too, was a trite note. This letter had been in a controlled atmosphere for most of the last fifty years so the condition of the ink and paper was much fresher than the one that had been languishing on the floor in the Cologne Post Office. But he was sure the dot was there.

Photography was really taking off by 1933. Zeiss-Ikon was founded in Dresden by Carl Zeiss in 1926 and its technical director was Emanuel Goldberg, the inventor of the microdot process. Goldberg had the good sense to move to Paris and then on to Palestine before the gathering Nazi storm had fully developed but it is sure that the technology for using microdots (Mikrat nach Goldberg) was known to the Third Reich and that microdots were used for clandestine communications back in the 1930s. Walter Zapp, another photographic genius, had formed Minox in Riga, Latvia, at about the same time. The war effort delayed his little Ur-Minox miniature camera from being produced until 1936 but no self-respecting spy of the '40s, '50s, or '60s would be ever caught without a Minox. It was about the size of your thumb and could take several dozen high-quality photographs under pretty low light conditions.

Eric was positive that the little sparkles were microdots. There must have been a relationship between Himmler and Schneider that had never been brought to light and the clandestine nature of it made it all the more fascinating. Cologne Wool Goods was a major company that came about due to the war economy, but was not really a participant in the Reich. Along with Krupp and others, the war made them rich, but they avoided the stigma of the Nuremberg Trials.

Who did Eric know with the equipment to read a microdot? Like iron wire recorders and vacuum tube radios and other technologies that are replaced, microdot reading equipment was not even mentioned in catalogs or directories. The technology was dead. But wait. The lithography equipment used in making Integrated Circuits could probably blow up the microdot to letter size with very little distortion. Which of his college buddies went into IC Chip design? He remembered...Christoph Klein.

Eric picked up the phone, called the last number he had and hoped that Christoph was still at the same extension at Philips IC. Sure enough, on the other end of the line was the usual breathless voice, "Extension 450, Christoph here."

"Hey, Chris, it's Eric...Eric Raudebusch." Have you got a second? I have a little project that might be interesting to you." They exchanged greetings and Eric wanted to know if he could help him. Christoph, a young guy, somewhat of an idiot savant with what some might call a compulsive behavior disorder, had dirty blond hair, thick glasses fogged from fingerprints, and wrinkled clothes. He said he would. Exasperating as he was, he would discover subtleties in problems that others would miss, so the company kept him around. Eric planned to see Christoph early the next morning.

Eric arrived at Philips at about a quarter to 7 and was eager to see if he was right. Christoph offered him a cup of coffee from the vending machine and they went down the hall to the lab. The lab was already set up with the equipment to look at the letters Eric brought. Eric slid them out of the manila folder and handed the first one to Christoph. It took a few minutes to get the lighting and magnification right, but the image was still sharp. Good exposures were captured. Carefully, they watched the drying enlargement of the microdot found on the 1941 letter to Himmler lost at the Cologne post office....

Formatted to fill a circle, as a microdot, they could read:

Heinrich—

I had hoped that it would not come to this but this is what I remember from mother, Stefanie's confession that evening. My brother was conceived in Vienna in 1907 when she met Hitler by chance at a coffeehouse there and was charmed by him even though he was depressed for some reason. She moved to Berlin and Karl's birth was recorded at St. Stephen's Church there in Berlin on July 20, 1908. The Christian name given was Karl Bergman Hittler. His parents were listed as Adolph Hittler of Linz, then Vienna, and Stefanie Bergman, my mother's maiden name. I think that it is just a numerical entry in the church records and the certificate is sealed in a wall in the basement, perhaps a mausoleum. Mother thought it was #18, the 18th birth recorded that year. I doubt that it was ever recorded with a magistrate. At any rate, Mother was amused that she misspelled his name as Hittler, the more common spelling in Linz. If it is in the civil records it is probably spelled that way. I have not been able to discover any formal adoption documents but Karl was raised by my parents along with me. As far as I know, he never knew of his infamous origin. He was active in the company for a few years but died in 1931. Regards, August

From the un-posted letter in the Himmler archive on the SS letterhead...

10 March, 1943
Herr Schneider,
I am glad that your wife is better. All is going well for the Reich as you have heard. The Russians are in full retreat and the only problems are in the Pacific. But they will soon be over.

Thank you for the cigars.
HH

From the "i" above Schneider in the letter, also formatted to fill a circle, as a microdot.

August—It is time. I must pull out all stops to save what I have worked for. Why have you not answered? If I cannot engineer a coup or gain some other advantage before Stalin and his hordes reach Berlin I may have no hope to escape their fury. I have lived up, even more than lived up, to our pact and you hold out. Do not test me too far. Heinrich

Eric and Christoph considered these "missed communications" from the end of the War. Christoph looked confused. Then Eric had a revelation. The new rising star in the Christian Democratic Party was Karl Schneider. But he was formally referred to as Karl Schneider II. The Karl in the letter would have been about 22 when he died and could have had a son between 1926 and 1930. The son would be about 60. Karl Schneider did not look 60 but looks can be deceiving. Could Karl Schneider actually be Hitler's grandson? That exquisite rush from knowing something important that no one else in the world knows swept over him. "I think Karl Schneider is Hitler's grandson," came bursting from his lips. Christoph still looked perplexed. He responded with, "Gee man, I'm glad I could help."

Eric gathered up his letters and papers, thanked Christoph, and headed back to the university to figure out what he should do next. His hands were shaking as he exited the building.

Not quite appreciating the ramifications of the new information, Christoph went to lunch at noon in the Philips IC Foundry cafeteria. When he joined his group at the table, he told his manager, Peter

Warren, about meeting with Eric and what they discovered, but he didn't know what all this meant. "I'm sure I haven't a clue," Peter answered weakly. But he worried, "could this revelation be quashed or could it even be true?"

Peter Warren was a good engineer, but like many engineers, had little or no experience in the arts or in any other field except electronics, for that matter. He had voted for the Christian Democratic candidate in the last several elections and he knew this rumor could harm the party pretty severely. He felt it was his responsibility and duty to tell someone.

3. THE REAGAN YEARS

It was June 1987 and the American President, Ronald Reagan, was in West Germany. A state dinner was planned and Karl Schneider was invited. By this time, Karl, though a nephew, was to August and the Schneiders what Jack Kennedy was to Joe and the Kennedys. Handsome, articulate, worldly. He had traveled the world, spoke perfect English, German, French, and passable Russian. Helmut Kohl, the conservative Christian Democrat, was still the Chancellor, but he had lost some of his majority and was anxious to show Reagan that the country was still essentially conservative.

President Reagan was always pleased when he could meet a regular citizen of the place he was visiting and Andy Becker was on the committee that suggested the names for this assignment. Karl was chosen overwhelmingly. His years in Scotland and the US along with his lively style and knowledge of American sports made the evening memorable to both the Chancellor and the visiting President and Mrs. Reagan. His success in this assignment did not go unnoticed by the Chancellor.

President Reagan's challenging speech at the Brandenburg Gate was at 2:00 the next afternoon. The ending of the speech was dramatic: "General Secretary Gorbachev, if you seek peace, if you seek prosperity for the Soviet Union and Eastern Europe, if you seek liberalization: Come here to this gate! Mr. Gorbachev, open this gate! Mr. Gorbachev, tear down this Wall!"

Most of Europe, as well as even some on Reagan's staff, were shocked at the bluntness of the remarks, but Karl Schneider, having had the opportunity to know the man a little, was not. "I think politics is getting to be fun!," he remarked to Sonja that evening during dinner.

Karl Schneider II, Stefanie's grandson, had dabbled in politics since his early 50's. He was of the wealthy Schneider family who had deep roots in Berlin and Cologne. His great-grandfather, Sebastian Schneider, was the founder of Schneider Fabrics that produced much of Europe's woolen fabric. His grandfather, Johann Schneider, Stefanie's husband, took over the company upon Sebastian's demise. When Johann died at the age of 39, Karl Sr. took over. He had the company name changed to Cologne Wool Goods AG and expanded the operation but died in an airplane accident after only a few years. Johann's other son, August, then took over. The company prospered for several decades and the family became very rich. They owned homes and apartments all over Europe and had factories both in Cologne and Berlin. All the Schneider children and grandchildren married well and though there were some sad and untimely deaths, the family held its own and hung together.

Karl II received his degree in Political Science from the University at Edinburgh, Scotland, during WWII and did his Masters and Doctoral work in the United States before coming back home to Cologne. He had taught at the University of Cologne but his conservative views alienated him from most of the faculty and he developed an itch to play the political game instead of teaching it. He was married to a beautiful woman named Sonja with champagne blond hair and long legs, who had been Miss Sweden in 1944, and was also the poster girl for Cologne Wool Goods.

The ranking Member of Parliament from Cologne died in the December following Reagan's visit, only a few months after his re-election and with Kohl's influence, Karl Schneider II was appointed to fill the remainder of the term.

Parliamentary life fit Karl and Sonja like a glove. Karl's capitalistic conservatism was more than balanced by the Swedish socialism of Sonja. Karl and Sonja were, however, good-natured about their philosophical differences that lent a degree of civility to discussions that otherwise could get very heated. The two were immediately embraced by the German political society. Karl Schneider II was on his way up. There would probably be an election called in early 1990. He started building a campaign organization that would, hopefully, land him this seat formally and give him a hand in shaping the future of Germany.

The day-to-day operations of Cologne Wool Goods were handled by Karl's cousin, Johann, and Karl was mainly the public face of the corporation. Karl enjoyed the limelight and part of the company's success was due to his high profile. He wanted to make a difference in Germany and, hopefully, see her reunified and the Soviet occupation ended.

Karl persuaded Andy Becker to join his effort as his public relations adviser with the proviso that all things political and personal might be involved. He was sure that his common sense and insights would benefit the people.

4. THE BUNDESTAG APPOINTMENT

A reception and dinner was held to welcome Karl into the society of Bundestag members. Part of the evening's entertainment was a "get to know me" question and answer session with some of the more senior MdB's and a moderator from the Press.

Martin Stutz, the moderator opened with an imaginative "Who is Karl Schneider?"

Karl was a little irritated. Everyone should know that he was Karl Schneider, by God. He decided to go along. "Well, I was born in the Wool Family that you know, but I moved to Edinburgh when I was 5 years old. My father had been killed in an airplane accident when I was only three. We went to Edinburgh so that my mother could expand our business to include buying from the woolgrowers in Scotland. The War started and we were kind of trapped there until it was over. Then I moved back to Berlin and married this lovely woman to my left. She is pretty far to the left, by the way."

There was mild laughter.

"When Berlin was blockaded, the whole Schneider family came to Cologne and Sonja and I have pretty much lived here ever since except for my two years in America. In the last few years we have been trying to establish trade with the rest of the world for Cologne Wool Goods. Germany has been very good for us and we would like to give back in service a token of what we have received in riches."

The audience applauded enthusiastically.

"Minister Brandt, you have a question?"

"Yes. Karl, how do you keep from fisticuffs with the lady on your left? You seem to agree on nothing political."

There was laughter again.

"Minister, we have only two principles on which we disagree, and they neither can be proved or supported with any logical rigor. Sonja, stop me if I go astray."

"Sonja believes that capitalists and big business are based on greed and that the little guy will always be stomped on unless government is there to restrain the greed. This is the main impediment to success for the little guy and production of the goods and services we all need at prices we can afford. Since the government does not rely on profit margin, per se, it is the best source of management decisions such as salary and allocation of resources. The general welfare of the citizens is its only concern."

"I believe that the greed for money in capitalists and big business is not as great a danger as the greed for power in the government bureaucracy, which I have just joined, by the way. With only minor meddling, the government can foster competition among the capitalists so that a business that is not run efficiently or that treats its employees badly will soon find its market share declining and be eliminated. Unfortunately, in our effort to foster competition we have made a financial environment where clever capitalists can subvert the system, sometimes for several years. During that time, their greed is unchecked and they cause the people to suffer."

"A greedy bureaucrat, on the other hand, not only can send government business to his friends, he can make the rules that facilitate this corruption. I am sure that no government can be sustained in a democracy if the corruption is too great, but it only takes a few greedy to do great harm. The other problem is that while a capitalist that runs a bottling plant usually knows almost everything there is to know about bottling, a bureaucrat appointed to run a bottling plant may have as his only recommendation a friend in the government. How could he possibly make it run efficiently?"

"The 'Invisible Hand' of economic competition is a really vague principle to trust. The inherent goodness of five hundred parliamentarians is, in my mind, an even more unlikely situation. Our only argument is that Sonja just thinks the reverse and that the latter is more likely."

There was a short silence then mild applause.

Stutz then asked another. "Why did you go to America to study? We have great schools here."

Karl was again irritated. He thought, "This guy will never be on my guest list."

"Let's see. The country that won two world wars it didn't even want to participate in. The country that essentially had no war machine and built one from scratch in two years while helping Britain and the rest of the world the Reich had not occupied. The country that developed an atomic bomb and used it only as a last resort and only twice. The country that, even right after the war was over, was strong enough to be feeding and rebuilding us from the mess Hitler left. And doing the same for Japan. It seemed like a place I wanted to see and learn from."

"What did you learn?" Stutz was a little taken aback but kept at it.

"I learned that most Americans don't realize what they have."

"Democracies were installed here and in France and even in Japan essentially by the United States. I think that they have the stamp of some of the frustration that U.S presidents feel in their American version of democracy. The U.S. Constitution went so far in trying to prevent the success of the mythical greedy bureaucrat that their president saw himself as far too weak. The truth is, that because he is elected in a national referendum, he just doesn't need to be subservient to the Congress over there. The chancellor over here seems able to get things done better, but that's because his friends elected him. The people might well have chosen someone else, given the choice. So President Bush may have trouble getting things done, but he doesn't owe the Congress anything and they can't easily toss him out. I had the honor of meeting President Reagan last year. His philosophy and concerns were refreshingly free of worries about the politics of America. He looked at the Soviet regime that had murdered twenty million souls as evil and that was that. Most importantly, the things he wanted to do were from his heart and in line with spreading freedom and with creating a positive legacy. I guess he owed something to the 'Party,' but not very much to the members of congress. I seriously doubt that Roosevelt or Truman or Eisenhower or any of the others would have been chosen chancellor if they had a chancellor. Somehow the independency of their president seems to be one of the sources of their strength."

The audience was silent, but then applauded.

Stutz ended the show. "Thank you, Karl. We can tell that you were a professor. Ladies and gentlemen, the dinner is being served. Please try to arrange your chairs so that the wait staff can serve."

Andy was in the audience. He knew that he would be very busy that next day.

5. THE LETTER AND THE LEFT

NOVEMBER 1989, JUST AFTER THE DISCOVERY OF THE MICRODOTS—

Eric Raudebusch's father, Walter "Wally" Raudebusch, was a volunteer in the Social Democratic Party in Cologne. The Parliamentary Election Campaigns were in full swing and Karl Schneider was their opposition's candidate. While Eric was not willing to contribute time and effort to his father's cause, perhaps this 'microdot' tidbit might be useful in his contest.

Wally Raudebusch thanked Eric for his efforts and told Eric that he could take the matter up now. Eric told his father to 'go at it' as he wasn't interested in pursuing "it" further.

Wally called and asked for a meeting with Carrie Schmidt, the local leader of the Social Democrats in Cologne.

Karl's opponent was Gerhard Mosel, a professor of history at the University of Cologne, one of the oldest and most prestigious schools in Europe. Karl had been a professor there briefly after the War. Carrie was managing Mosel's campaign.

Mosel wanted to see Germany reunited, but preferably under a more socialist government than the present administration. He was furious that the Kohl initiative was not to support the East German political machinery and gradually introduce the system that had grown up in the West since 1949. But the cultures were so different that it was hard to imagine that this scheme could be more successful than the cold-turkey capitalism of Kohl.

Mosel's wife, Soo Li, taught mathematics at the University. Soo Li had come from Communist China to East Germany in 1958 as an 'alien worker' to teach in Dresden. She met Gerhard at a U.N. sponsored educational conference there in 1971. While Gerhard was not a member of the Communist Party, he certainly was sympathetic. They were both idealistic and impetuous and were married before the conference ended. They grieved over whether to stay in the 'People's Paradise' of East Germany or return to Cologne where Gerhard had been offered an Associate Professorship at the university there. As much fun as Dresden was in the seventies, Cologne won out. As Gerhard's wife, she had no trouble emigrating and eventually receiving West German citizenship. The university also needed mathematics teachers after the WWII brain drain from the Reich to America and Britain.

Wally Raudebusch and Carrie met that evening.

"Herr Raudebusch, how can you come to me with such a tale?" Carrie almost thought that Wally was kidding.

Carrie was a talkative auburn haired 18-year-old woman who had never married and was totally devoted to whatever job she had at hand. While not a Socialist zealot, she was conscientious about doing the best job she could for her candidate. Dependable, organized, and trustworthy were her main attributes and she was like a watchdog on guard for any dirt that might be thrown her candidate's way. Eric's father was not totally without credentials since he was the local expert on Himmler, but the story was far-fetched, to say the least. "The 'covert' documents you show me are barely more than a rumor and we would be destroyed by the media if we went public with such a story on such a flimsy basis. Why has the story been hidden for so long? Did absolutely no one know?"

"Well, if the story is true, then obviously old August Schneider knows, but he certainly would not want it generally known. I think he is pretty senile now since we have not heard anything about him for several years. The Schneiders are a very close-knit family, so it is likely that they could keep this a secret." Wally was also groping for answers.

"All we need is a contest between a guy related to Jews and a guy related to Hitler." Carrie was still skeptical.

"Is Mosel Jewish?"

"His mother was Jewish so I guess Talmudically speaking, he is. But he has been an academic all of his life and doesn't belong to any congregation, Jewish or otherwise, that we know of."

Wally was still surprised. "Just let me check it out. I'll find the church and, with any luck, the records will be intact and the story verified or denied within a day or two." Carrie agreed and Wally Raudebusch caught the evening train to Berlin to look up St. Stephen's Church.

In 1907, there were eight Catholic churches in Berlin. St. Hedwig, St. Michael, St. Sebastian, St. Paul, St. Matthew, St. Pius, St. John, and Heart of Jesus (Herz Jesukirche). There was no St. Stephen's church, but there were about 25 smaller chapels, several of which were possibly known as St. Stephen's at the time. The major churches were still there, but several were severely damaged in the bombing of Berlin during the War. Since the War, about forty years of development and growth had razed and re-razed many neighborhoods. This might not be as easy as Wally had hoped.

Most of central Berlin had been destroyed by bombs during the War, especially Mitte, the "middle" province. St. Hedwig, the Cathedral, was destroyed by bombs and fire twice. Then it ended up in the East German sector. With the end of the Wall, it was uncertain exactly where to start to look for records from 1907. But Wally had never been to the Eastern sector and figured that St. Hedwig would be as good as any place to start the search. The Underground subway was not yet unified so he took a bus to the Staatsoper stop and walked over to the Cathedral of St. Hedwig.

Father Pfaff, the Curate was not too helpful. The disintegration of Communist rule was clearing the way for many theological restorations and everyone was overwhelmed by the task of becoming a real Cathedral again instead of a token allowed by the local regime. All records had been destroyed by the bombing and consequent fires except those since 1944 and no effort had been made to reconstruct them. However, he would introduce Wally to someone who might help. A Monsignor Anselm was still alive and lucid at the ripe old age of 92 and might remember some of the structure from that era. It was probably about the same from 1907 until he took his vows in 1918. The Monsignor came for Evensong on Thursdays. Perhaps Herr Raudebusch could drop by then. Wally thanked the Curate and decided to continue his search, using the Monsignor as a backup plan. He visited several other churches with even less success.

He called Carrie and dutifully reported his lack of immediate success. To his surprise, she urged him to persevere and gave him the name of Ernst Wollweber. Wollweber was the thirty-something-year-old nephew of the former head of Stasi, the East German version of the KGB. Ernst was only about 5'6" and had a slight limp. He told everyone that it was from a skiing accident but, in reality, he fell off his Vespa when he was 14. He cultivated a slight Russian accent although he had never been further east than Vienna. His dark eyes and black straight disheveled hair made him seem more dangerous than he could possibly be. He did, however, know how to negotiate the hodge-podge trail of records in the former East Germany and was friendly to the Socialist cause. If anyone could find St. Stephen's, Ernst could. Maybe.

Ernst Wollweber was intrigued by the tale related by Wally Raudebusch and asked for a few days to try to find the missing St. Stephen's Church. Raudebusch considered the fare back to Cologne and the rate in a local hotel and decided to stay in Berlin a few days longer.

On Thursday, Wally asked to take Monsignor Anselm to dinner after the service. When they walked out of the church a limo was waiting for the cleric.

Monsignor was the second son of a Prince of the Austro-Hungarian Empire. In those days the first son inherited the title and land, the second son went to God, and any following sons went to war. The title, of course, went away, but the land included a fine Riesling vineyard that still was owned by his family. The old priest got a taste for wine honestly.

Fr. Anselm suggested a French restaurant pretty much outside Wally's budget but fortunately Carrie was footing the bill. The waiter came over and greeted them. "So nice to see you again Monsignor. What will you have this evening?" Wally tried to set an example by ordering the veal cutlet, a house salad, and a glass of the house red. The old priest assumed an impatient, almost shocked look and sort of took over the meal. "No, no, no, Pierre. Cancel that. We will have Vichyssoise to start and then Escargot. Your marvelous whipped potatoes with shallots and truffles, steak au poivre rare, endive and mint salad, crème brûlée, then cashews soaked in Courvoisier."

"Very good." Pierre left to submit the order. Wally tried not to look shocked.

The restaurant obviously knew what was expected of them. Each course was with a different wine, which Monsignor lavishly described with comments such as "blackberry nose" and "lingering caramel and cherry aftertaste" obviously from the heart. After the dinner when he requested a Cuban cigar, Wally spoke up, "Not for me, please." When he lit the Montecristo, the table became surrounded by a thick cloud of smoke. Wally suppressed a coughing fit and listened carefully.

"St. Stephen. Yes, there were at least two St. Stephen places. Maybe three. An Orthodox church in Kopenick District was a converted Roman Church of St. Stephen. The Russians just keep trying to take over here. And a beautiful chapel in the North, in Wedding or maybe Pankow District was dedicated to St. Stephen... Have you been to St. Stephen's Cathedral in Vienna? I was ordained there, you know. It was on Easter in 1918 but it was warm, like Spring had already come. Did you know that St. Stephen's Cathedral faces exactly the rising sun on St. Stephen's day of December 26? The Bells! The 23 bells. Each has the name of a saint and I used to know them all. St. Mary is the largest and it is huge. It weighs more than twenty thousand kilos. You should hear the bells... It has been so long." Slowly, he dozed off. The cigar fell to the table, burning a hole in the tablecloth. An observant waiter extinguished the smoldering cloth and cigar with a damp napkin. The Monsignor started snoring loudly. Wally figured the evening was over. His driver was still outside so Wally saw that the Monsignor was safely put into the car and on the way home. When he went back to apologize for the damage, the maitre d' just smiled and said that it was not unusual for the Monsignor's evening to end in such a fashion. Wally signed the check and went back to his hotel.

On Friday, Wollweber called. He had not been able to find anything concrete about St. Stephen in 1907, and suggested the typical intelligence agency approach. Follow the opposition's guys. Bribe the opposition's employees. Ply an opposition worker with booze or babes. Wally was fairly certain that the Schneider organization did not know of the tale and, as such, there was probably no one to sully in this fashion. Elections were in nine weeks and the window of opportunity would not be open long. He went back to Cologne.

6. LET'S KEEP IT FAIR

Peter Warren from Philips had a problem. He was philosophically aligned with the Conservative Cause of the Christian Democrats, but he knew no one at all in the organization. The information he had was sensitive and should only be related to a dedicated and trustworthy person in the organization. Peter didn't even know anyone in the organization. The campaign was in full swing, so he went and bought every magazine and newspaper that featured election coverage. He had to find a name of someone he could trust. Philips as a corporation was pushing the non-political image this year, so it was doubtful that anyone in his Company would be helpful.

He narrowed the names mentioned in the media to two: Helmut Grainger and Andrew Becker. Grainger was the Christian Democrats' District Chairman for Central Cologne and Becker was Karl Schneider's Public Relations point man. He called the office of Grainger first.

Grainger, he found, was insulated by several layers of receptionists, administrative assistants, and other associates. He got past the receptionist by offering to volunteer to work for Schneider. This led him to an assistant in charge of staffing. This was not exactly the optimum place but he had to start somewhere.

"My name is Peter Warren. I would really like to help elect Karl Schneider, but the reason I am calling now is that I have uncovered a plot to seriously damage Schneider's reputation and qualification for the office. It is quite sensitive and I need to meet with someone appropriate to handle this kind of information." It was not the best sales pitch, but maybe this guy would want to check it out and maybe be a hero.

"Herr Warren, I have known Dr. Schneider for almost twenty years and I assure you that there are no skeletons in his closet. He is from one of the most respected families in Berlin and Cologne and any lies or innuendos will be handled quickly and efficiently. Would you like to work on a telephone bank or addressing envelopes?"

Peter's first contact was not working out. "Telephone bank is good. I have Wednesday and Thursday evenings free."

"Thank you, Herr Warren. I will transfer you to an operator who will take your contact information and maybe some personal information to help us decide where you might be most effective."

He offered his information to the operator and then called Andrew Becker. To his surprise, Becker himself actually answered the phone.

Andy Becker was Karl's main man. He had known Karl and the Schneider family since he was 14 years old. Andy was now fiftyish, 6' tall, of average build with thick silvering brown hair and brown eyes. He was a rather handsome type and struck a good figure in front of the cameras. He gave off a trustworthy appearance and knew how to run a good, clean campaign. His father, Alton, had been First Assistant in the Foreign Office for Konrad Adenauer after the war. Adenauer acted as his own Foreign Minister during most of his administration, so Alton was in the thick of diplomatic negotiations and Andy developed a passion for politics. When Karl decided to make a political career for himself, Andy was the first one he called to come on board.

With Andy on the other end of the line, Peter Warren tried a different approach this time. "My name is Peter Warren. I have always been a Conservative and I have recently overheard a plan to show that Karl Schneider was only a Schneider by adoption. Perhaps we could meet and I could lay it out and, with a little heads up, you could be ready for such information."

"Really, Herr Warren. This is pretty low, but the opposition is known for this kind of slander. Do you have any documentation or other proof, either real or forged?"

"I don't know for sure, but I have heard that there are some kind of papers in Berlin where his father was born—in a church. I will give you what I have." This time, Peter did not want the story to seem too fantastic to believe or too vague to be ignored.

"Can you come by my office this evening, Herr Warren?" Becker was pretty sure that the elder Karl Schneider's birthplace was not generally known. Early ties to Berlin were not helpful to politicians. If he could nip this thing in the bud, his PR career would get a real boost.

"I will be there." Peter now had to get copies of the documents and microdot text. He called Christoph into his office.

"Tell me all you know about this affair with the microdots and Himmler."

Christoph replied that he knew nothing except what was on the copies of the two letters and the microdot enlargements. "Eric took the originals back with him but I have copies." He went to his desk and retrieved what he had.

"Please do not talk about this to anyone else, Christoph. No good can come from opening old wounds from that black time." Peter Warren was hoping that the information was still limited to himself, Eric and Christoph.

7. THE RIGHT GETS THE LETTER

Peter arrived at Becker's office at about 8:00 PM Andy Becker's office was spacious, neat, and efficient. Anna, Andy's girl Friday, showed Peter in and told Andy to lock up when he left as she was leaving. Becker was on the phone. Peter was relieved to see the various pictures on the wall of Becker with Kohl, Becker with Thatcher, Becker with Reagan, and others. Becker seemed to be permanently connected to the conservative cause and, hopefully, could be trusted. The picture on his desk was of a striking light-skinned African girl autographed to Andy.

"Please pull up a chair. Show me what you've brought." Becker was now off the phone.

"Thank you for seeing me, Herr Becker. I hope the information I have is valid and that you can head off the storm it could cause. It is a bit fantastic."

"Please call me Andy," offered Becker. "Let's see what you have."

"These are copies of documents in the Himmler Collection at the University here in Cologne. The first is the letter found in the seventh district post office during its renovation last week. You may have seen it mentioned on the local news. The second letter is from the original Collection. They are between Himmler and, apparently, August Schneider of Cologne Wool Goods. They were clandestinely communicating using something called microdots. Schneider is, of course, Karl's uncle. Is he still alive? They are, I think, discussing Karl's father." Peter handed over the documents and sat back in his chair. He waited, expecting a stunned look, or, at least, a pensive one.

Becker studied each individual page. A slight smile on his face slowly expanded into a look of complete ecstasy. Peter was confused.

"Fixing this is the kind of PR challenge I dream of, Peter." Becker was almost jumping up and down. "Who else knows of this?"

"A file clerk of the collection is all, I think," said Peter. "A fellow named Eric Raudebusch."

"Please keep this confidential, Herr Warren. I must check out this Raudebusch."

"Please call me Peter, Andy."

"Thank you, Peter. You have been a great help to all of us," said Becker. "Please excuse me while I make a few calls. This cannot wait."

Peter hoped that he had done some good. He left and went home.

8. IS IT POSSIBLE?

August Schneider was now 79, but only lucid now and then. Andy had spoken to him at several functions over the years and had been to his home numerous times. He decided to start at the best source he could think of to check out the story. He called the Schneider Estate in Berlin and was told that August was not well and was not receiving visitors. Not even important political visitors. He then called Karl Schneider and pleaded with him to get him an audience with his uncle August. Karl was somewhat put off by Andy's vague reason for the meeting, but agreed to call his cousin Johann and see if a meeting could be arranged.

Johann told Karl that he would not burden August with a political meeting, but he would get back to Andy directly and tell him to try another tact. When Johann called, Andy was disappointed that he could not interview August. This would have been his best shot. He invited Johann to lunch that same day hoping to probe and see if Johann knew anything.

Andy, knowing that the best way to earn someone's confidence was to ask a favor, waited until they were about finished with lunch and explained that he was compiling a personal history of the Schneiders to be ahead of the media and to be able to respond to questions. Could Johann perhaps fill in a few blanks?

Johann said that he would if he could.

"Lets start back a generation, Johann. How did your grandfather, your namesake Johann, and his wife meet?"

"Well, Johann died long before I was born. But grandmother lived until 1952. I just remember her as a wonderful grandmother. She used to let us kids get by with a whole lot of stuff and she was very loving. I do know that she traveled a lot and was always writing. Mom traveled with her sometimes and said Steffi kept a diary of everything. She even started my mother off keeping a diary. They didn't have much else to do, I guess, since the housekeepers did all the work. My mom, Karen, I think, knows where Steffi's diaries are because she happened to mention them only a couple of weeks ago. They were very close, my mom and my grandmother."

"Steffi briefly lived in an apartment above one of our sales offices in Berlin. Johann came to check on it twice a week and that's how she met him. She fell in love with him at first sight and charmed and trapped him even though she was not from wealth or Berlin. I had an uncle Karl, our Karl's father, who died just after I was born. Dad seldom spoke of him. I got the feeling that there was some kind of disagreement that kept them from being close. Karl wanted to expand the company into aircraft and other really risky enterprises back in the 1930s. He actually died in a plane crash. They said he was going to buy the company that made the fatal plane. Aunt Emma, Karl's mother, died about five years ago."

"To be honest with you, Andy, I don't know a whole lot else about the old family history, but I'll bet you can learn more if my mother will let you borrow grandmother's diaries. She might say 'no' but I doubt it. She would do whatever it takes to help Karl and she knows you."

Andy felt he had fallen into a goldmine. He knew the family well, but he didn't know all the intimacies the family might have had years before his time.

Karen, Johann's mother, was lovely to Andy on the phone and apologized that August was indisposed and could not see anyone. She agreed to let him take the diaries for a short time, but only if he kept them very private and would take the utmost care, as they were quite special to her. She said she had never even looked through them herself. They were kept in Stefanie's closet in her wing of the castle and had not been moved except once when the painter came and Johann would know where they were, if Andy would kindly put him back on the phone.

Johann finished his conversation and told Andy to follow him home. Johann said it was not that far away but it was further than

Andy figured. Andy was just glad he would have the opportunity to look at some personal accounts of Stefanie's life. When they arrived, Johann asked Andy to step in while he ran up to get them. "Give me just a few minutes. Women's directions aren't always that clear."

Shortly, Johann reappeared with a beautifully tied box that smelled of dried potpourri. Karen said to tell you that there were several diaries, but she had not counted to see how many. Andy thanked him, said he would take the best of care of them and would return them as soon as he was finished.

Andy nervously placed the box on his back seat and decided that the apartment would be the best place to look at the books. The last thing he wanted was someone looking over his shoulder asking questions. He almost felt like he was taking Stefanie's corpse home with him instead of her belongings. It was a funny feeling.

Johann was getting into his car but Andy thought of one more question. "Oh, by the way, Johann, do you have any idea of where the old sales office was? It would make a wonderful human interest 'aside' to find the historical beginning of the Schneiders of this century." He thought a good place to start besides the diaries might be to pin down a neighborhood for the elusive St. Stephen's Church.

Johann thought for a moment, rubbed his chin and more or less remembered. "She actually showed me the building once when we were in Berlin. I was only about 10. I haven't any idea where it was. 1910 was a long time ago, but the address is probably in the company archives."

"It would really help Karl to find out. Could you inquire?"

"Better than that. Let's go over to the old factory building. The records are probably there."

It was only about a 10-minute drive to the original location of Schneider Fabrics. The grounds were still immaculately kept and the office neat and clean.

"Good afternoon, Herr Schneider. What brings you to this office today?" Miranda, the secretary, was glad to see anyone except the maintenance staff and security detail. Miranda had been with the company forever. At least, she had been working for the Schneiders for as long as Johann could remember. Miranda's father was the son of Jules Feinstein, a chemist hired by Johann's grandfather right after World War I. He had been killed in the bombing of Cologne when she was only 3. Jules and his wife took Miranda and her mother into their home but her mother was so traumatized by the bombing that she thereafter had trouble relating to anyone except Miranda and her in-laws. Some of the social deficiencies of her mother were evident in Miranda so Jules brought her into the company when she was 17. Miranda was bright, functional and trustworthy. She just couldn't deal with courting or dating.

"Miranda. I would like to know where our offices in Berlin were in about 1910."

"I'll be right back." She vanished down the stairs.

"Miranda knows where everything is filed and, Lord knows, this company has never discarded an invoice, receipt, contract, pay stub, or check. Let's see how long it takes her." Johann had a brotherly affection for Miranda and was always fascinated by her efficiency.

It only took Miranda about five minutes to return with a lovely, leather bound ledger engraved in gold with "Real Estate 1906–1910." The entries were by city, Cologne, of course, and Berlin, Hamburg, Vienna, and Paris. In Berlin there were two locations listed, one on Knesebeck Strasse and one on Luckauer Strasse. "That was quick. You are amazing, Miranda." Johann looked to see if Andy was impressed. He was.

"It is the same volume the reporter asked me about yesterday, sir." Miranda was happy to please.

Johann looked a little upset. Andy was showing mild panic.

"There was a reporter here? From which organization? Did you get his name?" Johann was getting irritated. Andy was more like alarmed.

"He signed the visitor's log and I checked his ID. He was from the university. He said that he was researching growth of the wool industry over the last century." Miranda was nervous that she had done something wrong. The name in the visitor's log was Walter Raudebusch.

"I don't think it was a reporter. Probably just a student writing a paper." Johann was ready to let the subject drop.

"Was he also interested in Berlin sites of the company, Miranda?" Andy remembered that the other person who knew the tale was a clerk of the Himmler documents named Raudebusch.

"Yes. Really odd, don't you think?" Miranda seemed relieved that Johann was not upset any more. Andy knew that his quest had just become a race.

Andy thanked Miranda and Johann again and drove back to his office. He knew he was running against the clock and to sort it out would take a little time. If indeed, it was an ugly rumor, it had to be stopped in record time. He wasn't sure what he would do if the story turned out to be true. He would cross that bridge later. He didn't even want to tell Karl or Helmut until he had something concrete to tell. He knew tonight would be a very long night.

9. WORK TO DO

Andy decided to wind up things quickly at his office before going to the apartment. He would be incognito for the rest of the day and evening, but really had to check in before going home. He greeted Anna as he quickly walked past her, but poked his head back around to see if he had any calls while he was away. He seemed terribly antsy. Helmut Grainger called, a few volunteers had called but nothing pressing, she said. And no, Larissa had not called. Damn! He knew she was mad and well she should be. He wasn't very attentive.

Andy had been married once in his late 20's, but his wife left him because she claimed he had no time for her. He tried to explain his driven life before they ever tied the knot and she pretended to understand, but she didn't. She could not tolerate his pace and she didn't enjoy the limelight that he was always in. He never remarried because he knew no other woman would put up with him either so he devoted his time to politics. That didn't mean that he didn't have an encounter or two every now and then. Larissa was his most recent and had been a constant for some time. She weaved in and out of his life, too, it seemed.

Larissa was a real beauty. She was 5'9", half African and half Italian and lived in Paris. She looked more like a model than a singer. Andy met her when she was only 16. Her father's jazz trio played for one of the political functions he attended and she was his girl vocalist. She was extremely talented, but extremely young. Andy would have liked to have knelt at her feet in adoration then, but he didn't. He could not have gossip floating around the political circles, so he kept his distance. They did exchange addresses, however, and corresponded at Christmas and at birthdays. The correspondence stopped when Larissa was about 19 and Andy figured she had found that special someone. He was sad but he chose not to think about it. He was becoming too set in his ways anyhow. But, when Larissa was 22, she danced back into his life. He was in Paris and saw that the group was playing at a club on the Left Bank and he was in the mood for some good jazz. This would be a good time to inquire about Larissa too.

As Andy walked up to the club entrance, he saw Larissa's picture on the marquee. What an incredible looking gal! He paid the cover and took a seat in the club as close to the bandstand as he could get. He hoped he had not changed too much and she would recognize him. As she finished her song and the audience applauded, she looked around and squealed almost into the microphone. And no, she had not gotten involved with anyone and was ecstatic to see Andy. After the shows, they went to an intimate all night café a few doors down from the club for coffee and decided to start seeing each other. She had finally reached an age where he wouldn't be considered a child molester. They both laughed about it. They knew that a commute back and forth to Cologne, then to Paris, sometimes Berlin and who knew where else, would be tough, but they agreed to try it for a while. Andy had two apartments, one in Cologne and one in Berlin. Larissa would keep her Paris apartment. They would each keep clothes at all three apartments. They figured they could make it work. She had to finish out a contract with her father that would end in just three weeks. She had been singing for two years straight without a break and needed to give her throat a rest and think about her life. She would be taking a three-month sabbatical.

Andy tried Larissa's number at the Paris apartment before putting on his coat, but her answering machine was on. He left a syrupy message, but knew she was pissed. This was the only woman he really cared for, but he just didn't have the time, at least, not right now. She still had clothes at the Cologne apartment so he knew she had to come back at some point. And this cat and mouse type of affair was getting to him too.

Andy told Anna to lock up, that he was going home early and don't refer any calls unless they were urgent or Larissa.

10. STEFANIE'S DIARY I: WWI

Andy took the box from his back seat and carried it in like a piece of crystal. His Cologne apartment was not huge and the one bedroom served as his office away from the office and for sleeping. He didn't have a housekeeper at the moment and needed one desperately. He never entertained there, so he only cleaned about once every two weeks. Stuff tended to pile up and that meant clothes mixed with papers, and because he smoked too much, he didn't empty the ashtrays as often as he should.

He set the box on the bed until he cleared some of the mess away. His best thinking and speech writing occurred late at night and in the wee hours. His public office, he considered, was just a front. He got rid of the stale coffee, note pads and overflowing cigarette butts and wiped his table clean before setting the box on top of it. He promised Karen he would be careful and he was.

Andy popped a frozen dinner into the microwave and took a warm shower while it was cooking. He had a penchant for comfort and needed to get himself situated before delving into the books. Pulling on some stretched out jogging pants and a loose T-shirt, his body was at least covered in case he had to answer the door. He quickly ate dinner such that it was.

The ribbon on the box was tied into a bow that had gone flat with time. It was a bit faded but still smelled of the delicate dried flowers that were inside. Andy carefully untied it and removed the lid. There were five books in all. He bent down to smell the net filled bags of potpourri packed neatly next to the books. Sweet memories of

Stefanie, he mused. There were three rather flat bags filled with the nice fragrances and he wondered how long they had been in the box. They were stacked to one side and the books were tightly fitted in next to them. There were no numbers or dates on the covers of the diaries. They were all soft black calfskin but of slightly different sizes and all were about 3/4" thick. Andy wondered which was the proper order of events. The earliest one was the one he had the greatest interest in. He opened the first book and it started with The New House 1930. Andy thumbed through the book and it seemed to be describing the house that was being built in Berlin. He knew this was not the one he was looking for. He picked up a second book and it was dated even later. He picked up the third and then the fourth and was sure the revelation, if there was one, would be in book number 5. Book five started with Sebastian's death in 1914.

Andy was confused and wondered if Stefanie had started her diary earlier than 1914 and the book might be missing but who would have taken it? Maybe there wasn't a number one and she mixed all her memories into the books that were there. He started over, thumbing through the diaries. He got up and poured himself a drink and decided to begin with the earliest one. He wished he had taken one of those speed-reading courses.

March 4, 1914, Wednesday
Sadness is filling the house. Sebastian died today. God bless his soul. He was a good man and liked me. I liked him too. Sharon is planning the funeral and Johann is helping her and trying to keep her strong. Johann has called on Fritz and Franz and some of Sebastian's associates to be pallbearers. I am trying to keep the boys calm. They tend to make Sharon nervous, especially Karl. I am sending notices to close relatives and friends of the family. Funerals are always painful. My job is to plan a menu to give to the cooks. There will be people in and out of here the afternoon of the funeral. Maybe we should have a large ham and peas.

Sebastian Schneider lived to be 72 years old. Johann took over the company just as WWI was starting. Johann had been steeped in the wool business since he was a young boy and had run the whole operation for the duration of his father's illness. Nothing changed much upon Sebastian's death other than it left a great sadness in Sharon's life. She only had her husband and her son as the infant daughter she had given birth to before Johann had died at birth.

Sebastian was buried next to the baby girl beside the chapel on the estate in Cologne.

September 1, 1914, Tuesday
Today, Karl and August started to school. Karl is in the second grade and August is in the first. Because there are only a few teachers, they may have classes together. I need a break from them. Karl is so wild. I hope his teacher doesn't pull out her hair. And, I hope he doesn't get thrown out of school.

Stefanie and Johann raised Karl and August in Berlin. Even at a young age, there were obvious differences in their characters and attitudes. While the boys looked a lot alike except that Karl had darker hair and August was blond, Karl was the more flamboyant adventurer. August was much quieter and careful. Karl often tore up the toys that belonged to August causing friction between the two youngsters. Karl seemed to demand more attention from his parents than his younger brother, but August learned to be a bit cunning in order to hold his own with his older brother. As Karl led the way through lower and middle schools, August found that everyone remembered Karl and so little had to be done to be remembered. Some of the teachers seemed a little disappointed that August was somewhat passive and was not as strong a character.

Andy skipped over some of the entries that did not yield any early information. But he kept reading.

June 28, 1919 Saturday
The war ended today and Johann may want to celebrate. I love it when he is in a good mood. Maybe we will have guests in or dine out. Places will be mobbed tonight so we should have guests here. I will talk to the cook. Sharon does not like to dine out much anymore. Keeping her happy is a real chore.

The War officially ended on June 28, 1919, with the Treaty of Versailles. The German Empire became the Weimar Republic and, surprisingly to all, was not occupied or carved up into chunks to be claimed by the victors. Serious reparations were imposed which caused financial woes and inflation but Germany was allowed to rebuild although with limited military presence. Karl was 11 and August was almost 10.

Industrialists were encouraged to hire cashiered soldiers returning from the war and Johann hired a promising young chemist named

Jules Feinstein who had been a lieutenant but had not actually seen any action. This had two very positive effects on the company in that Jules developed some very dense and very durable dyes for wool and Johann found that Jules' father, Stefan, turned out to be as gifted in finance as Jules was in chemistry. Stefan became what is now called the Chief Financial Officer for the company. With Jules and Stefan in Cologne, the factories were in good hands and the Schneider clan pretty much lived in Berlin exclusively.

July 10, 1922 Monday

Karl is giving me a headache today. He likes speed and is begging Johann to take him to the races. August shows no interest. I will not go, myself, but I think he is talking Johann into it. Johann is a good father and he has so little time to spend with the boys. Karl takes advantage of Johann's weakness for saying 'no'. Thank goodness August is not so wild. Karl told August there were bedbugs in his bed. August hasn't slept well for a week.

The Grand Prix racing tour resumed in 1921 after the War's hiatus. Karl was obsessed with the romance of the formula cars and drivers. In 1922 the French Grand Prix was held in Strasbourg on July 16. Strasbourg is on the French-German border and Karl persuaded his father to take him and August to the show. Road races are not really exciting spectator sports unless one sees a serious spin-out, but Karl insisted that they stay for the full 60 laps which lasted almost 7 hours. On the 51st lap, the left rear wheel on Biagio Nazarro's Fiat 804 flew off and, although his mechanic was thrown clear of the wreck and survived, Nazarro was killed in the ensuing crash. While Johann and August were appalled with the spectacle, Karl was just amazed and excited. Later, on the 58th lap Pietro Bordino's Fiat 804 had a similar failure but he managed to keep enough control to survive. The winner of the race was Felice Nazarro, Biagio's uncle, also in a Fiat. The three Fiats were almost an hour ahead of the next two drivers in Bugattis. Only three cars, Felice's and the two Bugattis, actually finished the race. Later it was learned that the Felice's winning Fiat had cracks in the same axle as the other two Fiats and probably could not have gone many more laps. But Karl, at the ripe age of 14, decided to become a race car driver. Johann was not impressed.

In 1923, Karl's best school friend, who was one year older than Karl, received a bright red Simson Supra roadster for his birthday.

Simson was a company in Suhl, Southern Germany, which mainly made small arms for the army and police. They also made a few two-place sports cars and a few four-place touring cars. The Supra was the sports model and could go 135 km per hour on the straight-away. It was really fast for its day. Karl wanted a car of his own but could not persuade Johann that he should have one. Karl managed to talk his buddy into letting him drive from time to time but, since Karl always pushed the car to its limits, Willy was not too thrilled.

One Sunday evening, while they were driving along the Spree River south of Berlin, Karl came into a turn much too fast. Willy screamed, but it was too late. The car flew off the embankment and into the river. The river was deep and the roadster sank immediately. It was dark and no one saw. Karl swam to safety but Willy was trapped in the car. Karl escaped blame for the tragedy because the authorities assumed that Willy was driving and Karl never said differently, even to Johann. Johann hoped that Karl had learned a lesson about speed and the fragility of life. But Karl took from the experience that accidents happen to other people and that Karl Schneider led a charmed life.

September 22, 1923 Friday
Today is very rainy. I received a note from August's mathematics teacher who says he has scored very high on one of his tests. He seems to be coming out of his shell and doing well in school. He loves music and I love to hear him play. He has Johann's talent. He has such a gentle feel for the music. He seems to be two different people sometimes - a quiet, sensitive musician, but then, an aggressive power-loving individual. I guess he is a typical Schneider.

In the upper school, August was an honor student, an excellent athlete, and showed considerable promise as a pianist. He began piano lessons at the age of 5. He enjoyed the "Three B's", Bach, Brahms, and Beethoven as well as the "Two M's" Mendelssohn and Mozart. But he also had a keen ear for Jazz. He resolved to keep music as a hobby, though, and prepared for the family business.

Berlin in the '20s was spectacular. Einstein was director of the Physics Institute. Humboldt University was the best in the world and the school to which Karl matriculated. He was not a particularly good scholar but did find some business courses interesting and useful. August also started at Humboldt and eventually was graduated cum laude in textile engineering.

Andy was almost to the end of the first book and was certain there wasn't anything dramatic. He carefully placed it on the table beside the box. Should he read word for word or just skim them? He would do both...

11. STEFANIE'S DIARY 2: BETWEEN THE WARS

July 24, 1924 Thursday
Johann took a day away from the office and we went shopping. The world is changing and the new trends are wonderful. Johann said he liked the new shorter dresses. He said I looked sexy as I tried one on. I'm sure Sharon would think I have taken up being a floozie if I came home with one of them. She tends to be such a stuffed shirt. She bosses everyone around and continues to act like I should be grateful to her every day of the week. Johann told me to ignore her.

The Bauhaus Movement in art and architecture blossomed. Architecture and furniture of Behrens, Gropius, and Mies van der Rohe were in demand all over the world. Music by Berg and Schoenberg and Weill were universally acclaimed. Buber and Weber with their new philosophical insights and the Institute for Social Research with its reliance on Freud and "Critical Theory" were definitely the wave of the future. Sharon Schneider, however, stayed Victorian. She considered the new movements decadent and unworthy. While Sharon had the last call at the mansion, Stefanie and Johann proudly were of the next generation. They looked on the new trends as exhilarating and inspiring. Stefanie continued to be reserved in fashion, however, and shunned the 'Flapper look' for the timeless designs of Mariano Fortuny and wore his dresses like the Greek goddess he intended them for.

March 20, 1925 Friday

I am packing for Venice. I need a new dress or two from Mariano and while Johann is in the mood to buy them for me, I have to jump. He is so good to me. Sharon and the nannies will watch the boys. I will only be gone less than two weeks. It will do Sharon good to pay some attention to them. She has such a stick up her ass most of the time. I need to check on the apartment (she should be grateful) and be there for fittings. I love Venice and I need to get away. I need some time to think. I wish Johann would go but he says he can't leave right now. I don't like to travel alone. Maybe I can convince him to go... I need to write to mother.

Mariano Fortuny had designed some of the most incredible fabrics and dresses of his time. He resided in Venice and his studio was located on the ground floor of the Palazzo Orfei where Stefanie had the pleasure of meeting him. Fortuny was truly a Renaissance man who was an inventor, a painter, a sculptor, a lighting designer and eventually became a master of fabric invention and dress design. He understood anatomy and loved the way the Greeks mastered the human form in art. He designed his dresses to mimic the Greeks and his famous Delphos dress became legendary. The colors he chose for his fabrics were breathtaking and most of the pigments he used, he mixed himself. He understood beauty in every form and Stefanie adored what he stood for. She had the good fortune to know him well since the Schneiders' owned an apartment on the Grand Canal. She also had the figure to do justice to his magnificent silk and velvet creations and Johann encouraged her to purchase whatever her heart desired since she represented Schneider Fabrics at trade shows all over Europe. He wanted her to look her smartest. Some of Fortuny's dye techniques were also an inspiration to the Schneider Company.

July 28, 1925 Tuesday
I am packing for Paris. Karl is going with me. He is so handsome but looks a little pale at times. People will think he is my gigolo. I need to spend some time alone with him and I feel protected when he is around. I hope he will pack the right clothes for himself. He is spoiled and doesn't get a lot done. He needs to take his new shirts and a few ties.

In 1925, Johann sent Stefanie and Karl to Paris to attend the huge Exposition des Arts Decoratifs, an assemblage of the latest avant-garde designers and manufacturers of fabrics and home goods from around the world. Schneider Fabrics registered for the Exposition but their application had been lost. When they resubmitted, it was too late and all spaces had been filled. Johann still thought it worthwhile for Stefanie to attend and show the flag of the company. She could possibly distribute literature to some of the exhibitors explaining their latest dye processes. Schneider Fabrics was growing and Stefanie made a good showing wherever she went. People remembered her as she was warm and gracious and outgoing, not to mention, beautiful.

August 5, 1925 Wednesday

Karl and I have just arrived in Paris. We are staying at the Grande Paree Hotel. It is gorgeous. This has to be the most incredible city in the world. I am supposed to give out brochures for the company. I will after I have had a look around. Everything imaginable is represented here. Karl doesn't like looking at the clothes. He only wants to see new gadgets. Everything you can imagine is here. It looks like a giant carnival.

August 5, 1925

Today, we started at the northern most end of the exposition and worked our way toward the middle. I could not believe that I saw someone I know. Elizabeth Watts-Moore was in the crowd. She still thinks she is the queen of England. She is totally self-absorbed but she has a cute daughter. Karl seemed to like the daughter more than I like the mother. Tomorrow, Fortuny. I can hardly wait but this place is ghastly huge and my feet hurt today. I am listing some potential customers for Johann...

Stefanie was surprised to see a socialite she had met at Fortuny's studio the year before named Elizabeth Watts-Moore from Aberdeen, Scotland. To bump into an acquaintance at such an enormous event seemed as fate would have had to intervene. Lady Watts-Moore introduced her daughter Emma to Stefanie and Karl. Emma had just made her debut and was happy to meet someone her own age in Paris. The Exposition covered 72 acres of land, had 12 monumental entranceways and spread throughout the Grand Palais, the Petit Palais, Cours la Reine, the Pont Alexandre, and the Esplanade des Invalides. Elizabeth Watts-Moore apparently attended every fashionable event that would guarantee her a newsworthy mention and the Watts family money allowed her to do it.

Both ladies were dedicated clients of Mariano Fortuny and were anxious to see his latest fabrics and styles as well as those of other designers who were exhibiting. Art Deco design was the rage both in home and clothing design. Stefanie was glad to see the trend toward dresses that were no longer fitted. She found it harder to keep her 22-inch waistline as maturity set in.

Emma Watts-Moore was a stunning young woman, a bit boyish in manner, and much more tailored in dress than the average girl Karl had taken up with. Her mother's passion for style had not rubbed off on her. Since the war forced some women to take on men's chores during its duration, many women took on men's style of dress, as well. Emma understood frills but liked comfort more and the unencumbered clothes that allowed her to participate in the athletics she so loved. She played tennis and golf, loved horses and was enamored with sports cars and all the wild stories Karl had to tell her. While she wasn't sure they were all true, they were definitely entertaining. And what better place could a girl hear them but at the base of the Eiffel Tower where they met several nights in a row for sodas and sandwiches while their mothers mused over fashions. By the end of the week, Karl and Emma were holding hands and sneaking kisses. Both Stefanie and Elizabeth took note but neither mother said a word. Six months later, Karl sent a telegram to Aberdeen asking Emma's hand in marriage.

February 1, 1926 Monday
Karl has asked Emma Watts-Moore to marry him. He was totally smitten with her and I must say, her family has money and she will not be marrying him for his. I guess two family fortunes are better than one. We have a lot of planning to do and they want to get married this year.

The wedding in June of 1926 was the social event of the season. There actually were two celebrations, one in Scotland and one in Germany. Emma's parents and three aunts came for the celebration in Berlin. Not wanting to be outdone, Emma's parents insisted on a second repeating of vows in Edinburgh in July. Stefanie and Johann attended the lavish Scottish festivities and were treated well by Emma's family. The couple, however, chose to take up residence in Berlin and Stefanie saw to it that her son and his wife were properly situated in German social circles. She worried about Karl's rebellious nature that was not a trait of the Schneiders and hoped that it would not cause strife in his marriage. She prayed that this marriage would calm Karl down.

February 8, 1927 Tuesday
Johann keeps me up all night with that hacking cough. I have given him warmed honey and whiskey but it doesn't seem to help. He smokes too much. I try rubbing his back and he says it relaxes him but that cough worries me. I am scared that he may have TB. Dear God, help him! I love him so much.

In February 1927, Johann became ill with a nagging cough that would keep him awake at nights. Stefanie was concerned that he had lost so much weight. He tried not to bother her with his problems but he could not seem to fight off whatever malady he had. Home remedies were totally ineffective and Stefanie begged him to get professional help. Johann had always had a sporadic cough but he attributed it to too much smoking. Some days were better than others and he would make an effort to go to the office, but only to turn around and come back home. Stefanie suggested that he go to the retreat in the Swiss mountains for the cleaner air, but Johann refused and took to his bed instead. Stefanie called for the brightest and smartest doctors from the university to come to the house to care for him. Johann's bedroom became a hospital room. The treatments, they had the feeling, were started too late. As his cough worsened and chest pains developed, doctors were at a loss as to what to do for him. Attendants were hired for 24-hour shifts. Stefanie tried to assist but all she seemed to do was grieve. Sharon was devastated as Johann's body became vulnerable and frail. Johann fell into a comatose state. Stefanie would not leave his side. She was told that there was not a lot more that could be done for him. Her beloved died on May 21, at the age of 39 of lung cancer.

May 24, 1927 Tuesday
Today is the saddest day of my life. We buried my beloved angel. I think I cannot live without Johann. He has been my rock. I can't even write tonight. I just want to die. The boys are so sad too. Karl gave a beautiful eulogy at the funeral. He loved his father and Johann loved him. August is still young and the loss has not hit him yet. Mother looked terrible today. She is sleeping in the room next to me now, but I would love to cry on her shoulder. Maybe she is lonely. Now, I will understand, too, what "lonely" is. I am going to try to get her to stay with me a while. She and Sharon are still at it and she probably will want to go home in the next day or two. I think I am going to die tonight anyway. My heart wants to crawl out of my body and hide.

Stefanie's mother came from Linz for the funeral. Her younger brother had been killed in WWI leaving Cora to come alone. Stefanie was shocked to see how pale she looked. Was it sadness she felt for her daughter's loss or was she, too, really ill? Cora had also lost considerable weight and had complained of headaches for the last few months. The tension that had escalated between Cora and Sharon through the years was still there and exacerbated Cora's condition. Stefanie could feel it. Each thought the other was too dominating and, even in the setting of a funeral, the iciness was evident.

June 10, 1927 Friday
I am on the way to Linz. I don't understand why all of this is happening to me. I don't have any strength left. Did I offend God so terribly that now I am being punished?

Stefanie's fears were well founded. Cora suffered a stroke on the train ride back to Linz, was hospitalized, and died one week later. It took two days for Stefanie to get word. Another blow was almost more than she could handle...two deaths, one on top of the other, of her loved ones. The stress of the visit may have pushed Cora over the edge, but Stefanie really did not understand the depth of the dislike between the two mothers. It was normal for a woman to join the family of her husband, but Cora could never come to grips with it. But it was over. Stefanie and her severe grief went to Linz where she had a small funeral for Cora with only the closest friends in attendance. She was buried next to her son.

July 18, 1927 Monday
Karl may take over the leadership of the company although Sharon doesn't trust that he can do a decent job. He is still quite young. I am too confused to think and I don't care, one way or another. My spirit is broken and I am not in a state of mind to voice an opinion. Karl may wreck what Johann has built up for all I know.

Johann's passing left a great void in the Schneider Fabrics management. Sharon, of course, did not believe anyone could replace her Johann, especially Karl, the wild one. She tried to get Stefan Feinstein, their long-time business manager, to find an executive to help him run the company. Stefan and his son Jules, however, both saw leadership in Karl emerging from the irresponsibility of his youth. Stefan agreed to stay at least five years to keep the company on course if Sharon would agree to Karl taking charge. She raised his salary accordingly.

August 30, 1927 Tuesday
Karl is doing OK with the company so far but he has just started. Sharon's face is still puckered but I think she realizes Karl is capable. He is putting on the dog though. I hope he doesn't go through all the money. I am still heart broken.

Johann had tried to bring Karl into the company culture for several years with only modest success. Karl, it seemed, was only interested in enterprises where he was the boss and Schneider Fabrics did not seem to be such a place in the foreseeable future. That all changed with Johann's untimely death. Karl, only 18, soberly but enthusiastically took over the company. With the help and guidance of Stefan Feinstein, Schneider Fabric, AG became Cologne Wool Goods, AG. Three thread-spinning factories, a contract sewing and manufacturing operation and several sheep farms were added to the holdings.

September 11, 1927 Sunday
My life is horrible. I am so lonely I think I will die. I wish I would die. I have no one to talk to and no one I want to talk to. All I do is talk to these stupid diaries. And, who cares?

After Johann and Cora died, life became an empty abyss for Stefanie. Johann had been a loving husband and friend and she had never really had to function in the Schneider family without him. Karl was married and had his own wife to take care of and August was concerned with his studies. He was still too young to understand the full impact the emptiness Johann's death had left in his mother. Besides dealing with her grief, she had the responsibility of caring for Sharon who was becoming increasingly bitter because her only child was gone. Stefanie went into mourning and only occasionally was seen out in public.

Andy was into the second book and had not found anything that he didn't more or less already know or that was damning in any way. All Stefanie seemed to talk about was her grief. She referred to

Johann as Karl's father over and over so...so far, so good. He decided to make himself a pot of coffee and continue reading.

12. STEFANIE'S DIARY 3: KARL SCHNEIDER I

May 21, 1928 Monday
Emma went into labor this morning. She was rushed to the hospital. Karl
was nervous. Emma gave birth to the prettiest baby boy, 3.8 kilos, and they
named him Karl Emanuel Schneider, II. He was born at 10:50 AM. I wish
Johann was alive to see him. I just got home and will visit her tomorrow again. I
will take Sharon with me if she is feeling well. Now, there are two Karls. I
wonder if his temperament will be the same as his father's.

Karl and Emma's first and only child, Karl II, was born on the
one-year anniversary of Johann's death. It was hard to say whether
Karl was more excited about his son's birth or the landing of 'Lucky
Lindy', Charles Lindbergh, in Paris that May 21. He had toyed with
the idea of funding an effort to win the Orteig Prize for the first solo
New York to Paris flight. Now this upstart Lindbergh had won it. It
wasn't the $25,000 US that attracted him, but the romance of the
effort and the publicity for the winner. The day ended in a
bittersweet mood, however. Since Emma's delivery was three weeks
earlier than expected, they were not completely prepared. Still, she
had gotten to the hospital on time and the birth itself was without
serious complications. Because there were some postnatal problems,
Emma was told that it would be dangerous for her to conceive again.
Karl was not happy with the news but satisfied and thankful that
Emma had presented him with a healthy son. Damn that Lindbergh
fellow!

June 3, 1928 Sunday
Ludwig and Sarah came by and brought a beautiful blue bath set for the
baby today. We have had quite a few callers. Sharon actually smiled today. This
baby is so adorable. He looks a lot like his father with that beautiful dark hair.
I hope it doesn't all fall out. Such memories…

Karl II's arrival brought joy into the Schneider household and did
wonders for Stefanie's attitude. Little Karl was a wonderful baby and
for the first time in almost a year, she was able to smile. Well wishing
visitors were invited and welcomed into the house and life was
beginning to return to normal.

December 28, 1928 Friday
Sharon fell today and we had to call the ambulance. We don't know what
bones are broken yet. She is in a lot of pain. I will stay the night with her.

Normal lasted until great grandmother Sharon fell and broke her
hip and was hospitalized for several weeks. The strain of a broken
bone and the on-going grief over her son's death proved to be too
taxing for her already fragile condition. Sharon Schneider died in
January of 1929. Her death was both sad and a relief for Stefanie as
Sharon had been a wonderful mother-in-law in so many ways, but a
very controlling woman in others, often leaving Stefanie to feel that
she had married Johann and his mother. Her generosity, however,
would never be forgotten.

January 16, 1929 Wednesday
We laid Sharon to rest. God bless her soul. She has gone to be with
Sebastian, my Johann and her baby girl. May she rest in peace. It has been a very
long and exhausting day. Sadness seems to follow me around.

Sharon Marguerite Schneider died with a heavy heart. She lost her
beloved husband and the son she almost worshiped. She was a good
and kind woman who opened her heart when her kindness was
needed. She was buried next to her husband, her son, and her infant
baby girl.

January 25,1929 Friday
I guess I am now head of the Schneider family. It is a responsibility that I take on lovingly and hope, with God's help, to perform wisely and with dignity. I will always try to do what is best for this great family.

Stefanie learned to trust Karl Sr.'s leadership and settled in as grandmother, the Schneider Matriarch and social organizer. She became active in charity organizations and volunteer work when she wasn't traveling to Venice or cooing over baby Karl. She, like her son, relished seeing her name in the society columns. While she had offers to be taken to dinner by some of the available and appropriately seasoned male aristocrats, finding another mate was just not on Stefanie's horizon.

February 1, 1929 Friday
I am discretely trying to find a girl for August. He is a wonderful son. How lucky can a mother get? He is shy, but he has Johann's coy grin. I almost cry when I see it on his face. And those beautiful teeth. I can't let him settle for just any of those silly girls he calls on. They are so shallow and stupid. And their families don't have nearly enough money for my August. He doesn't know it or even suspect it, but I am trying to find just the right one.

Stefanie made it her mission to connect with the 'right' families who had marriageable daughters for her beloved August. August was outgrowing his awkward teen years and becoming a handsome, well built young man. What Karl had in personality, August had in looks. His blond hair, his 6' 2" frame and wide shoulders made young women swoon, but Stefanie wanted assurance that he would marry well. She managed to vet each young woman who came around. She had to keep her matchmaking to herself as August would not like her meddling in his life. It was not an easy task but she knew she had to do it.

February 12, 1929 Tuesday
I think it might be working. I am so conniving and such a good keeper of secrets. If my brain or my heart were taken apart, I wonder if someone could find all my secrets, even my very darkest secrets.

August had struck up a lively conversation with a pretty Miss Karen von Bismarck at Karl and Emma's wedding but did not ask her out. He liked her right away, but had too many irons in the fire following his father's death to do much socializing. He also had his mother to contend with. Karen took the initiative, however, and sent a hand delivered request to August asking if he could be her escort for the formal debut which she would be making May 18th, a Saturday evening. She hoped he would accept. She would send him all the particulars if he would say "yes." August accepted, Stefanie was pleased, in fact, more than pleased, the debut was extraordinary and in November of 1929, Karen became Mrs. August Schneider.

Stefanie adored her new daughter-in-law and saw a lot of herself in Karen. The two became close and Karen was very much the daughter she didn't have. Strangers even thought she was Stefanie's daughter because of a very close resemblance. Karen confided in Stefanie often and there were times, Stefanie almost confided in Karen, but she and only she, knew that her deepest secret would have to remain her secret only.

February 12, 1929 Tuesday
My big Karl is doing a good job with the company and everyone seems pleased with him. He acts like a big shot though and August resents him a little. He needs to back way down. He spends too much money on himself. Self-control is one thing I have not been able to teach him.

Much to their surprise, Karl proved to be competent enough as the head of Cologne Wool Goods AG. He was a savvy young businessman and quite capable of wheeling and dealing. Stefanie and August worried, however, about his big ego. He made certain everyone knew that Karl Emanuel Bergman Schneider was now the head of Cologne Wool Goods. His goal was to make the company and himself famous. He somehow managed to always play the role. He knew he had the looks and the flair. He never allowed himself to be seen without fine English clothing and fine Italian shoes. He ordered shirts and suits by the dozens from London. While Paris was the fashion center for women, London was it for men. Karl liked the idea of a London label under his lapel.

Andy stopped to make another pot of coffee. His heart was pounding thinking about what secrets could Stefanie have been hiding? He waited until the coffee was brewed before he read anymore. He needed a moment to digest the thing about "secrets"...

With three books down, he wondered if he would find anything more revealing. He had to push himself to stay awake long enough to finish. Woman talk is so trite sometimes...

13. STEFANIE'S DIARY 4: AUGUST SCHNEIDER

Friday 14, 1929 Thursday
Today is Valentine's Day and I miss my Johann. The boys and Emma did bring me chocolates. Karl has surprised Emma with a trip he is arranging to America. Karen bought me a lovely brooch pinned to a silk red heart, so lovely. I bought chocolates for everyone and a toy boat for baby.

Karl planned a trip to America as a present to Emma celebrating the birth of Karl II. It was to be the most memorable trip he could arrange. The Graf Zeppelin had made its first flight from Friedrichshafen to New Jersey in October 1928. It and its sister airships sporadically made the crossing whenever there were enough passengers to pay the premium fare. Karl signed up for a crossing in December. And, without consulting anyone, he ordered a Duesenberg roadster to be picked up in New York. He never even mentioned it to Emma.

December 3, 1930 Wednesday
Karl and Emma left for America. It will be quiet here for two weeks except for Baby Karl's screaming once he realizes they are gone. I will entertain him as much as I can but he can be a real monster just like his father was. I guess it comes naturally. August and Karen announced that they are expecting a baby. We certainly have room for more little ones.

Karl and Emma were astounded that the flight was different from anything they had ever experienced. It was much quieter than the airplanes of the day and the food was superb…and the views! When they landed in Lakehurst, New Jersey, a limo was waiting to take them to the Waldorf Astoria Hotel in Manhattan, New York. Emma could not believe the next day when the Duesenberg arrived for them at the Waldorf. She was getting used to the excitement of Karl's planning. All of the rich and famous from Clark Gable to the Duke of Windsor would soon drive Duesenbergs but Karl was proudly ahead of the curve.

The Duesenberg representative spent a few days instructing Karl on the care and feeding of the machine and some of the new technologies in its manufacture. On Friday evening, Karl took Emma to *Die ägyptische Helena* at the Metropolitan Opera. Emma knew that Richard Strauss had written the part of Helen of Troy for Maria Jaritza who was singing that night. At the debut of the opera in Dresden, the impresario had refused to pay her rate. Not that Elisabeth Resberg did a poor job at the premier, but Karl wanted his wife to see the prima donna Strauss had in mind

The shopping in New York was incredible. Emma found sports outfits that were not available in Germany. Toy trains, toy blocks, toy bears and toy horses were bought for baby Karl. Boxes upon boxes were delivered to the Waldorf awaiting the cargo truck to take them to the ship for transport back to Germany.

The German luxury liner Bremen had just set the speed record for transatlantic crossings and Karl booked passage on it for their return to Berlin. The trip back with the Dusey would take less than a week. Life for the Karl Schneiders was exciting.

December 20, 1930 Saturday
Karl and Emma just got back from America. There are so many toys under the tree I'll bet they bought out FAO Schwartz. Karl doesn't know when to stop the extravagance. This will not sit well with August and he will bitch for weeks. Something funny happened while they were gone… Baby Karl has given himself a new name and that is 'Manny'. He can be a real stinker. He gets into everything. He put my lipstick all over his face today. What a mess.

Amidst the activity, everyone noticed that Little Karl II was becoming a handful. Perhaps he wasn't coping well with his parents on the go so much of the time. He was an extremely smart child, saying his first words at the age of 10 months old. By the time he was one and a half, he knew every family member's name and could count to 20. He was a full time job for the two nannies who chased after him as the walls of his nursery became marred with crayons and drawing pencils. When he was called down for bad behavior, he would be referred to as Karl Emanuel. When asked what his name was, he would respond with "Manny." From then on, the family called him Manny.

December 25, 1930 Thursday Christmas Day
I miss Johann. He would have loved seeing Manny play with all the toys. 'Spoiled' he would have called it. Today was pleasant enough. Mary and others came calling. Ludwig stopped by as he is lonely since his wife Sarah passed. He asked me if I would have lunch with him sometime. I am not interested in him, not even a little. I think I have had enough men in my life. I have two lovely sons. What more do I need?

January 9, 1931 Friday
Karl is getting big ideas about the company. He wants to expand and everyone is afraid he may make some very bad decisions. He acts like he can tell everyone what to do and when. He gets angry when anyone crosses him. He frightens me sometime.

Karl became convinced that something even bigger than Cologne Wool Goods and more prestigious than the wool business should be contemplated. A lasting place in history for the Schneiders was his new goal. He had the money and searched for opportunities with more romance than the rag trade. Airplanes were starting to be big business when the depression hit in 1929. Some of the companies were highly leveraged and when money dried up they could not survive. Curtis-Wright picked up Travel Air in Kansas City for a song. Travel Air had been formed a few years earlier by Clyde Cessna, Walter Beech, and Lloyd Stearman. There was a lot of talent there and these guys deserved success but they didn't get it in 1929.

Anthony Fokker was in America producing a wooden frame Tri-Motor for the passenger airline market as Ford started production on their aluminum version but most of the smaller companies couldn't handle the cash flow and folded. Karl was fixated on using the success of the wool company as a springboard into aircraft production. His original idea was to start with smaller private aircraft that could be developed quicker and for less money. He would then move into the smaller passenger transports. Determined to follow through with his plan, he looked around for a company to purchase and use as a base.

March 14, 1931 Saturday
Karl wants to purchase a large piece of land to build on for the house and offices, a 'compound' he says. I don't know if that is a good idea. He is looking at a site right here in Berlin. He is going crazy with spending and he and August are at odds. I can feel the tension and I don't like it.

Karl read about a property in the Spandau section of Berlin that had been one of several barracks there during the War that was now for sale. Without much ado, he acquired it to become the Schneider Compound. Aside from the barracks buildings themselves, it had a few medieval out buildings, access to the river, and enough roadway to really open up the Duesenberg. A gatehouse just inside the property had a nice garage that he would use as the home for the Duesy. It would be safer than storage near the mansion on Savignyplatz.

August 10, 1931 Monday
Karen went into labor last night and another boy came into the Schneider family named Johann Sebastian after my beloved Johann. August is so happy. He is smiling from ear to ear. The baby is the cutest little red wrinkly thing I ever saw. He is a tiny baby and so adorable. I am very happy they named him after his grandfather. Johann would have been proud.

Johann Schneider was an extremely good-natured baby. The two nannies on the Schneider staff had their work cut out for them each day running from the new baby to Manny and trying to keep some order in the nursery. Although Karen loved being a mother, she did not mind the nannies doing most of the caring for young Johann. She and her brother had been raised by a series of nannies throughout their childhood and they found them less demanding and more fun than their own parents. She felt no remorse for not seeing her parents more as it also seemed to insulate her feelings about death when her father passed.

November 2, 1931 Monday
Karl is unmovable about purchasing an aircraft company. August and the board think it is too far-fetched and so do I. I can't say anything because I don't "understand business." I have to keep my mouth shut. Emma thinks Karl can do no wrong. She is totally crazy about him.

After several false starts in finding a company suitable for Cologne Wool Goods to purchase, Karl interviewed a prospective inventor/engineer who had a struggling organization and agreed to take a flight as part of his evaluation of the operation. He had heard about this guy but needed to find out what he had to offer. As they were taxiing down the field, Karl remarked that the motor did not sound as smooth as he thought it should. Before much else was said, they were airborne. The flight only lasted two minutes and got to about 800 feet. There were no survivors. Emma was devastated. Karl II was only three years old.

November 18, 1931 Wednesday
My Karl is dead. Dear God, dear God, dear God. I can't take anymore. I cannot continue to give up my loved ones. The family is trying to support me but this is more than I can bear. I knew Karl's life would end some tragic way. He was just too wild. Did he feel he was immortal? I tried, in so many ways, to tell him but he wouldn't listen. May he rest in peace. I'm devastated.

Karl Schneider Sr.'s death broke Stefanie's heart. She could not understand why he was so reckless and didn't value life more than he did. He left a child who would always wonder about his father. Stefanie knew the difficulty that lay ahead for Emma. The loss of Karl so soon after Johann's death and at such a young age… She would ask herself just how many more deaths she had to endure in her lifetime. She considered herself a strong woman to deal with so much tragedy. Stefanie developed an unusual attachment to little Manny after the death of Karl Sr. Family members thought she was trying to recapture Karl, but then, they figured, it was her way of dealing with grief.

December1, 1931 Tuesday
August has taken over the lead at the company. He has a great business head and everyone likes him. I know he will do well. I miss Karl so much. My heart is

*heavy laden and I keep paying for my sins over and over. Does one spend a
lifetime paying for even a single sin?*

August Schneider took over Cologne Wool Goods on the death
of his older half-brother in 1931. His education and qualifications
were impressive for the post. While he had not planned to run the
whole show, he certainly prepared himself for the job and the
company did even better without Karl's excesses. Expansion plans
into areas where they had no experience were terminated. His
guidance avoided the drastic woes resulting from the financial world
meltdown of 1929. Stefanie was always proud of them both, but, if
truth be told, August was her favorite. The only comfort she took
was in her grandsons and in the success of August.

January 20, 1932 Wednesday
*Emma is so depressed. She can't stop crying. I understand her sadness more
than anyone. She feels like an outsider and I know that lost feeling. I wish I could
do something for her. Nothing can soothe the wound of losing your dearest. No
one can fill that void. It is a deep chasm of pain and bleakness. How many times
have I....*

The loss of Karl was even more than the loss of a loved one for
Emma. She suddenly was adrift in the Schneider family without a role
and it did not help that she was Scottish and her family were all still
over there. Her exciting trips were no more and at parties and social
gatherings she was "Karl's widow," a poor soul to be pitied. Stefanie
was the Matriarch and August and Karen ran the show. Even Manny
seemed to be taken over by Stefanie in an effort to replace the void
left by the loss of Karl and Johann. Emma really did not "need"
anything material and was not "needed" by anyone. She knew that
she had to make a change in order to survive.

Her family had financial interests in many fields in Scotland so
she asked August about the possibility of importing wool or wool
products to add to the lines offered by Cologne Wool Goods. He
was impressed by her initiative and together they decided to start
with raw wool. She wrote to her uncle for help in setting up a
brokerage for wool in the Aberdeen–Edinburgh area. He replied that
he would have it running by the time she crossed the channel. It took
a little longer than that.

June 20, 1932 Monday
Today is another awful day. Emma left with my little Manny for Scotland. I don't know if I can bear not having him around. I understand Emma's situation. Life is a constant disappointment.

When Stefanie heard that Karl's family was leaving she was upset, but pretty sure that she could see them often. She still had Karen and Johann. Emma and Manny moved to Aberdeen in June of 1932.

July 1932
We received word from Emma today. They arrived in Scotland and she had much to do getting Manny in school and herself to work. She already missed us all but would keep in touch. She said my boy was doing fine.

The Watts-Moore estate in Aberdeen was not as opulent as the Berlin mansion but it was large enough for the new guests. Emma's mother, Elizabeth, welcomed her daughter and grandson warmly and tenderly, but without much fanfare. She was not quite sure how Emma would take to the role of a single working parent and she wasn't ready to present her again to society.

Emma hit the ground running, however. She found a school that would teach Manny the King's English without the Scottish brogue. She found office space and arranged for furniture and letterheads and a sign. Her uncle had most of the incorporation of the wool brokerage in place and she would be able to handle transactions in a few weeks. She found that an old school chum, Ian McKeon, was in the wool business already and had sources but not many customers. Ian was struggling to succeed but the depression was not quite ended. Since Emma had a really big customer but no sources, they decided to form a partnership. Ian's wife was pregnant and they had a son about Manny's age. Molly was jealous of Emma, the rich widow, at first, but soon came to accept her as a friend and her husband's business partner. She didn't realize that Ian could never live up to the excitement of Karl anyway.

With their business on fairly solid ground Ian and Molly could finally relax with enough income to feel secure.

November, 1932
Emma wrote again and said Manny was a little hellion. He was so lovable but tried everyone's patience. I guess they just don't love him as much as I do. Or maybe, he is just a chip off the old block...

Elizabeth wanted to take care of Manny but it soon became obvious that he was a little too much for grandma. The school was complaining that Manny wanted to be in charge of every activity even at the tender age of six. A nanny with a proper London accent was hired. The nanny also was just under six feet tall and weighed in at 80 kilos. The civilization of Manny was accomplished without torture or cruel restraints but these were often mentioned in the discourse.

The one unstoppable habit that young Manny had was the drawing. Manny drew on his toys, his furniture, the walls, his books. Anything that would accept crayon or chalk became decorated. The only way to confine the artwork was to designate things or areas as "not here or you will loose the crayons (chalk)." That seemed to save the rest of the home. And, Manny never got along with Ian's boy. In fact, Manny seldom seemed to like any of his peers.

December 1, 1932 Thursday
Karen and I are in Venice offseason. Getting away is doing me some good. I forget myself. Is that good? I don't know. Karen loves Italy and loves shopping. Karen loves everything as far as I can tell. She has a bee up her butt to meet Mariano. She is fascinated with his collection. This girl is so kind to me and I do adore her. August and I did well... Karen told me she was pregnant again. I hope this traveling will not hurt her. She seems to feel good. The weather is gray most days and the water looks threatening but this is Venice. After so many years, it is still here.

Karen loved August and she loved her child but she liked her freedom too. She also felt a closeness and responsibility to Stefanie and wanted to be the one Stefanie could rely on through these hard times. August became occupied with running Cologne Wool Goods. Karen thought traveling might help Stefanie take her mind away from her sadness so Karen asked Stefanie to go with her to Venice. August had not yet taken her there and he certainly didn't have time now. Karen, too, loved everything Italian and she knew they would have fun shopping and sightseeing and it would be something for Stefanie to do besides mope. Stefanie was fascinated that Karen knew so much about early Italian furniture and art objects. Although she loved anything Italian too, she learned from Karen. Karen's father had been a big collector and would spend time, what little he had of it, explaining to his children how to recognize the 'good' stuff. He was a collector of fifteenth and sixteenth-century Italian and Gothic furniture. Karen's mother still had the furniture collection and one day, it would belong to Karen and her brother.

The apartment in Venice had plenty of important furniture and objects that had been collected by the senior Schneiders, but it was fun adding new additions. Stefanie and Karen became fixtures in Venice and took pleasure visiting with the shopkeepers for the three weeks they were there. Their Italian improved and they liked being included in the gossip of the day. It was mainly "antique" gossip or shoptalk. Stefanie's thoughts would turn back to Johann and Karl, however, and she would become disenchanted with Venice and ready to go back home. Karen would honor her wishes and they would head back to Berlin.

Venice was hit hard in early 1932 by the Depression. Many of the banks went bankrupt but the very rich stayed rich. The Schneiders were able to keep the apartment and visits there were infrequent but purchases made during this time were good ones as the Venetians were hungry for money.

December 5, 1932 Monday
August is really brilliant. He is trying to branch out into new avenues with wool. I remember when I used to meet with clients to impress them with our new techniques. Those were the days.

As his confidence and leadership skills improved August realized that Cologne Wool Goods would have to change to stay competitive in the textile business. His technical education made the path to modernization pretty clear. The company needed a source of rayon and equipment to blend the new "miracle fabric" with traditional wool. He found that a small munitions factory that had been closed by the Treaty of Versailles was available just South of Cologne in Bonn. Much of the equipment was appropriate to be converted to the manufacture of rayon. Soon, the new Schneider factory was producing high quality rayon fiber that they called "Sebron" after Sebastian. August personally devised modifications to the spinning equipment to allow the introduction of the rayon fiber into the virgin wool thread and yarn. He hired chemists to develop dyes for the new fabric blends and processes to make creases and seams more durable, a problem with early wool blends. His designers and tailors were encouraged to design piece parts that would efficiently use the whole bolt of fabric. Methods of matching dye lots as well as tracking them and tying them to production dates were implemented. Unfortunately for Stefanie, this meant that August would spend most of his time at the Cologne estate. The Berlin mansion with the two women and two children and two nannies was stressful, to say the least.

December 16, 1932 Saturday
I feel so drained of my strength. Nothing seems to make me happy anymore. I don't feel well. I am not eating properly and cook tries, but I can't eat. August told me I have to eat. He gets pushy. I guess he is just concerned. I am really ill. My fever was raging last night. My fever is getting higher again today and I can't get out of bed except to go to the loo. I can't write anymore... I have to tell August the truth about Karl...that he was really his half-brother. This will be hard. I have to. I am so sick. I can't die without the truth...

Stefanie had dragged around for a month or so, not feeling like herself. She eventually came down with a terrible Influenza. She was extremely ill and almost certain she would die. She called August to her side, took his hand, and, with great reservation, she told him the truth of his brother's paternity. With what stamina she had, she tried to explain the tryst in Vienna with the sketches and poems, and the birth record at a church, St. Stephen's, she thought...it was foggy. She couldn't remember. Already Adolf Hitler was definitely a force to be reckoned with. Stefanie seemed to fade in and out. Her fever was extremely virulent.

August was dumbfounded. Hitler was well on his way to being Der Führer and absolutely nothing was known about his past. He was either from Austrian aristocracy or a beer fortune. His father was a lawyer or maybe the governor of an outer province. It was rumored that he caused his childhood acquaintances and contacts to be "eliminated." Was Stefanie in danger? She insisted that Hitler never knew of his "love child," but Stefanie's abrupt exit from Linz might have been a clue to him. Yet, could Hitler take vengeance even on his own flesh and blood? Who knew?

January 15, 1933 Sunday
I am feeling better but I have made the gravest mistake of my life. I told August. Now I may not be able to face him. Maybe he will think I was talking while in a delirium. Was it a delirium? It all runs together and now I am not even sure. My whole life may be a dream. I don't know.

Stefanie did not die but fully recovered. She pleaded with August to keep her secret. He said he would. She tried to pretend it might have been a dream because she was so ill, but August just looked at her. She and August were at least glad that Manny and Emma were situated in Scotland. No one would look for them there.

****

Andy was deflated. "Oh Christ, oh Christ, oh Christ, oh Christ!" That bitch really did sleep with Hitler. But she says it might have been a dream. "I need proof." He kept mumbling to himself. It was 2:30 am and he was pacing. Maybe the last book, she really will spill her guts. Maybe she was totally out to lunch and she was imagining all of this. Andy couldn't take any more coffee. He was a nervous wreck as it was. Perhaps a glass of milk…maybe a glass of chocolate milk. He wished Larissa were there to rub his neck.

14. STEFANIE'S DIARY 5: RUMBLINGS OF WAR

May 1, 1933 Monday
Everyone is so busy and the house is too quiet. August is gone most of the time, staying at the factory in Cologne. Karen reads a lot when she is not in Cologne. I am bored. I am invited to the Behrens' for a dinner party on the 20th. I need to go through my wardrobe and decide what to wear. She said it was early eveningwear. The flowers outside my bedroom remind me of Linz. Maybe it is only because I am feeling better that I would like to go out. I need a project. This house no longer fascinates me.

In May of 1933, Heinrich Himmler came to call on August Schneider. Himmler had spent the past six years building the Schutzstaffel or SS from a few hundred men to over fifty thousand.

The SS was, however, still a part of the Sturmabteilung, the main army known as the Storm Troopers or SA. Himmler was determined to make the SS his own independent force to balance the power of the SA. A major step in his plan was new uniforms. The SS would have new black outfits to differentiate them from the "brown shirts" of the SA. Could Cologne Wool Goods design and provide samples? Could they be trusted to do it in complete secrecy? "Of course," August agreed.

Hugo Boss, a small manufacturer of work garments in Southern Germany at that time had a designer named Walter Heck who would work on the design with August and provide liaison with Lt. Karl Diebitsch, Himmler's aide. Himmler would arrange everything.

Besides the contract at hand the men found that they had common interests in, among other things, harpsichords. The two became friends. No mention or even thought was given to the Vienna intrigue and little Karl's heritage.

July 2, 1933 Saturday
Karen gave birth to a baby girl last evening and she and August named her Heidi Marguerite. She looks exactly like August. She is the first girl to be born into the Schneiders for several generations. What fun it will be to buy pink for a change. I wish Johann could see this beautiful little girl.

Johann was glad to have a new sister. Since Manny had left, he needed someone to play with. Stefanie was not burdened with grandmotherly chores, however, unless she wanted them. Two nannies were continually kept on the Schneider payroll.

August 10, 1933 Thursday
I think I need to get away from this house. I am starting to hate it. It is going to be torn down eventually anyway. We might as well leave gracefully before we are pushed out.

Back in Berlin, Stefanie decided that the old Victorian mansion held too many bad memories for her and she needed a project. She had met the architect Walter Gropius several times at social functions. She had mentioned to him the barracks site and that eventually they would like to build something special there. Their mansion was one of only about eight which were still in Savignyplatz. Knesebeck Strasse was being consumed by apartment buildings for the new gentry. Stefanie was not quite ready to give up the luxury of a private home for the new life style of apartment living. The problem now was to convince her conservative son August to commit to starting the barracks project.

September 19, 1933 Tuesday
August seems so preoccupied and jumpy when I say anything to him. He says he is tired from going back and forth. I try to stay out of his way. Karen says he is edgy around her too. We can't figure him out. Maybe the news we hear on the radio depresses him.

The uniforms were designed and a few hundred manufactured and delivered. They were a huge success but when time for the major production came, August found that Cologne Wool Goods was underbid by another firm. Ever the salesman, he began to think about how could he use this friendship with Himmler to tip the scales back in his favor. Perhaps the "love child" story would be usable. He would have to be very careful to keep such a tale under his control or the SS might just "eliminate" the ones with knowledge of the truth. Six-year-old Karl II was still in Edinburgh and essentially unknown. He would probably be safe. August Schneider went home to Berlin with a plan.

Schneider and Himmler occasionally met for a drink at a bar near the Brandenburg Gate when they were both in Berlin. Himmler often spoke of Hitler like a buddy or partner. At a lull in the conversation this particular evening, August ventured, "So he never had another love like Stefanie, did he?" Himmler's eyes narrowed quickly and he looked around to see who might be able to hear their conversation. He recovered just as quickly. "Stefanie who?" he asked. August knew that he had touched a nerve. "The girl from Linz. He is supposed to have written her poetry. Not much like him now, do you think?" "Let's go outside," Himmler said.

They strolled into the park behind the Gate. "All information on Stefanie has been purged. Her mother died years ago and she disappeared." Himmler was cautiously probing.

August took a deep breath and plunged in. "Heinrich, it may be hard for you to believe but that girl from Linz named Stefanie is my very own mother. I only learned the story recently because she is very ill and not expected to survive the month. She told me to assuage her guilt before she dies." It did not seem to be appropriate to reveal the truths that August had known the story for some time and that Stefanie was in remarkably good health for her age.

"But she was Jewish," Himmler said.

"No, Catholic for several generations."

"And you are sure? Der Führer is paranoid about the story of him and a Jewess."

"There is more."

"What could top this?" Himmler was noticeably turning pale.

"I had a half brother who was Hitler's son. He died in 1931."

They sat down on a bench in the park for a few minutes.

Himmler chose his words carefully. "Is there any proof?"

August chose his words carefully as well. "Yes. If this is something you could use perhaps our conversation could also cover the SS uniform production."

Several more minutes passed.

"We must be very careful in this matter, August. The Nazi Party power structure is becoming ruthless at every level. I have enemies and I am also trying to secure a place at Hitler's side in the coming World Order. I may even have to destroy some competitors in this endeavor. The risks are high but the rewards are infinite. I cannot even think of a situation where I would try to pressure Hitler by exposing the past that he so completely has hidden but the ability, no, the possibility of having this kind of trump card is fascinating. I will be in touch."

Heinrich Himmler vanished into the Autumn Berlin night. August Schneider returned to Cologne the next Monday.

A week later a steamer trunk arrived at Cologne Wool Goods, addressed to August Schneider with the note "For Room 209." Now, Room 209 was the secure area where the design and prototype production of the black SS uniforms was accomplished in secrecy. Schneider had the trunk taken to the area that was unoccupied at this time. He went in, closed the door, and opened the trunk.

The trunk opened into a compact optical and photographic station that could create microdots and view them. The note from Himmler read:

Herr Schneider,

Only the SS has this equipment so we can continue the conversation started last week privately, as between friends. Look above the "i" in your name.

HH

PS. Please only use the enclosed linen stationary and supplied ink. The product is expressly designed to blend with this combination.

So the correspondence started.

The next day, Schneider got the first production order for sixty-five thousand uniforms.

He immediately telegraphed Emma in Aberdeen and asked her to send all the wool that she could find.

Emma pressed Ian to find people to help him buy, but he was convinced that he could find all the wool they needed. Why pay someone to do what you can do yourself? Then they would need a larger office...the utility bills would increase and what if business might not always be this good?

Emma was disturbed as the increased workload took its toll on Ian. He was slender to begin with and still lost weight. Molly would call the office asking what day he would be home not what hour. After two months, Emma rented the adjoining office, furnished it and ran an ad for sales help. When Ian got back from a two-week buying trip in September, she confronted him and he finally relented. One of the new-hires was experienced enough to be sent directly to Perth and Glasgow. Ian would take a week off then take the other new-hire on his next buying trip to meet the sources up near Inverness. Ian made as much money in four months as he had in his whole previous lifetime. He would just have to learn that you sometimes can make even more money by spending a little. Emma had her hands full arranging for shipping and tariffs.

When Stefanie heard of the order back in Berlin she knew that she could finally abandon the old mansion and start to bring the Schneider clan into the modern era. She called Walter Gropius and started the process.

October 30, 1933 Monday
I have spoken with Walter Gropius today. I told him about the property and our plans. We scheduled a meeting for Nov. 6th at Amadeus, 11:00 AM.

Walter Gropius was one of the leading architects and designers around Berlin after the war. Before going off on his own, Gropius worked for Peter Behrens who also employed Mies van de Rohe and Le Corbusier at the time. He left the Behrens firm in 1910 to form a partnership with fellow architect Adolf Meyer in Berlin. He was called to war, almost killed, but returned to Berlin. He gained a fine reputation for the advancement of Modernism and, after the resignation of Henry van de Velde, a Belgian, Gropius was offered the position of Master of the Grand-Ducal Saxon School of Arts and Crafts in Weimar forming the Bauhaus school. Stefanie had raised money for the academy. Gropius continued to do work for the private sector and agreed to do the plans for the new Schneider Compound, which would be in Spandau, on the property that Karl Sr. had purchased.

November 6, 1933 Monday
Today I met with Walter. He seems quite nice and receptive to doing our
project. I like his attitude and his willingness to work with us. I must speak with
August about giving him a retainer to start. The lunch was lovely and he treated.

Stefanie's meeting with Gropius was an exciting one and she told him that she and the family wanted something that was on the cutting edge of new design, somewhat controversial and yet classical and totally comfortable. Money seemed to be no object for the Schneiders as long as they got what they wanted. Gropius was confused by the request of "modern" but "classical." He read between the lines and knew that Stefanie wanted something unique and he would make sure that he would be the one to design it for her. He also knew that clients, more often than not, didn't know what they wanted until they saw it.

There were definite requests, however. The Compound needed to house the offices at one end of the property and Stefanie saw the main house in the center. There would need to be a wing for August and Karen and the children as well as accommodations for Karl Jr. and Emma when they came to stay. She, herself, needed a private suite with ample dressing rooms for her growing collection of clothes. She wanted another guesthouse for visiting clients and friends, tennis courts, a large pool and pool house and beautiful landscaping. The Servants' Quarters and Coach House were to be on the bluff overlooking the river. One of the medieval buildings was to be restored to house some of the Old Masters and furniture from the mansion. The rest of the important furnishings were to be sent to England for auction after Emma's family took what they wanted. The project was a large one but one that was exciting to Gropius as well.

The Compound Project took two and a half years to complete and gave Stefanie a new reason for living. The office front was exquisite with its winding staircase enclosed in a wall of glass with two additional glass towers. The old entrance to the property was closed and a new road cut to the main living structures of the Compound. The new iron gate and gateposts were followed by a winding drive, tree lined, perfectly planted and dotted with modern bronze and stone sculptures. The asymmetrical plan of the main house contradicted the classical style Stefanie requested but was so superb that she asked that Gropius design some of the furnishings for the house itself. She worked hand in hand with him to appoint the house with the finest and most appropriate furnishings. She became interested in the paintings of Klee and Kandinsky who were on the faculty of the Bauhaus academy. She found herself loving the work of the Modernists. Her traditional style would be saved for Venice and Cologne. She secretly wanted to feed the press something interesting and controversial to write about anyway. Ultimately, she found Klee's early pencil studies exhilarating and the colors of Josef Albers unique and playful. She made a decision that the Compound would be a place to exhibit works of famous artists and a vehicle for upcoming artists to get a start. Art and fashion shows became a regular feature of the Schneider Compound.

****

Andy skimmed over the next two years of entries, which were entirely about the Compound.

15. STEFANIE'S DIARY 6: WWII

April 1935

What has come over Adolf? He is scaring me to death. He doesn't know how much he has had to do with my life. He never reappeared and Glory be to God that he didn't. He has turned out to be a totally insane and depraved madman. I will never, ever let him know about Karl...not ever! I think August has all but disowned me. And Manny must never know. Dear God, please don't ever let Manny know.

Stefanie watched closely the Hitler phenomenon in Germany. As it became more ruthless, she became more and more troubled. When his Nazi party took power in 1933 and he became Chancellor the whole country was in a kind of euphoria that the pain of the Versailles reparations and the worldwide depression seemed to be ended. Now, however, things were going too far. One of Hitler's first acts was to eliminate Jews from all government jobs. A year later, government purchases from Jewish businesses were restricted. In 1935, the Nuremberg Law was enacted making Jews "subjects" instead of "citizens." Intermarriage with "citizens" was outlawed and many professions restricted to "citizens."

Although it was not official, Himmler protected Cologne Wool Goods from these and later War measures. The Feinstein family was not persecuted and the rayon output not confiscated. August was occupied with the fast growth of the company and chose to ignore the special treatment given to his operation but Stefanie could not ignore the course that Adolf seemed to be taking. What had caused him to become so tyrannical? Who was this total lunatic? Certainly not anyone she would knowingly have associated with... She was outraged by her sense of compassion and care. And it would get worse.

December 1936
So, Manny has his first crush. At least, she is getting him to learn. I hope he has settled down. I didn't know he liked older women. August said that Emma and Manny are both doing OK. Thank goodness. I miss them so much.

For the first few years of his school life, Karl Emanuel had little use for classmates or teachers but then came Miss Cox. Terry Cox was a 24-year-old red-headed knockout that taught Social Studies. She was passionate about freedom and democracy, but she was also passionate about music and art, physical fitness, and fun in general. Twelve-year-old Karl Emanuel was smitten.

Miss Cox noticed Manny's sketching and made him the "class illustrator." She had him draw Victoria and Napoleon and Chamberlain and Churchill and Hitler and Roosevelt. As he was sucked in to the subject, he learned history and current events. He had been born with an interest in and a talent for drawing but he had never known how fascinating power was in the hands of the world's leaders. Even Miss Cox did not see the pattern. It seemed that every single leader had at least one or two flaws that could cause the whole system to collapse. Of course, some of them had really major flaws. Manny became interested in the world situation.

At the end of the semester when Miss Cox announced her betrothal, Manny was crushed, but the start of war changed his focus.

July 1938
Adolf has taken total leave of his senses. He is either on dope or has gone completely nuts. I thought he was strange but not this kind of strange. I hate him! I am tired of crying. He is killing people, innocent people. If only I could stop him, I would. Maybe seeing him again would stop him. No, I am too scared. I wouldn't care if he killed me, but Manny? He may not even remember me and I would put my whole family in danger. He may be too far gone. Insane men like him usually can't be stopped. I would ruin this family if they knew what I am thinking. All I feel now is humiliation. How could I have been so naive and so stupid? Youth sometimes yields a lifetime of regret.

In 1938, Jews of Polish citizenship were banished and dumped at the Polish border where refugee camps were set up but conditions were inhumane. Soon "Slavs" were grouped with Jews, cripples, homosexuals, and gypsies to be eliminated. Western Poland was occupied in 1939. The first death camps of Auschwitz and Treblinka were set up in occupied Poland but the task was just too great. Buchenwald and Dachau were built in Germany. The list of "undesirables" grew. It now included Soviet POW's, Jehovah's Witnesses and political dissidents and others at Hitler's whim.

Propaganda released to the world denied it but the inner circle of German society heard horror stories of the "Final Solution." August seldom had contact with Himmler. August thought of him as "nice enough for a Godless, power-hungry psychopath," but on those rare occasions where they met, Himmler was obviously bearing a heavy burden by supporting all of Hitler's insanity. At one meeting, Himmler just sobbed and eventually left without saying a word. In private, Hitler's chief executioner was not completely comfortable with his work.

The Schneider Compound was fairly far from any strategic targets in Berlin, including the psychological target of Mitte where most of the museums and theaters were. In November 1943, the Imperial Guard barracks, only four kilometers away, was severely damaged and on that night a single bomb exploded a dozen meters from the Compound office building. Many windows were broken but there were no employees inside at the time. No one was hurt. The war had not come that close to the Compound until then and it was terrifying.

Manny was now attending Aberdeen Middle School, one of the oldest and best prep schools in Britain, founded in 1257. He spent his free hours in their formidable library studying history and governments. He read everything he could find about the internal politics of Germany and the Axis and Britain and the Allies. London and Birmingham and Manchester were being destroyed. Berlin and Frankfurt and Dresden were being destroyed. And the insanity continued.

When the land of your birth attacks the land where you live, it is confusing. The effort to save France from Hitler collapsed at Dunkirk in May 1940. The bombing of Britain started shortly after in August. Aberdeen, in the far North of Scotland, saw almost no action in the War but it was an excellent place from which to observe. London and Glasgow were being pummeled and soon so were most of the major cities in England. Shipping was next to impossible due to the U-boats and mines from Germany. Germany was the villain. How did Germany think it could take over the world? How did Italy agree? How did they both think they could control Japan? Even to a teenager, it was madness.

Manny finished high school and continued his education at Edinburgh University still trying to figure out how it all happened.

In June 1944, the Allies had amassed almost a million men in England, about a fourth of them fighting soldiers, and sent them to the beaches at Normandy to start liberating France. More than ten thousand were killed or wounded that Tuesday. The Germans responded by launching the terrifying V-1 unmanned rocket bombs, about a hundred a day. They randomly rained down on London and its surrounds causing another 25,000 civilian casualties. As the Allies disabled the launch areas for the V-1's in France, the V-2's from more remote launch pads started. They were supersonic and had guidance. They struck essentially without warning.

From 1939 to 1944 contact with Karl and Emma in Britain was sparse because of the War. Mail exchanges were almost useless as they took up to a year to get through if they even got through at all. Stefanie craved to get news from her grandson. Of course, she feared for his safety during the bombings of the Battle of Britain. She wanted so terribly to see him and loved him far too much for him to grow up without knowing her. Unfortunately, the politics of the time was an insurmountable barrier.

May 25, 1944
My little Manny should be finishing his degree about now. I don't know since I hardly hear from them. I have missed that boy so much. He will never know just how much. Emma has been doing a good job, August said. She includes a letter once in a while, but it has been awful.

As the war was coming to a close, Manny was completing his studies at the University of Edinburgh and was graduated in 1944 with a degree in Political Science and a minor in Art. As a present, Emma promised him a trip to Stockholm to celebrate his finishing school and to get away from war ravaged Britain and the many evacuees who were coming to the surrounding cities to avoid the bombings in London. Sweden, which remained neutral throughout the war, was a safe place to visit. Emma had also received a special invitation to the grand opening of Berns French Dining Hall in Stockholm. It was making its debut in Berns Concert Hall. It was to be a grand affair featuring celebrity entertainment and foods from all over France prepared by its eight full time chefs. Emma accepted the invitation for her son and herself.

It was on this trip that Karl met Sonja Svensen, the reigning Miss Sweden. She was one of the guests of honor. Sonja was the most beautiful young woman Karl had ever seen. She far surpassed any of the girls he had dated in school or anywhere in Scotland or England. It must have been love at first sight because the electricity between the two of them was obvious and they vowed to keep in touch after Karl returned to Edinburgh. Emma felt Karl's infatuation and told him that the first moment she had laid eyes on his father, she felt the same way.

In April 1945, the war ended in Europe and the uncertainty of the post-war arrangements set in. The Americans appeared to be forgiving of the German population in general but the Soviet Union was out for blood. The Compound ended up in the British sector of partitioned Berlin that became part of West Berlin. It seemed it might fare well in the beginning but West Berlin ended up a thorn in the Soviet world and a status symbol for the West. Life in Berlin was becoming a duty more than anything like simply living. The Schneiders persevered and tried to make their existence more or less normal. They desperately wanted to put the trauma of war behind them.

May 5, 1945 Saturday

I cannot believe I just got word that Manny and Emma are coming home to stay. I have not been so happy in years. I will plan some kind of celebration. Thank you, God, for taking care of them. Let them get home safely. I have much to do.

When Stefanie received word that Karl and Emma were coming home, she was overjoyed. It had been a long time since she felt excitement and their homecoming would provide her with something positive to look forward to. Her "baby" would be back and the wing of the house that had been constructed for them and unoccupied for so long would now be opened and made ready for their arrival. The tennis courts that had not seen much activity since the Compound was built would be a welcoming sight for Emma. And Stefanie would, without question, have to introduce young Karl to Berlin society. Part of being the doting grandmother was to make sure he was accepted and quickly by all the important people.

May 8, 1945 Tuesday
I am overwhelmed. There is so much planning that has to be done. I almost need to dust my address book. Who can I invite? This must be a real blow out. It can't be anything less than fabulous. Music, champagne, caviar, flowers, good food, right people, photographers…we must have it all.

Berlin was in need of a party and this was the perfect time to have one. The war had left such recent scarring on everyone's psyche that a joyous distraction might be welcomed. Stefanie and her staff planned the guest list, the menu and the entertainment. She wanted this to be a "newspaper worthy" event, this time more sincerely than ever, as war stories were all that people had to read about for far too long a time. Wine from France and beer from Belgium and lamb from Alsace and fruit and vegetables that June brings in abundance were to be served. The Bosendorfer had to be tuned and a chamber orchestra contracted. The silver was polished and the chandeliers were cleaned, crystal by crystal. The grounds were manicured with not a single dead branch or wilted leaf in sight. Four trunks arrived on Monday with the clothes and other personal effects of Karl and Emma. They were moved to their wing of the house.

May 16, 1945 Wednesday
Karl and Emma arrived on Wednesday.

Stefanie frantically hurried from room to room, barking orders and hyperventilating. The staff could not understand Stefanie's erratic behavior and as the limo pulled up to the house, Stefanie adjusted her hair and looked around to make sure everything was perfect. She hesitated before opening the door, hoping that Karl would recognize her. They had left Berlin before the Compound was built and this was the first time they would see it and Manny had been just a baby. When the bell rang, Stefanie's heart pounded and as she opened the door, squeals and tears poured from all directions Karl and Stefanie grabbed each other and both just clung and cried. Stefanie then turned to Emma who was crying too and they embraced.

Karl was touched by her emotional outbreak and glad to see her looking so well. She was always lovely but he was surprised that age had not changed her much. Stefanie was surprised by his obviously English accent. Of course, he only had Emma to speak German to for all these many years. He was tall and much taller than his father. Karl was amazed as he peered around the vestibule of the house. The house was grand. "Is that Johann?" He flashed his wide smile as his cousins Johann and Heidi, who were all grown up, had come into the room. Heidi ran to greet them with laughter and hugs and kisses. They were genuinely happy to be together again. Standing beside Johann was a pretty girl that Karl did not remember. Stefanie held out her arm and said "Yes, of course. And this is Hannah Junkers, Johann's friend." As Johann walked up he and Karl shook hands and gave each other a manly embrace. Hannah, wanting to be a part of the greeting party, grabbed Karl and gave him an extended hug. The frown on Johann's face only lasted for a second and then vanished. It was just a warm welcome, he figured.

May 16, evening
Today was exhilarating. My loved ones are back. I wish that Hannah had not clung to Manny so long. That was not good right in front of everyone. I will never forget the look on Johann's face. I am so happy my Manny is back. He looks like Karl, only taller.

As the group settled in, drinks were served and conversations were mixed in German and English. Everyone had a story to tell with one story bigger than the other. Johann noticed that Karl was especially animated, using his hands to make his stories more lively. Political training must have taught him to do that. Stefanie interrupted and borrowed Karl and Emma long enough to take them up to their wing of the house and show them around. The dinner bell rang, everyone found the dining room, and dinner was served. The cooks had outdone themselves as the food was superb and August and Karen were brought up to date on the missed years apart.

Emma had matured into a real Schneider and was thrilled to be with the family. She was eager to visit but the long hours of travel were catching up with her and the absence of Karl Sr. sitting with the family made her sentimental. She apologized and asked to be excused. Manny remained lively until late into the night. Johann walked Hannah to one of the guest cottages and kissed her goodnight. She did not seem as warm to him as she usually was.

Hannah Junkers' great-grandfather, Hugo, founded Junkers Aircraft in 1919 but his pacifist leanings kept him in constant confrontation with the German government. He was placed under house arrest in 1933, on a trumped up charge of spying for opposing some of Hitler's policies. He died a year later. Under pressure from the Nazis his wife, Therese, sold his interests and patents to the Reich for twelve million Reichmark, only about a third of their value, but enough to maintain their lifestyle. Hannah's uncle, Klaus, was still in the courts trying to regain what he felt was stolen from the family but to little avail. Hannah never suffered from the travail and was bored by financial problems. She had never known hardships.

May 28, 1945 Monday
That Hannah Junkers is causing strife between the boys. She snuggles up to Johann and then cuddles with Karl. And Karl seems to enjoy it! The nerve of him. Hannah is Johann's girl. Has he no shame? August is not taking kindly to her or his behavior.

After Hannah met Karl, she became undecided as to whether Johann or Karl was the better choice for her. She was something of a flirt and unashamedly dated them both to Johann's dismay. August noticed the problem and, ever the planner, decided that the Sonja he had heard so much about would be a better wife for Karl and Hannah was the perfect wife for Johann. He set about facilitating the matchups. Stefanie, Emma, and Karen were not oblivious to what they saw, but bewildered by the situation.

August 18, 1945 Saturday
August is one smart cookie. He will not let Karl mess with his son. I guess I don't blame him. He has decided to hire "Miss Sweden" to represent the company and asked Manny to get her here as soon as possible. He is going to fix Karl's little red wago…or Hannah's.

Sonja Svensen, with her champagne blond hair and her incredibly long legs, was invited to become the poster girl for Cologne Wool Goods' new advertising campaign, "Warm Enough for Lappland." Sonja was from Malmö, Lappland, Sweden, nearly at the Arctic Circle. She was anxious to see Karl again and the Compound she had heard so much about, so she accepted the invitation. The flame that was ignited in Stockholm the previous year was rekindled just as August had planned.

****

Andy was about in the middle of Book 5 and wasn't sure he would find any more dirt. He had to finish. Geez, he was cross-eyed. He didn't know if his digestive system could take another cup of coffee. More than ever, he had to have his guns loaded. He was having tachycardia. He didn't know if it was from the revelation to August or the caffeine. A Valium would only put him to sleep. He had to finish.

****

May 10, 1946 Thursday
It is less than a month until Manny's wedding. I am exhausted. I don't feel well but I keep going. The doctor has prescribed some vitamins to build me up. I think I am just taking on too much responsibility.

Karl and Sonja were married in June of 1946. The large wedding and elegant, not to mention costly, reception took place at the Compound with 200 guests in attendance. The newspapers were there. Sonja's parents were there. And once again, Stefanie, the ultimate party planner, pulled off another fabulous affair. Johann asked Hannah to marry him during the midst of the celebration.

December 9, 1946
I am getting too old for such large functions. I'm going to Venice. I'm sure the apartment needs attention. I may ask Karen to go with me. Emma has a golf seminar she is attending and everyone has someplace to be. I will spend Christmas in Venice. Maybe Karl and Sonja could come later.

In December 1946, Sonja, the poster girl, was sent to Paris to represent Cologne Wool Goods at a trade show. This was her first assignment and Sonja was eager to be a part of the company. The trip also provided her an opportunity to see the first "bikini" bathing suit ever shown to the public in Paris the previous July. During the same month, Johann found it necessary to go to Dresden to rescue their new Angora processing mill from being "nationalized" by the new Soviet-style government set up in East Germany. Karl and Hannah found themselves alone in the house except for August and Karen in their wing and Stefanie who was busy packing for another trip to Venice. They figured that this might be their last chance before Hannah and Johann were married to see what, if anything, they had missed. It was quick and passionate and afterwards, neither felt guilty, but both agreed that the family and fortune depended on following the path they had both committed to. They never noticed August in the hall. He had come to this wing to ask a question of Karl but discovered the lovemaking. Worries about Karl's heritage came down on him as he went back to his study. He never mentioned the incident to anyone, but Karl's betrayal of Johann was a bitter pill.

January 20, 1947
Another wedding. And I am so tired. At least, this one was small. It was a pretty wedding and I am glad we had it catered. Hannah and Johann seem happy enough. They received a lot of beautiful things and they didn't even have a shower. Being a Schneider seems to guarantee presents.

Johann and Hannah were hurriedly married in January before Lent started. Hannah thought she was pregnant but surely by Johann and if they waited until after Easter she would probably be showing. Their wedding was a lovely but rushed affair, and included only the immediate Junkers and Schneider families and a few intimate friends. It was still news in all the Berlin papers.

September 10, 1947
Another boy. I am surrounded by boys. This little guy is a love. He is so perfect. I haven't held him yet but there is lots of time. He certainly came quickly. I am suspecting that some messing around happened before the wedding. Who am I to talk? They named him August after his grandfather.

Little Augie was born in September. He had a small crescent-shaped birthmark on his right shoulder. God in Heaven, August had seen that mark before. Emma, Karl's mother, noticed the mark too. No one said a thing. In later years, Emma felt that it was not so bad that Karl and Sonja had no children. She got to dote a little on Augie. Strange it was that Manny did not have the mark that Karl, Sr. had.

****

Andy was coming to the end of the book. He knew the rest. He would read it anyway. The phone rang. "Good grief," it was 4:00 in the morning and he was beat. He told Anna not to let any calls through so someone must have the wrong number. He let the machine pick it up. It was Larissa. He grabbed the receiver and said, "Hello, babe." She couldn't sleep and she missed him. She would be in Cologne tomorrow morning if he would want to see her. He told her he looked like death as he was attending to some important business but to come straight to the apartment. He really needed her more than ever.

Andy tried to read faster but his eyes were getting blurry. Coffee, it must be. He found a piece of stale chocolate brownie in a baggy in the back of the fridge. It was from last week but it was sugar and he needed something.

16. STEFANIE'S DIARY 7: OCCUPATION

January, 1948
Manny and Sonja are moving to the USA for two years. Karl is unhappy
with the way things are here. He is wishing he could fix them. It will be a long
two years while they are gone. My kids are constantly moving in and out of my
life. I guess that is the life of a mother. Maybe he will come back with new
insights. He always seems disgruntled.

As bickering over how to govern conquered Germany continued
between America, France, England, and Russia seemingly without
end, Karl lost patience with life in Berlin. He decided to take some
post-graduate work. Michigan State University had an advanced
degree program in Political Science that seemed appropriate. It was
time to see America anyway. Karl and Sonja moved to the US for the
two years of 1948 and 1949. Between his studies, America was their
playground. They took excursions from Ann Arbor to New York
City, Hollywood, New Orleans, Washington D.C., and San Francisco
with brief visits to Chicago, Dallas, and Houston. The cities were all
so new and the country so big!

Hollywood fascinated Sonja. Back in Sweden she had dreamed of
being a star. Clark Gable was at the height of his career on the silver
screen and Sonja found that she could playfully annoy Karl by
commenting on Gable's exceedingly good looks. Karl was convinced
it was mostly the moustache. It took several starts to keep it going as
he had always shaved his upper lip first in the morning. If he was not
completely awake the moustache went the way of the drain

automatically, but eventually he grew a respectable version. Sonja began to kid him by bragging to her friends that Karl looked just like Gable. He did not. Karl discovered that America truly was a melting pot of cultures. He imagined a world completely like it.

The Soviet Union became more and more oppressive over the areas they were given and West Berlin became an island inside a Communist country. The darkest hours for Berlin were, of course, the time during the Blockade. From June 24, 1948, until May 11, 1949, all road and rail service from West Berlin to the rest of Western Germany was denied. Although more than 13,000 tons of food and supplies were brought by air to West Berlin each day during this period life was still far from normal. Management of the factories in Cologne and access to customers from isolated West Berlin was so impaired that the family was forced to move to the Cologne estate.

The Schneider Berlin Compound was sadly closed except for a maintenance staff, which would keep up the grounds and knock the dust off of the covered furnishings that were to remain in the main house and the separate Medieval "museum." Some of the paintings from the museum were packed and transported to Cologne for safekeeping. The Duesenberg was forgotten in the old gatehouse garage. Most people thought that Berlin would again be normal in a year or two but it was more than forty.

May, 1948
I have never liked Cologne. In fact, I hate Cologne. It is a desolate city and without Johann and Manny, it is dreary. The castle is beautiful but what's a castle without a king?

When the Schneider clan moved to the Cologne Estate, they felt crowded even though the house consisted of about 30 or so rooms and had several smaller cottages and a beautiful chapel on the property. The area just East of the chapel was the family cemetery where several generations of Schneiders were buried. The "house" was actually an eighteenth-century Rhenish moat castle set amongst the most splendid of rose bushes and ancient trees. Sebastian's father had acquired the property back in the 1800s from a prince who had a gambling problem. This magnificent castle was at the other end of the spectrum from the modern Berlin Compound. It was believed to have been designed by Michael Leveilly, a French architect who was in the service of the Cologne elector, Prince Clemens August. It was an enchanting two-storied rectangular structure of plastered brick with perfectly preserved interior Rococo stuccowork covering the doors and walls. Johann senior had purchased two of the magnificent tapestries that adorned the living room and dining hall walls. The senior Schneiders had been in love with the place the moment they set foot inside the huge entry doors and Stefanie's Johann had grown up there. The style of the interior was a bit fru fru for Stefanie's taste, but because Johann had so loved the place, she could not help but feel sadness as she moved her personal belongings into the home. The largest problems she could foresee would be making the antiquated kitchens functional again for day-to-day living and cleaning up a few leaks in the roof. Bathrooms and dressing rooms had been added in about 1900 and were still in proper working order. Through the years, structural repairs had been done and any cracking stucco, decorative or otherwise, had been restored. The Schneiders saw to it that the castle had been kept in good repair up until the war. None of them knew how long they would be staying there but a house staff would have to be interviewed and hired. One of Cologne Wool Goods' secretaries who knew more about Cologne could take care of that.

December 10, 1949
Karl and Sonja came back home today. I was horrified when I looked at Manny. He scared me out of my wits. He has changed. Maybe America changed him. Sonja looked almost the same, maybe a little older. My stomach is still uneasy. I just have no appetite and I am weary. Why am I not even excited to see my Manny?

Karl and Sonja came back to Cologne from America in late 1949. Sonja had hoped to come home with a baby but even the specialty doctors in America could not figure out why she could not conceive. She so wanted a child but Karl did not seem to care, one way or another. He loved Sonja and he liked his life and it certainly wasn't from their lack of trying.

The day they arrived, they received a lukewarm welcome from Stefanie who took one look at Karl and said, "No way, that thing has got to go!" "Karl hugged her and responded with, "What has got to go, Steffi?" Karl had not taken off his coat yet nor set his luggage down.

"It makes you look just like Adolf!" Stefanie composed herself, cleared her throat and repeated, "It makes you look just like Adolf Hitler!" Stefanie started to cry and ran into the next room.

Emma and Sonja looked at each other with raised eyebrows. They couldn't figure out what triggered Stefanie's outburst. Emma squinted her eyes and looked at Karl again. She pursed her lips and agreed with Stefanie. "I guess you need to shave it off, Manny." Before Karl could even think about unpacking, he asked to borrow a razor from Augie, took one last look at himself in the mirror and mockingly held out his hand and said "Heil, Hitler" and removed the bushy growth.

Dr. Karl Schneider II was offered and accepted a professorship at the University of Cologne in the field of political science. He was an excellent teacher and his courses were popular with the students and always filled to the maximum capacity. Karl enjoyed having a captive audience in his classroom to listen to his views on politics. That was fortunate as the position did not pay much. Karl did not need the money.

The "old man of Cologne," Konrad Adenauer, was selected by the Allies as the new Chancellor of West Germany. He had been the mayor of Cologne for many years, helped write the "Basic Law" or new Constitution, and was the overwhelming choice of the American diplomats. Mainly due to his wishes the little town of Bonn, just South of Cologne, was chosen as the new capitol since Berlin was not accessible. It soon became known as the only capitol in Europe with no nightlife whatsoever. Adenauer had known August and his father before him and even Sebastian before that. On Sunday afternoons, Adenauer would come by to visit with Karl and August. He never ran out of stories from his long political life. They would play bocce or just sit and drink Brandy and smoke cigars. Karl was fascinated by his insights and started to have a real desire to play the political game instead of teaching it.

On a few occasions the Chancellor brought Alton Becker, his assistant in foreign affairs to the afternoon sessions. Alton usually was accompanied by his precocious son Andrew. The 14-year-old was fascinated by politics and bocce and Sonja, the beauty queen, and almost everything. Karl and young Andy formed a lifelong bond.

There were no more entries in the book, only notes and a few scribbles on the last blank pages. Andy knew the family after that and knew that Stefanie had a bad last few years. He remembered her pretty well and he had made small talk with her when he went to see Karl. She would always tell him he was turning into a handsome young man, but he remembered she always looked sad. The family said the last couple of years of her life were strange. They saw her writing when she sat out on the lawn, but they thought she might be writing poetry because she loved poetry.

Stefanie was bored with life in Cologne and was beginning to feel depressed. She did not enjoy participating in family conversations anymore. One member or another would often find her aimlessly walking around the grounds, by herself, with a distant stare. She had a book with her but they didn't know if she was reading it or writing it. She didn't often answer when she was spoken to. Emma and Hannah were only a little less bored. They tried to jump-start the social scene, but it was not totally successful. They planned a couple of dinners but there were precious few interesting or influential people to invite. Cologne would never compare to Berlin.

17. HEIDI

Heidi, the youngest of the Schneider clan, had a few young friends at school but she was more interested in music than partying with her classmates. She had inherited some of Johann's musical ability and Johann gave her first piano lessons. Her obvious talent led to more professional instruction. She continued piano for a while but took an interest in singing.

Heidi turned 17 and American Rock 'n Roll became the rage in Cologne. The fall of Germany politically was accompanied by a decline in popularity of all things German, including fashion and the arts. Fortunately for the Schneiders, good wool was still good wool.

Heidi had an operatic voice, light and lilting, reminiscent of Lily Pons whom she loved. Emma and Hannah listened one afternoon as she sat at the piano and accompanied herself to the "Bell Song," one of Lily's trademarks. Delibes would have been pleased with the performance. They agreed that Heidi should attend a conservatory for music and voice. Berlin was still inaccessible so they asked Stefanie if she had any contacts at the Paris Conservatory. The answer was "no" but that the company still owned a small apartment on the Left Bank. It was usually rented but the tenants had not renewed their lease, which would expire next month. Karen was talked into taking her daughter to Paris to check it out. Stefanie was invited to go but declined. Karen tried hard to convince Stefanie that it would be like old times. She reminded Stefanie of the fun they used to have traveling together and how Stefanie always loved Paris but Stefanie said "no and that was final." "No" seemed to be the only response Stefanie had anymore. Emma wrote to some of her friends associated with Covent Garden asking for advice on teachers and coaching.

Karen and Heidi arrived in Paris, Heidi appeared for her audition, a few strings were pulled and Heidi was accepted to the conservatory. After helping her settle into the apartment, getting a new piano delivered and making sure that Heidi had all she needed for her classes, Karen returned to Cologne, happy that her second child was situated.

Heidi had never really had to work very hard before. The local teachers in Cologne did not demand much in the way of perfection or precision. The conservatory was different. The courses were difficult and the teachers expected total dedication. There was music history, solfège, languages, music theory, violin, and oboe, orchestration and manuscript, transposition and composition as well as voice. She was forced to sing Mozart instead of Donizetti. Not that there was anything particularly wrong with Mozart, but she felt her real talent was being suppressed. And the competition among students was fierce. The one-upmanship reigned supreme and Heidi managed the first semester but seemed to be losing ground. She kept this up for three semesters and finally decided that music was a wonderful hobby but as a career, it was not for her. She was upset with herself for not wanting to put in as much effort as it required and somewhat afraid to tell the family that she did not want to do it any longer. The family was not fond of quitters. She had the talent but not the drive.

Heidi had met a handsome young conducting student named Jean-Claude Ramon. They dated for the last months she was in Paris but it was not to be. Jean Claude confessed he was gay…that he liked her a lot but not in that way. He had fallen for one young Philippe Orly. This was another low for Heidi's deflated ego but since she had not yet decided that Jean Claude was "the one," she closed up the apartment and returned to Cologne a bit wiser but not hurting.

18. R.I.P. STEFANIE

Karl continued to teach, Johann ran the firm, the wives tried valiantly to entertain themselves and Stefanie continued to be depressed as they waited for Berlin to become normal again. The time dragged and Berlin did not seem to recover.

Karl became involved in the politics of Cologne. His conservative views alienated him more and more from the faculty at the university. His students rallied for him but eventually he resigned. As international trade grew, he found that he was effective at opening new markets and negotiating trade alliances. With Sonja ever at his side they went around the globe promoting Cologne Wool Goods. He instituted designer days' at the factory where fashion designers from all over the world could come and suggest patterns and textures and weaves that they would like to utilize. The process engineers and the staff at Cologne Wool Goods would advise them on how to make the designs economically and, if a new process or method was needed, then a quotation for the development costs and an estimate of the production costs would be offered. It was very successful.

Slowly, Bonn, which was only about 20 kilometers from Cologne, became lively as the capitol. The recently elected representatives and appointed administrators occupied the newly constructed parliamentary buildings and supporting office and ministry buildings. From the chaos of the new constitution and procedures and extra-national control by America, Britain, and France finally appeared some organization and routine. Eventually, there was time for socializing and State Dinners and occasional celebrations. Lobbyists and the other influence peddlers begin to show up. Money started to flow and entertaining became fashionable again. "Party time" had come to Bonn.

"Party time" did not seem do much for Stefanie. The family noticed that she was staying more to herself and seemed to be sinking further into a loneliness that none of them could seem to fix or figure out. Stefanie, a woman of many words became a quiet woman with very few opinions. She kept seeing Adolf's features and psyche in Karl. Whenever she was at a function where he spoke, she heard the same charisma and persuasiveness that had brought Germany to ruin. She had nightmares about the death camps with her at Hitler's side, cheering. She would wake up in a cold sweat. Insomnia and a lack of appetite began to take their toll on her already slim frame. August and Karen noticed the decline but seemed to attribute it to her getting older. Emma, however, felt that it was something much more ominous. Karen tried to talk to Stefanie but to no avail. It seemed that Stefanie was determined to take her dark worries to the grave.

A friend of Sonja's family in Sweden, Werner Dankwort, was nominated to be Ambassador to Canada in 1951. A German intellectual, Dankwort had opposed Hitler and took exile in Sweden during the War where he met Sonja's family. Sonja persuaded Karl to host a send-off dinner for the diplomat. They asked Stefanie for her help in planning the dinner. She had always been at the helm of such affairs, but seemed not at all interested when Karl asked her to help.

Later in the evening, Sonja went to Stefanie's bedroom and tried to convince her. Stefanie started crying uncontrollably, grabbed Sonja by both arms and in a wailing voice, started in.. "Oh Sonja, Sonja. You must keep him good." Stefanie's grip became tighter. "Oh Sonja, keep him happy. I am begging you. Don't ever let his anger turn to hate. Please. I am so sorry…so sorry…" Then Stefanie's face went pale and her eyes became glazed. Her thin body slumped forward. Sonja screamed for Karl and they called for a doctor.

Stefanie slept fitfully for two days. When she awoke all she could remember were the days above the shop and the courtship with her beloved Johann. She continually called out for Johann. Emma and Karl tried to talk to her but all they heard were incoherent responses and inaudible mumbling. Karl held her in his arms and rocked her like a baby repeating her name, "Steffi." An ambulance came and placed her limp body on the padded gurney. Stefanie was hospitalized for several weeks without recognizing anyone or anything. The doctors said something had triggered a stroke and she would recover, but she never did. The family took turns staying at the hospital hoping for a positive sign. Stefanie died in February 1952.

****

Andy congratulated himself for staying awake. He felt his career might be over if he didn't figure out how in hell to handle this with kid gloves. So far, all he knew was an admission by a woman who was depressed most of the time to a son who had ratted a secret she said she had. This certainly was not proof that she really did have an affair with Adolf Hitler. Hitler knew nothing about it. Wouldn't a woman want the father of the child to know? Even if he was a maniac? It all didn't make sense. She never spoke of a previous pregnancy. Anyway, how would she get a man as powerful as a Schneider who could have had anyone, interested in a pregnant woman? Especially in 1908? Nothing was mentioned, so it still could be an imagined or made up story. After all, the woman was ill with a high fever. Fevers can cause hallucinations, delusions, and God only knows what all. Andy had to get some sleep. He didn't know what time Larissa would knock.

19. THE FAMILY AFTER STEFANIE

The party planning for Dankwort fell to Hannah and Heidi. Parties were not Emma's "thing" and while Sonja loved a good party, she had no idea how to go about planning one. It was the first Schneider function without the flair of Stefanie. She was sorely missed but, fortunately, it went well. Not everyone was in tuxedo and the band was mediocre but, all in all, society and style were beginning to come to Bonn. West Berlin was still isolated and the East German government was still belligerent.

Josef Stalin, the Premier of the Soviet Union, died in 1953. Under Nikita Khrushchev, the Soviets tried to lessen the tension in the world and the Berlin situation began to get a little better. The original principle was that there were four 'zones' administered by the four powers but the city of Berlin was not divided and travel and commerce in Berlin would be normal. It did not work. The East German intellectual and professional citizens began going into the Western zones and asking for asylum in the West. Over the years it became a flood. By 1961 about 2,000 citizens per month were defecting and East Germany was running out of its best talent. Walter Ulbricht, the East German Chancellor, was responsible for secretly planning a high barbed-wire barrier that went around West Berlin. He had it erected on one single day of August 13, 1961. Guards were posted and the exodus from the East was stopped. Eventually, the Wall became 12-feet-high concrete with watchtowers, gun emplacements, and mine fields. Twelve thousand troops were required to police it. American President Kennedy, the leader of the free world, was criticized because he seemed to think that the Wall was within the rights of the Soviets to protect their borders although it was clearly contrary to the treaties in place at the time. The world followed Kennedy's lead. Some think that Khrushchev was emboldened by Kennedy's limp response and the Cuban Missile episode would not have occurred if the West had shown more resolve.

Kennedy made an attempt to show more support for Berlin by visiting the city in 1962. His speech from the courthouse balcony stressed that free people everywhere were figuratively citizens of West Berlin and supported the city. He concluded with his famous phrase, "Ich bin ein Berliner," which formally translates to "I am a Berliner," showing solidarity with the citizens in his audience. Since "Berliner" was also the name of a confection, many took his phrase to mean "I am a jelly donut."

Adenauer stepped down in 1963 and was replaced by Ludwig Erhard, Adenauer's Minister of Economics. Erhard's economic reforms as Minister and later as Chancellor were instrumental in the recovery that West Germany and, indeed, all of Western Europe enjoyed.

In the early 1960s, American foreign policy was centered on containing Communism. World War III was being avoided by MAD or Mutually Assured Destruction. Each superpower had the ability to annihilate the other in an all-out conflict. In order to further their goals the Communists started several proxy wars, the most extensive being the Vietnam War. It was barely underway when Kennedy was assassinated in Dallas, Texas, in 1963. Lyndon Johnson was the American Vice President. When he took over, he felt obligated to continue and even escalated Kennedy's War. The war became very unpopular with the American public as well as becoming an economic drain on America and a diplomatic nightmare. It was such a disaster that, even though he won the 1964 election, Johnson didn't even try to run for a second term. When Richard Nixon was elected in 1968, he unilaterally stopped the fighting. Millions of Vietnamese were murdered in the vacuum created when the U.S. military left but it is hard to say whether any other outcome was possible. This was a battle to the death between the two regimes: the Communists in the North and the Dictatorship that America was trying to support in the South. The peasants minding the rice paddies just wanted to be left alone. The Communists won.

Nixon was much better at foreign policy than his predecessors. America had traditionally recognized the government of the little island of Formosa as the legitimate government of all of China, ignoring the billions of people on the mainland under the Communist government there. Early in his term Nixon sent his Secretary of State, Henry Kissinger, to Beijing to begin opening diplomatic talks with mainland China. This had two major consequences. First, by being recognized by America, Communist China suddenly had enough prestige to stand up to the Soviet Union and second, a massive trade package could start. Nixon also understood the plight of West Berlin. There were two major agreements about Berlin and East Germany that were negotiated in 1971.

The "Berlin Agreement" recognized the de-facto divided nature of Berlin and guaranteed citizens of West Berlin rights to their way of life and legitimized the Wall. The "Transit Agreement" guaranteed that the roadways and railways and telephone lines from Western Germany to West Berlin would be maintained and kept open. West Berliners were guaranteed a connection to the rest of West Germany.

20. BERLIN STARTS TO RECOVER

In 1972, Hannah decided and Karen agreed that the time had come to reopen the Berlin Compound. It would be much more comfortable for Karen and August. Emma and Heidi would enjoy both the facilities and the privacy of the place, and travel to Cologne, when required, would be easy and safe. That Hannah's family was still in the area also came into play. Johann was not anxious for the aggravation he knew would ensue but he tacitly agreed.

Johann became more enthusiastic after his first night with Hannah in the bedroom of their wedding night. They found themselves more inspired to make love than they had been in years. Hannah, at 44, found herself pregnant. Her doctor required her to take it easy the first few months and managing a major renovation was more than she probably should attempt. Heidi, who seemed to inherit her grandmother Stefanie's flare for design and style and who needed some direction in her life, was the natural choice to take over the details of the renovation.

The Compound was in remarkably good shape after more than 20 years but a sizable amount of restoration was necessary before the family could comfortably occupy it again. The interior needed work and with Karen, the new matriarch at the helm, the work would take a slightly different direction than was originally done in the utility areas and the personal bedrooms. While Gropius' architectural intention and integrity would remain, the kitchens and bathrooms had to be updated, the floors that had suffered some water damage needed refinishing, the entire Compound needed repainting, the tennis courts needed resurfacing and the pool and pool house needed modern maintenance. And lastly, some of the unused rooms had to be converted to rec rooms for the younger occupants and of course, a nursery had to be carved out of one of the bedrooms to welcome the new baby who would arrive in just a few months.

The furnishings that Gropius designed for the main house would remain with a few new additions. The original furniture, which had been triple wrapped before the Schneiders left the Compound years before, had been perfectly preserved. The original fabrics having been custom woven for the Schneiders were in mint condition. The chairs and sofas that were designed for certain rooms would remain. The draperies, though packed away, had gotten damp from water leaks and were faded and fragile and had to be replaced. Since Gropius and Stefanie together had designed the fabrics, the Schneiders wanted to duplicate them. This would be done by a top weaving firm.

The office building needed a more sophisticated repair from the bomb damage and Cologne Wool Goods wanted to stay in the forefront of design. They decided to replace all of its furniture, which would include new desks, tables and chairs, in the hi-tech mode.

The work on the Compound became a major challenge for Heidi who thought it would be all fun. She did not realize how much planning and selecting and overseeing would be required. August hired the architectural firm of Glocke and Glocke for the restoration as Luther Glocke was a friend of August's and the firm was very familiar with the Gropius house. They would be more than pleased to take on the Project. August explained that his daughter Heidi would be the one they would report to and they were instructed to keep her in the planning loop. The Construction company of Schuster and Schuster were hired to carry out the work.

The renovation moved quickly and on schedule, but Heidi, once again, had trouble staying focused. Luther Glocke reluctantly recommended a decorator to help select and assemble the colors, furnishings and soft goods. The Glockes had an aversion to "decorators" as such, because, according to Luther, they wanted to cover up an architect's masterful work with unsightly frills. Having three women plus Heidi in the Schneider Compound to deal with however, seemed to be a greater evil than the decorator. Karen had the last say, but could not make decisions. Emma did not really care, but did not want to be ignored. Hannah had strong opinions, but was "indisposed." Heidi was the contact, but was afraid of committing to anything... Luther decided to let the decorator handle the women and their politics.

The final phase of the renovation was exasperating, but eventually paint colors were selected, carpets were picked and installed in the bedrooms, new, tailored sofas were ordered for the rec rooms and a huge modern sofa was made for the den. Baby furniture arrived just in time for the appearance of little Catherine. The Italian designer Ettore Sottsass designed the office furniture for Cologne Wool Goods' lobby ands offices. The Compound took on a life of its own, loose ends were tied, everyone was paid and it resumed its original glory.

Hannah's pregnancy went smoothly for such an event so late in her life. Augie was already 22 and somewhat embarrassed to introduce his pregnant mother to the new friends he was meeting in Berlin, especially the girl friends. After Catherine was born she was often mistaken for his daughter instead of his sister. He was still "playing the field." Catherine was a bright little girl and tried to stay out of her older brother's way. As Catherine grew, out of love for her brother, she would introduce herself as "Catherine, Augie's little sister."

Augie had many girlfriends but could not settle on any one. On an afternoon in 1973, he was bicycling around the compound with Rose, his current amour, when they came upon the old gatehouse and its garage. He looked in the window and that is when he found it. The Duesy.

Through the dirty pane, Augie could only see what appeared to be an old car. When he tugged at the padlock on the door, the lock, hinge, and hasp all came off in his hand. The sliding door was embedded in a track full of dirt but he managed to slide it back far enough to squeeze through the opening. The rubberized tarpaulin over the car fell apart as he pulled it away to get a better look. Then he gasped. The brilliant blue paint was still fresh, but the leather seats, though shiny, were very dried out. He wiped the years of dust off the odometer, which read 4,326 km.

The car looked ready to drive. Upon closer inspection, he saw it was up on wooden blocks. Karl must have had it winterized during the fall before he died. The roadster was not the best car for a Berlin winter. It had been elevated to keep the tires from taking a set and becoming less than perfectly round. If they sat all winter in the same position then at 100 km per hour they would shimmy so that the car would be hard to control. The battery was on the bench behind the car to keep corrosion from the battery compartment. The radiator and gasoline tank had been drained. There was a checklist under the dust on the workbench. Even the plugs had been pulled and the cylinders oiled and turned over to prevent rusting of the walls and rings. He opened the glove box and found the key and the papers showing its origin in America. Augie just stood back and looked at the classic for a few minutes. "Wow! Wait till I tell the old man. Let's go." Then the two of them pedaled back to the main house. Augie was several steps ahead as they burst into August' study.

August looked up from his newspaper when Augie and Rose burst in. "Doesn't anyone knock any more?" August feigned annoyance but smiled broadly at his grandson.

"Uncle Karl's Duesenberg is still in the old gate house garage!" he exclaimed. "It looks brand new and only has 4,000 kilometers on it. I thought all those stories about Karl's father were legends or something since no one in this family could be so exciting. But his car is still there. Can we fix it up? It's beautiful."

August hadn't had an engineering challenge for many years and did not have to think very hard to say "yes." He remembered the race in Strasbourg and smiled. "Le Mans, here we come." Rose had been completely ignored for the past hour. Her seething was totally unnoticed by the two Schneider men. She had been upstaged by an old jalopy. She excused herself and never spoke to Augie again.

Augie and August went back to the garage, this time in the jeep. The 44-year-old car was definitely a classic. August remembered some of his brother's escapades and smiled. They would have to find a mechanic up to the challenge. This was not a project for a backyard tinkerer.

When they told Hannah about the find, she surprised them. She had a nephew in Bayraschzell that, although they had never met, was reputed to be quite the engineer and his hobby was restoring classic cars. He had a Bugatti and a Triumph TR and some other prizes. August had never heard Hannah talk about anything except fashion and cuisine and here she was with a little automobile history. Nephew Hugo was invited to the Compound.

Hugo Junkers, namesake of the founder of the aircraft company, arrived about a week later. They went over to see the Duesy.

Hugo had done his homework and identified the Duesenberg as a Model X Boattail. Only a few were built and only four other than this one were known to still exist. Straight 8 overhead valve Lycoming engine. Four wheel hydraulic brakes. Synchromesh transmission. The really tough things to replace like the body parts and trim were all perfect. The hydraulic seals and hoses would need replacing but they and most of the mechanical parts were either stock items or used in other machines from the era. Hugo could hardly contain his excitement. He had some classic cars but this was the mother of them all. He hardly noticed Hannah when she walked in.

"You must be Hugo. I'm your Aunt Hannah." Hugo ran over and embraced Hannah and planted a serious kiss on her lips. "Pleased to meet you, Aunt Hannah. This is the most amazing machine I have ever seen. When can we get started?"

Hannah pulled herself away from the excited Hugo laughing. "You will have to work that out with Augie. How is your family?"

Hugo ignored the question and turned to Augie. "Do you know of a really good machine shop? One that can handle a big straight 8?"

Augie and Johann were also laughing at his excitement. Johann said, "We will find one."

They tried but could not find a facility in all of West Berlin that passed the "Hugo Test." They were either too dirty or too small or dealt only in subway cars or something. Hugo wanted to take the car back to Bayraschzell on the Southern border of West Germany. Augie was not anxious to let his new baby go so far from home. He insisted on first seeing its proposed temporary home so he and Hugo traveled to Bayraschzell. The machine shop Hugo used was amazing and after he saw Hugo's collection and the meticulous work he had done, he agreed. The shipping and financial arrangements took about another week.

It approached a year for the Duesenberg to be restored, but when Augie got it back, it was spectacular. All Hugo wanted for his efforts was the opportunity to show the car now and again. Everywhere Augie went, it caused a commotion. He was in the magazines more than the Schneider parties. Girls, girls. Where did they all come from? Eventually he settled down to seeing only Polly Reinhart, a pretty petite brunette with pixied hair.

Augie met Polly at a sports car rally. Polly was there with her brother who had come to show a souped-up Karmann Ghia. The Ghia was cute, but the Duesy was the talk of the show and Polly just had to sit in it. She really looked good in it. Augie wanted to keep her in it.

In May 1975, Augie persuaded Polly to go with him to Monte Carlo for the Monaco Grand Prix Formula 1 race. That week in Monte Carlo, Niki Lauda, the Austrian, won the race in a Ferrari and Polly won the title of Frau August Schneider.

Augie was very busy for the next nine years. He earned an MBA and a law degree and he and Polly had four little girls before they had their son, Sebastian. Catherine was like their big sister. The Compound needed a larger nursery for the growing brood. The Duesy was a bit small for a family of seven or eight, depending on how you count, but it remained in the family collection.

Professionally, Augie was handling some of the legal matters for Cologne Wool Goods, but wanted a little more excitement. He was offered a staff position with Diepgen, the Mayor of West Berlin and decided to accept. Karl's fascination with politics was beginning to rub off on Augie. He saw no conflict in working for both the family business and Mayor Diepgen.

21. ANOTHER DIARY FOUND

There was a light tap at the door, but it awoke Andy at 8:00 A.M. He jumped up, looked at the clock and realized he had not called into his office. He hoarsely choked out, "Just a minute." He ran to the loo, gargled some mouthwash and brushed his hair, but his eyes were still half shut. With only four hours of sleep, he felt drugged. He opened the door and it was Larissa.

"My Lord, what happened to you?" she coldly asked as though she suspected he had been with someone the night before.

He hugged her lovingly and said, "No, nothing of the sort. You look beautiful and I've missed you too." Andy took her bags and her coat and invited her in.

Larissa saw the feminine box on the table and wondered what was going on. She sniffed and asked him again if he had had some call girl spend the night.

Andy replied with, "Do you think I would have told you to come on if I had?"

"Then what is that cheap whore smell? It ain't just cigarettes, honey."

Andy swore Larissa to secrecy. He made her sit down while he put on a fresh pot of coffee. After only four hours of sleep, he really needed coffee now. He told her the whole story, beginning to end. At least the rumor. He told her to go over and look at the books if she didn't believe him. He said Johann Schneider's mother, Karen, had lent them to him.

Larissa, for the first time in her life, believed Andy, and was sympathetic and said, "poor baby." She got up and stood behind him and rubbed his back as he was putting the coffee in the brewer and asked what he planned to do?

Andy said he didn't know yet. "You should read the one where she tells everything to her son, August. It still isn't proof, though. The woman was overwrought most of her life and I still didn't find anything other than that one admission and a few flutters here and there..."

Larissa walked over to the table to look in the box. She saw the bags of dried flowers and a feeling of sadness came over her. "Poor soul, she had a lot of grief in her life." Larissa picked up one of the bags to smell the flowers and she noticed there were three bags. "I wonder why she stacked three bags in the box? Maybe they were different flavors. Larissa carefully picked up another one, smelled it and gently put it down. Andy watched Larissa's long, graceful fingers lift the bags as though they were filled with gold.

"Andrew," she said in her singsong voice, "something heavy is in this bottom one." Andy put the pot in the slot and went to see what Larissa was holding.

They both chimed in at the same time, "There's another book." Larissa set it down and carefully untied the green satin ribbon that held the netting around the bundle. She tried not to lose any of the potpourri as she lifted the small journal from the bottom of the netting. It was not black leather like the other books but had a pale floral fabric cover and was thick but small. The pattern blended in perfectly with the dried flowers, almost like a camouflage shirt.

"What do you suppose," Larissa said in a deliberate tone of voice and handed the book to Andy. Andy was immediately awake. He opened the book to the first page and it was dated 1951. His heart sank for a moment and wondered what could be so important about 1951. That was one year before Stefanie died.

Andy started flipping the pages and said "Bingo."

The introduction read:

I know I haven't many days left on this earth. I have to confess to you, my loved ones, who I really am. I am not the pure woman you know me to be. I have deceived some of you and have carried the darkness of this deception with me all my life. The pain of my indiscretion has been in my heart for almost fifty years. The burden has been almost unbearable and yet I selfishly kept it to myself. I was afraid it would cause too much hurt. Perhaps now, it will still cause hurt. Please try to understand that I was young and Adolf Hitler was just an art student, not the monster he became. He never knew and I never imagined the consequences of what we had done. I beg your forgiveness.

I remember it like yesterday.

When I found that I was pregnant I went to Confession. Our Priest seemed, at the time, like the only one I could talk to. Before I left the church, he told me to find out everything I could about the young man who had gotten me this way. I told the Priest that his friend had given me some history when I asked him but I had not read it all yet.

I was so scared. I couldn't tell anyone. I had seen the same young man for at least two years almost everyday, watching me. He was cute, certainly not handsome, but extremely charismatic. He never even said "hello." He sometimes had a friend with him. My mother thought he was strange because he never spoke to us. Back then, it was not so common to meet each other. My mother thought I was too young for dating anyone. I was barely 17.

I went out of my way to find out everything I could about him. I tried to ask questions discretely but no one knew him. I finally got a few answers out of his friend. I swore his friend to secrecy and did not tell him why I wanted to know.

Adolf was only 14 years old when his father Alois died in 1903. Alois was retired from the Customs Service with a nice pension. The pension survived his death and allowed Adolf and his mother and siblings to live comfortably.

Although young Hitler was a lively, wide-awake young man, he was completely incapable of regular work or scholastic endeavor. He had the reputation of being extremely lazy. He was expelled from Realschule, a "modern" curriculum after previously failing at a more "classical" one. He hated school and despised all of his teachers. He chose to settle down to being an artistic genius in his own eyes, dressing the part, and generally becoming a fixture in the town of Linz.

Always decked out in his Sunday best, Adolf was a lanky, pallid and shy young man and often carried an ivory-tipped black cane. He was a loner with almost no friends. The exception was his long-time chum, August Kubizek. August might possibly have been the only one who would tolerate Adolf's crazy moods and rantings and ravings. August was the son of a local decorator in Linz and a very patient listener. The two teens had noticed each other at the theater where neither of them ever missed an opera performance. August, who paid for his opera ticket with money made from working in his father's dusty upholstery shop, wondered if Adolf might be from a wealthy family or was a student as he never seemed to have to work. They were both 16 years old.

The friends, who couldn't see eye to eye on anything, were complete opposites. August was a devoted violin and viola student and was the quiet one - mild mannered and introspective. Adolf was high-strung, somewhat sinister and often explosive. They, nevertheless, complimented each other and never tired of the other's company.

August, or "Gustl" as he was called, would all too often become Adolf's captive audience as Adolf convinced him to sit for exhausting periods of time while he expatiated about something. This could be anything. A boulder or any other platform served as his stage. With grand hand gestures and head jerking motions, he would speak in a harsh, piercing tone to get the point across. August would look around and notice that he was a crowd of one. He was never allowed to disagree with Adolf or an argument would ensue.

Politics became a tedious subject. August had very few opinions about the goings on in government and Adolf could not believe one could be so passive as to not have strong feelings one way or another. Adolf hated the 'Czech thugs' coming into Linz and robbing houses while the local police were ineffectual in stopping them. Adolf said someday this sort of thing would never happen because the 'Reich' would take care of it. The word "Reich" in Austria meant the German State, but Adolf took it to mean everything that was important to him. From then on, the "Reich" would take care of animals, the 'Reich' would construct beautiful buildings and the 'Reich' would assist people with problems and handle thugs and misfits. Adolf would see to it that he would be head of the "Reich."

One evening in 1905, Wagner's opera *Rienzi* was being performed at the Memorial Theater in Linz. Adolf and August were in attendance. Rienzi, an opera about a medieval populist figure who succeeds in defeating the nobles and raising the power of the people, affected Adolf deeply. The emotionally charged music and the plot itself terrified him and upon leaving the theater, August noticed that his friend appeared to be in a trance. As they walked in the moonlight, Adolf grabbed August's arm and spoke of a mission he would be given to bring his people to the heights of freedom. This behavior unnerved August and Adolf was never the same after that night. Adolf would often refer to the night it all began.

During his daily stroll through the center of Linz, Adolf regularly saw an attractive, fair-haired girl walk arm-in-arm with her mother near the Schmeidtoreck. He never missed the opportunity to see them as they came by each afternoon. Much to August's father's dismay, Adolf forced August to leave the shop unattended just to keep him company while he waited.

I learned that his name was Adolf. He would look me up and down when mother and I past him on our daily walks. I remember his eyes would just sparkle when he saw me. It was obvious he thought I was pretty. I tried to dress my best for him and even tease him a little. Mother said I was acting like a dance hall dolly but it was fun.

Adolf noticed that both mother and daughter wore only the best of clothing. The mother, and Adolf assumed it was the girl's mother, was a rather robust and tightly corseted woman who appeared to be well-to-do and dressed her daughter accordingly. The daughter, somewhere under the age of 18 or 19, must have acquired her father's good looks as she was taller, slimmer, incredibly beautiful, and more radiant than her older companion. Perhaps the huge hats with the stuffed birds, the bright flowers and the copious ribbons attributed to the larger silhouette of the older woman. The young woman seemed to not have an affinity for hats, however, as she wore her thick blond locks exposed. She usually styled her hair in a bun but often she would pile it loosely on top of her head creating an angelic aura of gold. It seemed that her favorite afternoon frocks were of filmy materials, pulled in at the waist, and trimmed with quantities of lace and handwork. In winter, she wore magnificent velvets. Being the observant artist that he was, Adolf took note of what this delightful creature had on each day. And the way she pushed the hem of her long skirt forward with her immaculate footwear drove Adolf mad. He could not help but notice that the parasol she carried was to get his attention because of the provocative way she tapped it on the pavement as she passed him by.

I used to tease Adolf just to see his reaction. I guess it wasn't very nice of me. I kept trying to get him to speak, I think…

From time to time, the young girl would catch the glance from Adolf. She would nudge the older woman and appear to whisper something in her direction, then turn her head to return the glimpse of a smile to the young gentleman. Adolf lived for these moments. But then there were times she ignored him completely. Adolf's world crashed. He would lash out at August as though he were to blame and the tirade went on for hours.

My brother, Herwig, would go on walks with us when he was in Linz. He had already gone away to law school in Vienna but visited us some weekends. He and I looked a lot alike but Adolf thought he was my friend. I could see the jealousy on Adolf's face. He would turn red and it was amusing to watch. He really did get jealous when other guys would ask to stroll with us or talk to me.

On several occasions, a good-looking young man appeared with the mother and daughter. Adolf's heart skipped beats with anger and his rage was ignited. He pleaded with August to discover the young man's name. A few days later, he was relieved to find out that the young man was the young woman's brother. Jealousy, however, became a regular part of his being, when at other times, he would see the two women strolling with handsome young officers in their snappy uniforms. It was obvious that the lithe young girl was flirting with them by the way she twirled her parasol. When a whiff of male cologne from the decadent perfumed men in uniform blew Adolf's way, he held his nose in an effort to display his total disgust.

The silly boy never would speak to me and it was not lady-like to ever speak to a gentleman first.

Adolf discovered that the girl's name was Stefanie. He never spoke to her but early on, he developed an intense romantic feeling for her. He once made August stand at attention while he recited "Hymn to the Beloved," one of the innumerable love poems that he wrote to the lovely Stefanie, but she did not know. August watched as young Adolf suffered. August tried to get him to speak to her, but he refused. He could never bring himself around to an introduction and chose to let her be his dream. He was sure the erotic looks he threw her way were enough to transmit his burning feelings of passion for her.

Mother and I didn't see Adolf for a few weeks. I thought he had taken a job or gone away to school. I sort of missed the attention. Of course, I would never let him know that.

In the spring of 1905, Adolf traveled to Vienna. This was his first time there. He wrote to August and told him that he was overcome "by the glory of the Ringstrasse that intoxicated him like the magic from the *Arabian Nights*." The Burgtheater had become his nightly hangout where he experienced the intensity of *Tristan* and *The Flying Dutchman*. The majestic music, he said "transcended him into sublimity." It gave him time to think about Stefanie and what he wanted to become. He vowed to move to Vienna and bask in all that this metropolis of Europe was. He returned to Linz after two weeks in the ever-dazzling city.

I will never forget that day in June, June 15th, I think, mother and I participated in the Flower Festival. We had decorated our carriage with wild flowers. Every other carriage chose roses or something common. We wanted to be different. And we had just gotten new outfits. We were anxious to show them off. I saw Adolf and I was glad he was there. I threw him a flower.

Adolf's interest in Stefanie peaked one Sunday in June, 1906, when a flower festival was taking place in Linz. Adolf waited for August to come out of church to take their usual seat at the Schmeidtoreck. A parade was to pass on the narrow street right in front of them. Adolf and August had a good view as the Regimental Band led the line of flower-decked carriages with their fine ladies waving to the spectators and tossing flowers of every type. Adolf was not particularly interested in the parade and only wanted to see Stefanie. He began to get bored as there seemed to be no sight of her. But coming around the curve in the road, a carriage adorned with wild flowers, poppies, blue cornflowers, and white marguerites, approached. Adolf pinched August's arm. In the carriage was beautiful Stefanie and her mother. The mother wore a grey silk dress and flashed a red parasol and Stefanie donned a stunning crème silk frock and held a huge bouquet of flowers that matched the ones attached to the carriage. Adolf had never seen her look so lovely. As Stefanie rode past, she caught Adolf's eye, flashed him a smile and carefully picked out a flower and threw it to him. When Adolf caught the poppy, he was momentarily transfixed. He repeated over and over, "she loves me."

It was beginning to be the fall of the year and I had not seen Adolf for a very long time. He was always frail looking and I hoped he wasn't ill. Maybe he went off to school for real this time, mother said. Mother tried to discourage me from thinking about him or talking about him because she said he would have spoken to me if he was all that interested. She also didn't want me to hook up with some hobo anyway. I don't know why she thought he was a hobo at that time. I still missed the attention.

Adolf packed his best clothes, his books, his sketchbooks and his drawings and moved to Vienna late in 1906. He commissioned August to keep him posted on the comings and goings of Stefanie. If Stefanie asked about him, August was instructed to say that his friend was not ill but had gone to the Academy in Vienna and upon completion of his courses, would spend a year traveling through Italy and then would return in four years to ask her hand in marriage. August wondered what girl would wait four years, but he knew he had to do what Adolf asked if they were to remain friends.

Adolf regarded himself a gifted sketch artist. He saw much beauty in the Vienna cityscape but much he considered unattractive too. He spent time sketching the "redesign" of the city. He thought it should be more interesting, coherent, and organized. This was the way the Vienna of the future would look and he would make it happen.

Adolf's funds, however, were beginning to run low. He needed to stay alive but regular work was offensive to him. He tried to sell his art but his drawings and watercolors only fetched small amounts of money from dealers who used them to put into empty frames that were for sale. He made posters for some of the shopkeepers, but Adolf knew his work was worthy of much more recognition.

Adolf's mother's landlady, back in Linz, was the aunt of one Alfred Roller, a stage director at the Hofoper and a professor at the Academy of Fine Arts in Vienna. She persuaded her nephew to recommend young Adolf to the Academy. The recommendation was soon followed by a cordial invitation to an interview. The Dean, himself, would see him. Adolf arrived within seconds of the appointed time, the very image of an artist-to-be. The Dean welcomed him into his conference room with a warm smile. Proudly, Adolf spread his portfolio on the magnificent mahogany conference table and stepped back for the Dean and the other members of the admissions committee to see.

As the committee looked through his work, he did not notice at all that their enthusiasm seemed to diminish. After a half hour or so, they thanked him politely and told him that he would hear within a week. He left the interview elated and confident. He would soon be in the company of Wagner, Goethe, and Feuerbach. He went back to his flat. That night he went to *Tristan und Isolde* and let the grandeur of Wagner wash over him.

The Vienna Academy of Fine Arts classification list in October 1907 was posted outside the Dean's office. It contained this entry:

"The following gentleman submitted unsatisfactory drawings and was not admitted to the examination:

Adolf Hitler, b- Braunau am Inn, April 20, 1889, German, Catholic, Father civil servant, upper rank, four grades of Realschule. Few heads. Samples unsatisfactory."

Young Adolf was devastated. "Not qualified to take the Admissions Test." The phrase burned in his consciousness even after the letter was burned in his small fireplace. How could the admissions committee be so shortsighted and oblivious to genius? The Academy of Fine Arts in Vienna would not long survive with this artistic bent. He put on his most superior attitude and went down to the coffeehouse.

Amanda and Jonathan had invited me to spend the weekend in Vienna. They said I could stay at their apartment. They had a nice guest room that had not been used. I also could pay Herwig a quick visit. He complained I never went to see him and that was a good chance. The trip was exciting because I was bored, bored, bored. I needed some excitement. Mother said I could go.

Adolf hurried toward his usual secluded booth on the left side of the Vienna Kaffeehaus. He was annoyed to see it was taken. Then he saw that it was occupied by the lovely Stefanie from Linz and another couple. He almost turned to leave as the sight of her made his legs go weak. But, he took a deep breath and proceeded to stroll over to the table. His heart seemed to stop.

"Stefanie, my dear. What brings you so far from Linz?" he said, in far too loud a voice. "She may not even know my name!" he worried after the fact. And now she would know that he knew hers.

I couldn't believe Adolf was in Vienna and at the same coffeehouse as my friends and I. I wondered if he found out I would be there. Maybe it was just sheer coincidence. I didn't know and never found out.

"Sehr geehrter Herr Hitler, I heard you were often seen here," she said jokingly. The surprise of finding her ever-so-shy admirer from Linz in a coffeehouse in Vienna left Stefanie at a loss for words. Then she said, "Please, won't you join us?" Adolf felt the stress of the Academy rejection fading. The romance from afar and the multitude of poems filled his head and he knew he was right about the knowing glances and her unspoken love for him. He could hardly wait to tell August.

After introductions, Stefanie's friends took the occasion to excuse themselves. It seemed that Stefanie would have a much better time with her friend, who now lived in Vienna, if they were not there.

Adolf sat down and it was the first time we had ever spoken to each other. He looked at me as though he had known me forever. He had very dark eyes. I thought it was very unusual to see him every day for years and then finally have him speak to me in a totally different city.

He made himself very comfortable at the table, leaning his elbow far onto the top and turning his body sideways so he could talk directly to me. Every now and then, he would pull at one of my curls and watch it bounce around my face. We talked until late into the night.

Stefanie and Adolf ordered strudel and coffee and talked. Linz. Art. Opera. Vienna. Plans for the future. And, finally, Adolf's rejection by the academy. Stefanie moved closer. Her closeness and perfume were intoxicating. She was so sensitive and sympathetic. They went back to Adolf's flat.

I don't know what made me go home with him. I knew better than to do that. Maybe the freedom from being away from mother made me feel all grown up. Maybe seeing Adolf again was exciting. I don't know what I was thinking. To this day, I don't know what made me do that.

The flat on Stumpergasse was certainly nothing to write about. A strange feeling swept over Stefanie leaving her to speculate just how successful this ardent admirer really was. It was a rather wretched little place, quite small with just the necessary furnishings to get by day to day. There was only one room with a bed, one tatty rug, far too tiny for the area intended, a plain fireplace and three crates with stacked blankets he said he brought from Linz. The assemblage formed something of a dilapidated bench. She could see the cuffs of a pair of trousers being "pressed" between the bed's mattresses. There were a few empty hooks on the walls that may have held paintings. Some were bent downward. She could see that Adolf was not illiterate as there were stacks of books, many with dog-eared pages, and a number of political pamphlets he had thrown about. The pamphlets probably were the free ones he had picked up at the local coffee shop. The flat's only saving feature was a Southern exposure. Artists do need great light most of the year. Of course, she wondered if this young man would stay long enough to take advantage of it. Oh, well. He really needed comforting tonight.

Adolf saw no need to apologize for the inadequacies of the flat. He knew in his heart that Stefanie had come looking for him. He had, after all, decided that this extraordinary woman was his absolute soul mate. She must already know everything about him... It didn't matter that he didn't have food or drink to offer her. He only hoped he had not talked too much at the coffeehouse. His big fear at this moment was if he had said the wrong thing, it might break the "spell" that was cast upon the two of them. The night was quite cool and he stoked the fire a bit. When he turned around, he saw Stefanie unbuttoning her blouse.

I had never been with a boy before. He knew that too. I'm not sure he had ever been with a girl. He kissed me and hugged me as though he never wanted to let me go. He had so much passion stored up in that thin body of his. For some reason, he was so desirable. I wanted to be with him. I couldn't stop myself. I didn't want to stop myself. I liked being with him. I am ashamed to tell but the fire in us burned hotter than the coals in the fire, which we lay in front of. It was as though we were both starved for love. He was only 20. I was just 17.

Stefanie awoke before Adolf. She crept out of bed so as not to wake him. As she dressed quietly, she noticed his sketchpad and a notebook. There were three very beautiful renderings of her in the pad. She was totally nude in two of them and had a sheer sheet over her modesty in the third. Her hair, loose instead of in the usual bun, formed almost a halo around her face. Stefanie carefully removed the less risqué of the three and put it in her purse. In the notebook were dozens of poems, some in various states of completion and rework. Most seemed to be about her. She had not realized the troubling degree of his obsession with her. She wrote a note. The next morning when Adolf awoke, Stefanie was gone. The note only said "You will do well, my secret."

I sneaked out because I couldn't face him the next morning. I really was horrified that I allowed myself to completely lose control. Maybe the desire had built up over the last few years of seeing him almost every day and not really knowing him. I tried to think straight, but all I felt was shame. I felt dirty, not physically, but mentally...I hoped I would not have to think about it again. I couldn't help wondering if he would come looking for me. I almost hoped that he would.

After she dressed and left Adolf's flat, she went back to her friends' apartment. She was pleased to find that they had already left for the day. Their knowing looks and nudge-nudge, wink-wink in response to her being out all night were not something she was anxious to endure. She let herself in and wrote a nice thank-you note, picked up her things, and left for the train station. She tried to remember the night before but really didn't want to.

Stefanie Bergman realized her indiscretion. She had come to Vienna to see her friends and pay a visit to her brother who was a law student at the University. She needed to get away from home, mother, rules, and the Linz gossip crowd. She just did not plan to be quite this wild.

I tried so hard to put it out of my mind. Mother asked if I had a nice time and I said "yes" but I did not go into any detail. I remember taking bath after bath, trying to get the soiled feeling out of my system. Adolf wasn't dirty. No, it was just what I had done that made me feel dirty. Finally, I quit agonizing over it and tried to get back to my humdrum life.

I didn't even see Adolf's friend, August, for a while. Then, I saw him once. I managed to get away from mother while she was talking to some friends she met on the street. I asked August to write down some things he knew about his friend because I was curious, which I was. I begged August to not mention anything about this to Adolf.

Adolf convinced August to move to Vienna. August, who had become an excellent violinist and violist, auditioned and was accepted to the Conservatory of Music in Vienna and agreed to move into the flat with Adolf. The place was uncomfortable but it would save money. He often tried to get Adolf to tell him how the Art Academy submissions went, but Adolf circumvented the subject. August knew something had not gone well. The music conservatory was demanding and while August applied himself, Adolf slept until noon each day and stumbled through life. He would never speak of school or of work. His day consisted of a casual stroll through the parks or the museums without a care in the world. At night, he entertained himself at the opera house, even if he had heard *Tristan und Isolde* 30 times. The music inspired him and freed his mind to think of his future and the greatness he would achieve some day. Adolf was sure that Stefanie would wait for him for as long as it took to make his "career." He would return to Linz for her, perhaps on a white horse, perhaps not, and only then would he deserve more of such ecstasy.

Adolf Hitler's fortune took a drastic turn for the worse. His mother, Klara, whom he worshiped, died in December 1907. He did not go back to Linz until after her death, nor did he tell anyone about his rejection by the Academy. Only lovely Stefanie knew. With Klara's death, the pension that had allowed him to live a frugal but passable life in Vienna ended. He was forced to stay in Linz for another year. He had no other relatives willing to support him and no marketable skills that would make him enough to live on. A career was out of the question. While he took on menial jobs and thought about other careers, he did not have the ambition to pursue them. He decided to return to Vienna, the city that had rejected him. Day to day living became a problem. He tried to enter the Art Academy once again and again, he failed. Adolf sadly spent the next few years in and out of homeless men's shelters, flophouses and ate from food lines and charity soup kitchens. The experience was dreadful. Out of desperation, he packed his belongings and moved to Munich to enlist in the Bavarian army. Stefanie was probably lost forever. He wondered if she would ever know what happened to him. This was too painful to even think about.

I was able to not think about Vienna for several weeks. Adolf never came calling after that. I felt used. I started to feel angry. It was my fault, I knew. He probably felt heroic. I didn't know what to think.

Things were pretty much the same as they had been in Linz. I was starting to think more about what I wanted to do when I grew up. I did not have any other gentleman friends that I even cared to think about. Women didn't really work back then so I was unsure about my future. Mother and I were two peas in a pod. I told her everything.

Back in Linz, life was about the same. Until she missed her second period, that is. Stefanie's mother was her best friend and main confidant and the only one she could really trust. When she ashamedly told her mother that she thought she was pregnant, she was surprised by the composed reaction and loving support she received. Stefanie's father had died several years before and she knew he would not have accepted the news so calmly. At least the affair had not been with a local boy. Linz was just too provincial for the unwed mother thing.

I couldn't believe it, but I finally realized I was pregnant because my menses did not come when they were supposed to. I was so scared. Mother had never discussed sex with me. I had lived in total ignorance about it. I blamed myself but I blamed mother too. I had to go into hiding somewhere. I was feeling terrible that I had disgraced myself and mother. Cousin Sharon, in Berlin, came to my rescue just in time.

They started thinking about how to handle the pregnancy when Stefanie's mother remembered that the Bergmans had distant cousins in Berlin. Berlin was a town that would not take much notice of Stefanie. The Berlin relatives were rich and successful. Stefanie and her mother had met them on a visit when Stefanie was just five. They were gracious and generous at that time and perhaps they still would be. A letter was written discretely asking for a place for Stefanie to stay for the duration of the pregnancy. They were willing to pay whatever the rent would be as long as it was in a safe and somewhat convenient location.

A few days later they got their reply. Cousin Sharon Schneider, the matriarch of the Berlin Schneiders, had an apartment over one of their shops that she graciously offered to Stefanie for her confinement. Stefanie could help clean the shop or assist in the office for as long as she was able in order to keep her from feeling completely like a burden. Sharon wanted no rent or other compensation. Stefanie was thrilled that she had found such support in her situation. She smiled for the first time since realizing that she was with child.

The Schneider family owned Schneider Fabrics, a manufacturer of woolen cloth. It was a lucrative business that allowed them to have a mansion in Berlin, an estate in Cologne, an apartment in Venice and a retreat in Switzerland near Lucerne. The main and original factories were in Cologne.

Mother helped me get ready for Berlin and the next few months. We didn't know what we would do once the baby was born. We would figure it out, but I had to get over the first hurdle.

After a tearful goodbye, Stefanie left for Berlin. Her mother had helped pack her bags with a few large garments intended to conceal a growing belly and tonics and potions to keep her healthy. No one else in Linz was aware of her "condition." Her mother told friends that she had taken a scholarship to study in Pretoria.

I moved into a sweet little apartment owned by Cousin Sharon's family above their business offices. It was very plain but clean and had everything I needed to live comfortably.

The apartment over the shop in Berlin was comfortable and in a quiet neighborhood. The building was used as a sales office for the woolen fabrics milled by the Schneider factories in Cologne. Franz, the salesman and bookkeeper, and Fritz, the stock manager, initially gave Stefanie simple chores to do such as minding the door and postal errands, but Stefanie had the energy and ability to do more.

I wanted Cousin Sharon to know that I was not lazy and I was willing to work for my keep. I also felt well enough to work, only a little morning sickness every now and then, but it would pass.

Johann Sebastian Schneider, the heir apparent to the Schneider Empire, came by on Tuesdays and Thursdays to check on the shop. He found Stefanie attractive, even radiant during her pregnancy. Being a smart dresser and a clever young woman, Stefanie watched her weight and managed to hide her growing body well. Even the staff of Schneider Fabrics suspected nothing until the very end of her confinement. By then, she had proved to be both valuable and instrumental in the showroom, setting up and organizing displays to show to perspective customers. Having an extreme flair for design and presentation, her efforts made sales a lot easier. Once the staff learned of her condition, no one bothered to gossip. Stefanie had become their friend.

I had so wished I wasn't pregnant because Johann Schneider was a very attractive man. He was Sharon's son and he was next in line to his father, who was head of the company. He was very cordial to me and I liked him a lot. He was soooo good-looking and nice. He knew I was in a motherly way and that's why I was occupying their apartment, but I still tried to hide my belly as best I could. I didn't eat a lot so I kept myself in good shape.

Stefanie soon learned Johann's routine and had coffee and a sweet of some kind waiting for him when he arrived. Johann was happy to talk of anything except the wool business and so enjoyed these afternoons. Despite her "situation," Johann found himself falling in love with Stefanie. He thought she was incredibly beautiful and extremely smart. Stefanie never spoke of the father of her child-to-be and Johann never inquired. Johann's mother, Sharon, liked Stefanie well enough, but was not really thrilled with the relationship that was obviously developing between the two of them. She had higher hopes for her only child.

Johann was the apple of his mother's eye. Sharon and Sebastian had brought a little girl into the world a few years before Johann, but because of shoddy and incompetent birthing practices, the child died during delivery and Sharon suffered excessive bleeding. Only by the grace of God was she spared. When she became an expectant mother for the second time, she and Sebastian spent her complete pregnancy looking for a midwife with a clean record. It was a nerve-wracking experience for both Sharon and Sebastian as Sebastian was 20 years her senior and they knew this might be their last chance for carrying on the family name. Thankfully, Johann was born healthy and it was an easy birth.

Johann was a good boy and an obedient child and earned praises from his teachers and mentors. He strived for good grades and wanted to follow in his father's footsteps. He was fast with figures and could talk anyone into anything. Sebastian took him into the business at a very tender age. This proved to be a wise decision as Sebastian fell ill when Johann was only 18. Johann basically inherited a larger than reasonable burden and did not have much time for friends and fun. Sebastian did what he could from his wheelchair, but as his strength diminished, Johann was saddled with more responsibility.

Johann had to be the sweetest person I had ever met. He had the most beautiful body too. I finally asked him if he had a girlfriend. He said, "Yes, I do." My heart sank and I almost started to cry. And then he said, "You're my girlfriend, are you not?"

The only recreation the young man had time for was an afternoon swim in the family pool at the close of the business day. His daily routine served to develop a well-toned body and sun-bleached hair. His big smile, his tanned square jaws and large hazel eyes took Stefanie's heart away. Everything about him was model perfect but he chose to deal with wool. And best of all, he seemed to be choosing her.

Sharon saw the writing on the wall and began planning how to bring Stefanie into the Schneider fold. She was apprehensive but Sebastian, in his wise but weakened state, convinced her that Johann was in love and was a level-headed boy capable of making his own choices. Stefanie was a very pretty girl, well-mannered and from a respectable family. He could certainly do worse.

My mother sent some adorable baby clothes, a bassinet and things to me for the baby. I wanted her to visit but she had my grandmother to take care of. Mother didn't like responsibility like that. I felt for her. I wrote back thanking her and I told her about Johann.

Stefanie's mother, back in Linz, was still trying to hide the unwed daughter thing but was increasingly burdened by her own mother's decline. Cora seemed resigned to let Stefanie make a new and better life on her own for now. She secretly, however, took pleasure in helping prepare for the arrival of the baby. Tiny clothing, a bassinet and a few necessities were addressed to Schneider Fabrics in Berlin so no one would ever suspect. She made sure that her daughter had been provided with enough money to deal with whatever situation might occur. She was satisfied that Johann was a good person, that he loved Stefanie in spite of her condition, and was from a well-off family. She was pleased that Stefanie had found happiness.

Little Karl Bergman Hittler was born in July of 1908, while the Schneiders were vacationing at their Swiss retreat. It was very warm that week in Berlin when Stefanie went into labor. She considered the terrible pains of childbirth and the oppressive heat in her small apartment to be part of the penance she had to pay for her wild and unexpected liaison. At least, she managed the birth on her own with the help of Mrs. Troutmann, a professional mid-wife hired by Johann and his mother.

I had not felt well for about a week and I called the mid-wife Mrs. Troutmann, the lady I had hired to help me with the birth, to come and stay with me if she could. She did and it was fortunate because I went into labor in the middle of the night. The pains were terrible and it was hot, and back then, there was nothing for pain and no air conditioning. I just had to endure it.

Mrs. Troutmann bore the reputation of being meticulously clean, diligent and welltrained. She possessed certificates for her formal medical education. She was a widow without children of her own who devoted her later years to practicing the art of a mid-wife. Stefanie felt blessed to have found this woman and placed the utmost confidence in her ability. The baby was delivered without complications. Mrs. Troutmann liked Stefanie and agreed to stay on for at least three weeks to assist her through her recovery.

I gave birth to a precious baby boy. He was so cute I couldn't believe he was real. He looked more like a little doll. Mrs. Troutmann cleaned him up, wrapped him in a new white blanket, one that my mother had sent, and placed him beside me on the bed. The only blemish on him was a little birthmark behind his shoulder. He looked at me with a questioning look. I told him I was his mommy and that I would take good care of him. He was already hungry.

Little Karl was beautiful, healthy and perfect except for a small, crescent-shaped birthmark on his right shoulder.

When Karl was a few weeks old, I took him for walks. We passed a church and could hear voices singing. I stopped in one Sunday for Mass. I tried to get Karl to look up at the pretty glass that was on the church window. We sat close to that window and the beautiful colors kept him fascinated. The figure was St. Stephen. He cooed out loud and made the lady sitting next to me laugh.

On Sunday mornings, Stefanie could hear a choir singing in the little chapel East of the apartment. During the winter, she had not even noticed the church. One Sunday, she took baby Karl for a stroll to hear the music. As they approached the church, she was attracted to a large stained glass window depicting St. Stephen. She reflected on how her trials and worries were pretty insignificant compared to St. Stephen's suffering. A priest came out and commented on her "beautiful baby." She knew the Church needed to have a record of her son's birth and asked the priest about the process.

After Mass, Karl and I followed the Rector into the church office and recorded his birth. I did not know how to even spell Karl's father's last name. I put two t's in it instead of one... "Hittler."

He invited her into the Rectory and together they recorded the baby's arrival listing his father as "Adolf Hittler of Braunau am Inn, then Linz, now of Vienna." She had confessed to the priest in Linz of her encounter and was assured of God's forgiveness. Her life seemed to be getting back on track.

Thank goodness, my waistline has come back quickly. When Johann got back he told me I looked beautiful. He even held baby Karl and bounced him on his knee.

When Johann returned to Berlin, Stefanie's girlish figure had returned and she was even more attractive to him than before he left. She found him sweet, handsome, and rich. In November, Johann proposed to her. She gladly accepted.

When Johann Sebastian Schneider asked for my hand in marriage I was the happiest girl alive. I could hardly wait to write to mother. And even Sharon was happy for us.

A society wedding was out of the question since Stefanie was already a mother. Sharon arranged for a simple ceremony in their home with a few friends. Stefanie, being the fashion conscious girl that she was, expressed the desire to have a beautiful gown even for a home wedding. And though it wouldn't be the traditional white, she wanted it to be close. She felt this was to be her new beginning. She realized she would not be dragging the train down a church aisle, but there was the huge Schneider mansion staircase and that would work for her. After all, Johann deserved a beautiful bride and motherhood did not affect her youthful feminine spirit in the least.

I helped design the most beautiful wedding gown that mother and I could afford. It was made by Hans Burgher, Sharon's dressmaker. He was marvelous. We ordered the fabrics from French houses and the newspapers made a big deal about the wedding and the dress. I felt like a princess.

Ecru was the color she selected. Stefanie's perfect figure fared well in any style but she chose a classic Edwardian pattern to be custom made by Sharon's couturier, a master craftsman. Stefanie wanted to be accepted by her soon-to-be mother-in-law and much to her own mother's dismay, she turned down Cora's suggestion of a Gibson Girl gown for a more conservative look which was Sharon's preference. Stefanie adored her mother and wanted to include her in the planning, but fitting into the Schneider family was now the most important thing she had to do. Cora would have to understand.

Sharon and Stefanie selected the fabrics and as with any family of wealth and prominence, the fabrics would have to come from France. The boned bodice of the gown would be made of fine French lace over silk, have a sweeping collar of ecru silk satin and puffed sleeves under the collar of pleated cream silk much in keeping with Fortuny's fabrics that Stefanie loved. The waist would measure a tiny 22 inches. This required Stefanie to corset herself in, a real challenge, she realized, since not all of the weight gain during her confinement had left her body. The skirt of ecru silk satin would fall gracefully over her slender hips hitting the floor in front and billowing out to form the long train in back. A gathered insert of French lace would flare over the center of the train. The gown would be a masterpiece. A simple headpiece of fresh flowers would adorn her golden hair. Glad that she had not overspent during her pregnancy, the making of such a spectacular garment was expensive and neither she nor her mother wanted to appear cheap.

The French fabric houses were more than pleased to work with the bride-to-be and the family as a Schneider wedding was great press for them. Stefanie thrilled to learn that the Paris papers had gotten wind of her soon-to-be wedding and published speculative drawings of her finished gown. It did not take long for the word to spread to Berlin. It became big gossip as to how the gown would be fashioned. Stefanie did not think that being a Schneider would change her, but the increase in respect and deference was hard to ignore.

I became Mrs. Johann Schneider and I loved the title. Johann and I received gifts from all over the world, I think. It took me weeks to send thank you notes. It was like a dream come true.

The "simple" event was to be easily the most elegant Stefanie had ever attended. The flowers alone would break most anyone's bank. She was formally introduced to the household staff. She marveled as her trousseau accumulated from the seamstress and Johann's friends and associates. She approved the menu and wine list submitted by Sharon. Johann spent several days acting like a tour guide as they wandered around the family home. To Johann's delight and Sharon's surprise, she seemed immediately at home with the luxury of her life-to-come. She already had a deep appreciation for the arts and music and having "old masters" around the house was a thrill she fully appreciated as well as the Victorian furniture and style of the home. After all, Kaiser Wilhelm, the German Emperor, was the grandson of Queen Victoria.

Johann wanted to adopt Karl. He said he didn't want to know who his biological father was nor did he care. He knew Karl's real father did not even know of my pregnancy. He said he would raise Karl as his own. I was the luckiest woman alive as well as the happiest.

Soon after they were married Johann asked to adopt Karl. The local rumor was that Karl was his child anyway, so Karl Bergman Hittler became Karl Emanuel Bergman Schneider, of the Berlin Schneiders. Stefanie wanted no snags in her new life.

I tried to change Karl's birth certificate to show Johann as his father but it wasn't allowed. The Priest was angry with me for asking. He pounded his clenched fist down on his desk and wondered how I could request such a thing. So I said I was sorry and explained why I had asked. He said he would separate the records out so they would be hidden away in a bottle and no one would ever look for them there. That was the best he could do.

On a day when she was able to get away from the house alone, Stefanie secretly went back to Kreuzberg to talk to the priest, Father Mark Gutenburg. She asked him for a change on the birth record of her son showing Johann Schneider as the father. The priest's answer was "no" and that it was "against all the rules." He would, however, separate the Certificate from the rest. He would secure it except for a numerical entry in the rolls referencing his action.

Father Gutenburg found an empty sacramental wine bottle, inscribed it with the entry number in the rolls, sealed the Certificate in the bottle with the original cork and sealing wax, then placed the bottle in a mausoleum niche in the wall of the church undercroft. Only God need know.

Stefanie and Johann decided that no good could come from Karl knowing that he was illegitimate so it was never discussed by them again. Their second son, August, was born in 1910.

Johann and I decided to never mention that Karl was not his real son. He loved him the same as his own and would take care of him as his own. I was so relieved and felt so fortunate. From that point on, we were all Schneiders.

The End of My Saga.

Dear Ones, I also have a scrapbook that I have kept for many, many years. I have misplaced it. There are things that you might want to look at in it. I will continue to look for it and when I find it, I will tie it to the bottom of the box. I love you all.

22. A STAINED GLASS WINDOW

Andy and Larissa looked at each other with solemn expressions. They put the books back into the box. Larissa carefully set the floral book on the netting and repacked the dried flowers around it, retying the frayed ribbon. She and Andy were without words. She felt very strange knowing the little book's contents. She put all the filled bunches back in the order they were found.

Andy just shook his head in disbelief. He still needed absolute proof. He told Larissa to call Anna for him while he showered to say that he was headed to Berlin. That something had come up concerning Karl's campaign and he would call in later. He knew they had to get there, pronto...

Raudebusch was probably already on his way. He asked Larissa to come with him since she was never very thrilled about his comings and goings without notice and he had missed her terribly. And besides, the shopping was great in Berlin.

Andy took the box, placed it in a large plastic bag and shoved it under his bed. There was no need to get it back to Johann this week. He would up the security on the apartment to make sure the box stayed put. He kissed Larissa and said that he would like nothing better than to make nice to her beautiful body, but that it had to wait until they were in Berlin. She told him she would throw a few things in an overnight bag for him. He looked too exhausted anyway. She might even need to drive so he could get a couple of hours of shut-eye on the way.

****

In Berlin, Larissa was dropped off on the main mid-town strip and they planned to meet back at the Berlin apartment at 6:00 PM. Andy drove off to find where Stefanie and Johann met. He knew that he was looking for a shop with an apartment above it instead of a residence. He went directly to #7 Luckauer Strasse. It was still a store, now a currency exchange, with an apartment above. If St. Stephen's Church was in the neighborhood, it would probably be annexed to St. Michaels, a few blocks north. He parked the car and started walking north toward St. Michael's across the rubble of the Wall and there, a block from the old Schneider office, was the blackened ruin of another church. Only part of one wall still stood. Curious, he walked closer. There, in the wall, still in the iron and leaded frame, in beautiful stained glass undamaged by strife and time, was the likeness of a suffering young man with an angel overhead being stoned by the citizens. The church may not have been St. Stephen's, but the window's subject was definitely St. Stephen.

A large gray and white cat strolled out from the pile of demolition. It stared at Andy with that aloof, "what are you doing in my church?" look. Andy spoke to the cat and assured him that he would not harm his house. Andy cautiously walked around the old church. Even to his unprofessional eye there was not nearly enough rubble to be the total structure. As he looked around, he saw some similar stone over where the wall had stood. A few hundred meters east, the debris from the wall had been hauled off and this area would probably be cleared in a week or so. Daylight was fading and it would soon be hard to see, so he rejoined Larissa at the apartment his company kept in Berlin to contemplate his next move.

Could there still be evidence in this obvious ruin? Could it have been moved to another location before the damage to the church happened? Or right after? He called Johann Schneider and asked if he knew an architect or engineer that he could trust. Someone who could look at the ruin and perhaps locate what was the undercroft or mausoleum.

Glocke and Glocke had managed the refurbishment of the Compound when it was reopened in the seventies and designed most of the sites for Cologne Wool Goods since then. Luther Glocke was a good friend of Johann's and lived in Berlin. Johann would call him and ask him to call Andy.

Andy and Larissa went to dinner. When they got back to the apartment, the phone was ringing. It was Luther Glocke. "Good evening, Herr Becker. I understand you are studying an old church somewhere around here."

"Thank you for calling. Yes, I am trying to put to rest the rumor of a skeleton in the Schneider closet. The answer may be in the undercroft mausoleum of this old church ruin with a window commemorating the Stoning of St. Stephen." How could Andy make the search interesting without revealing too much?

"St. Sophie's chapel by St. Michael's." Offered the architect. "Designed by Otto Glocke in about 1820. The narthex took a direct bomb hit during the war and only the back wall was left standing. It was abandoned like many chapels in the Eastern zone. I think it was partially salvaged to build that section of the Wall. Fine white marble at one time." Andy could hear him sucking on his pipe. "There isn't a lot of that church left."

Andy reeled. "I don't suppose you have the plans on file."

"No, no, it was a different Glocke. But I do know the structure. I did a sketch of it back when I was a student in the dim past. It was a charming little chapel."

"Did it have an undercroft?" Andy was pushing his luck.

"I don't remember it, if it did. But it did have a basement and a sub-basement, which was a little unusual for the area. My driver and I will pick you up at 8 in the morning. Let us see where the mystery leads us."

"I'll be ready." Andy poured two glasses of the Riesling always stocked at the apartment and they turned in for the night.

****

Wally Raudebusch was frustrated. He had been to every Roman Catholic Church near the Savignyplatz and there was no mention or clue to the elusive St Stephen's that he could find. He went back to the hotel and decided to check out the other location. Tomorrow was another day.

The next morning he found his way to #7 Luckauer Strasse. It was the currency exchange with a nail salon above. The structure looked nineteenth century. What a dreary neighborhood. He studied the Frommer's guide and saw that St. Michael's was a few blocks North. No other churches were in the neighborhood according to the guide. He mentally talked himself into an optimistic and determined frame of mind and walked briskly to the North.

He had to walk around the Mercedes limo to continue on his way. He only barely noticed the two well-dressed men climbing around what was left of the Wall.

He continued to St Michael's. He could tell from hearing the organ and choir that the morning service was in progress.

There was an artist in the platz with a good start on a charcoal sketch of the church tower. "Very nice," he commented.

"Shhh. I only have about ten more minutes of this light. Once it is gone, I have to wait for tomorrow, and they are forecasting clouds. I have the worst luck. I think I will have to move to Athens or somewhere where the weather is better. Could you stand over there? I have to catch just the right glare."

Wally, half amused, stood "over there." After a few minutes the artist started packing up his supplies. "Do you live around here?" he asked the artist.

"Around here, around there. It's all the same. So many church towers and so little time to capture them all. I'm already twenty nine. I don't think I can finish." His particular madness seemed harmless and even a little amusing. He had his beret laying on the ground with a few coins in it. Wally got out a 10-shilling piece and dropped it in. "Danke." The appreciation was overwhelming.

"Have you done the St. Stephen's tower?" Wally asked, fishing but half kidding.

The artist let out a yelp and dropped into a fetal position and looked around frantically. "Watch out for the rocks! Watch out!"

Wally stepped back. "Hey, I didn't mean to scare you. Do you know where St. Stephen's is?"

The artist looked up, then down the street toward St. Sophie's. "He's dead now, you know. He was so sad. Let's go cry about him." He picked up his kit and started briskly South toward the church ruin.

Fascinated, Wally followed. When they got to the window, tears welled up in the artist's eyes and he fell to his knees again. That was when Wally saw the window.

He did not know exactly who St. Stephen was, but he was pretty sure that the window depicted his fate. The limo was just pulling out. Wally wrote down the license plate number. The day had been so strange so far, maybe the VIPs in the limo were working on the same clues that he was.

Surely there was nothing in this ruin that survived since 1907. He looked around for a few minutes, not noticing that much of the remains were at the Wall site. The artist was still staring sadly at the window. He went back to the hotel.

****

Luther Glocke arrived a little early, about 7:20. Andy, fortunately, was ready and downstairs reading the paper. Larissa was still asleep. He heard Luther ask the doorman to ring his apartment. He went over and introduced himself to the architect.

Luther was a diminutive man with slicked down salt and pepper hair and little round horned rim glasses. "Sketching St Sophie's was usually an assignment when I was at the Institute. It had probably been sketched more than any other place in Berlin except the Gate. Too bad it's gone now. What, exactly, are we looking for?"

"A birth record from 1908." Andy answered as they climbed into the limo. "A question has been raised about the lineage of Karl Schneider and that question led to St. Stephen which led to St. Sophie. I don't suppose you know of another instance of St. Stephen in Berlin?"

"No, no other St. Stephen comes to mind, and I am pretty sure I know all the religious buildings in the area…sort of a hobby of mine. Of course, there's the Cathedral in Vienna. Are you sure that you should be looking in Berlin?"

"Let's say that I am more sure about Berlin than the name of the church." Andy studied his new acquaintance as the limo moved quickly through the lighter-than-usual Berlin traffic. Soon, St. Sophie's was in sight. "Here we are," said Luther. "Let's see if I can remember the place from what might be left of it."

Luther knocked the old ash out of his pipe and reloaded it as they walked over to St. Sophie's and paused in front of the St. Stephen window. The sun was shining through it and it really was a work of art. "Unscathed after all these years and bombings," Andy thought, "it's kind of a miracle." Luther was trying to re-assemble the structure in his mind and remember his assignment from long ago as he worked at lighting his pipe.

The first floor of the building was mostly gone so they stepped down into the basement. The remnants of some furniture and fixtures were strewn about. Luther made his way to the northeast corner of the building where the staircase that led down to the sub-basement used to be. A large section of the ceiling above had fallen, still intact, over the stairwell. "We will need help to clear this away," he told Andy. "I think I remember the record vault being down there."

They climbed back to the surface and went over to survey the Wall. Sure enough, significant parts of the church were evident, including part of the lower wall that included the mausoleum chambers, the altar and part of the porch. Luther was visibly saddened by the desecration. They went back to the car. They didn't notice Wally and the 'artist' by the window.

Luther Glocke called a friend at the Ministry of Buildings in East Berlin. They were still in business. Could he bring a crew to St. Sophie's and make sure the structure was safe for visitors? It had been in the no-man's-land since the sixties and now, with the Wall and all, probably it should be stabilized and checked out in case tourists started climbing around. The Buildings bureaucrat hemmed and hawed, so Luther offered a case of Macallan's 15-year-old as an inducement. It worked. Luther could pick up a permit the next morning. Andy picked up the tab for the Scotch.

Glocke arranged for a front-loader and several men to be at the church the following afternoon. He had the Scotch delivered to the Ministry official that evening. He and his wife and Andy and Larissa had a nice dinner at Lutèce, Berlin.

****

Wollweber called Wally that evening at the hotel. Was there any new development?

Wally disclosed that he might have found the church and gave him the license plate number of the limo he saw. Wollweber said he wanted to check out the limo ownership and would get back to Wally.

Wollweber called back excitedly about fifteen minutes later. "The limo is registered to Glocke and Glocke, the architects who do most of Schneider's work," he shouted in the phone. "We've got them.

We've got them!" Wally was less enthusiastic. "Where have we got them and how will it help us?" he asked the former agent.

"Now we have someone to lead us to the answers." Wollweber was ecstatic. "All we have to do is follow the limo. I'm on it!"

Wally took two antacids and went to bed.

23. THE BOTTLE IS GONE

Luther was meeting with other clients at his office the following morning so he had a messenger retrieve the permit from the Buildings Department. Luther did not notice Wollweber across the street watching the limo. After lunch, Luther got into the limo and picked up Andy and met the crew at St. Sophie's.

They affixed the permit to part of the structure still standing and started uncovering the stairwell to the sub-basement. It took about 2 hours to remove the debris and convince themselves that the structure was in good enough shape for them to go down.

There was about two inches of water in the sub-basement. There were also several file cabinets in various states of decay. Each was labeled. Births. Deaths. Marriages. Baptisms. Confirmations. Luther quickly discovered that there were significant numbers of church records that still could be retrieved. He told Andy, "We really need to let the staff at St. Michael's know about this. They will want to conserve as much as possible."

"Let's see if 1908 births are still readable, Luther. Then we can call St. Michael's." They approached the "Births" cabinet.

The bottom drawer was rotted and could not be opened. On the "Weddings" cabinet the bottom drawer was still marked "1820–1899." The second drawer was marked "1900–1915." The "Births" drawer labels were unreadable. They started working the second drawer of the "Births" cabinet trying to open it carefully but suddenly, the front of the drawer came off in Andy's hand. The folders and papers inside were discolored and curled but somewhat readable. One folder was labeled "1908." Andy carefully retrieved it and started thumbing through. The 18th page was smaller and yellower than the rest. On it was the note:

"By the Grace of God, this Innocent Bastard's record was reserved to the Mausoleum, sealed in a vessel which once held that which became Christ's Blood. Fr. M. Gutenburg, 12 July, AD 1909."

They replaced the folder without the note. Luther went to tell the staff at St. Michael's of the records they had uncovered. Andy went to the section of the Wall where the mausoleum remains still rested. On the way he accidentally dropped the note, which the wind carried eastward. A passerby saw him chasing the note and caught it. Andy ran up breathlessly. "Oh, thank you, my friend. The paper is really important to me."

"So glad to help." Wollweber handed the note to Andy.

Andy returned to the Grabnische segment. The niches were all empty now. It appeared that a row or two might be buried still and there was no assurance that this was the only Grabnische wall. He went back to the church and asked if the front-loader could be used to lift the mausoleum up and check for buried niches. The operator guided the machine over to the wall and attached a chain to the Grabnische. Slowly the stone was raised. It was obviously pretty close to the limit of weight the front-loader could lift but it managed. There were no more niches. One niche was odd in that the sediment had formed a cradle-like shape as though a wine bottle had been stored there. The bottle was gone now.

Andy saw Luther returning from St. Michael's with a priest. He went over to meet them. The priest was saying that he would have the papers transferred to St. Michael's and then probably to the Cathedral of St. Hedwig. Luther gave the construction crew instructions on stabilizing the structure and installing appropriate railings and signage. He said he would send over sketches and specifications the following morning.

On the way back to Andy's apartment he told Luther of the lack of any bottles or anything else of value in the mausoleum niches. They had seemingly come to the end of the road.

****

"By the Grace of God, this Innocent Bastard's record was reserved to the Mausoleum, sealed in a vessel which once held that which became Christ's Blood. Fr. M. Gutenburg, 12 July AD 1909."

Wollweber's years as a spy served him well as he memorized the phrase after only glancing at it. As Andy walked away from him toward the rubble of the Wall, Wollweber wrote down the phrase verbatim in his notepad before he even considered the meaning. He got into his car, pulled over into the shadows and continued watching what was going on. His targets did not seem to be suspicious of him. After they were finished, Luther and Andy climbed into the limo and as it took off, Wollweber followed it. It dropped Andy off at the apartment and then went back to Luther's office. At about 8:00 PM, Wollweber continued to follow the black car to Luther's home. After the last stop, the chauffeur took the car to the lot for washing and detailing for tomorrow's service. Ernst Wollweber continued to concentrate on the text carefully transcribed.

"...vessel which once held that which became Christ's Blood." "I think he is talking about a wine bottle, a sacramental wine bottle." Then the memory of the American with the rock and the bottle on the Evening News crept into his consciousness. The Stasi equipment was probably still recording all news broadcasts from West Berlin. And that was the day the Wall came down. Could it be?

24. THE STUDENTS GO HOME

Back at the Petersen house, Werther had enjoyed Alan's company and thought he was the right young man for Mary. "They're a lot alike." Elsie had to agree. They had had an exciting week to say the least. Everyone wished there could have been more time for visiting but with the Wall coming down and the crowds around the house, it was hard to concentrate on anything but the news.

Alan did do some sightseeing in spite of the massive crowding and some rioting. He and Mary took pictures of Dr. Hejduk's buildings and those of Mies van der Rohe and he got to meet some of Mary's friends, so that was good. Best of all, he got to know Mary's parents. That was the most important thing to him when he suggested the trip, and of course, the Silvermans were curious about the Petersen family.

Werther was an executive at Siemens and had considerable diplomatic privileges and Alan thought that was interesting to tell his parents. And Werther's charge was to keep the company's interests secure in Iran in the aftermath of the Iran-Iraq war. Iran blamed Germany almost entirely for Saddam Hussein's chemical weapons and keeping the German industrial giant's business on an even keel in Iran required diplomatic finesse that taxed the most talented of negotiators. Complaints had to be handled literally within hours and public apologies for transgressions, real or imagined, required a 24-7 dedication. Elsie was the Administrator of Special Education at a small private school. Her vacation included essentially the whole month of December.

At dinner on the last evening, Alan and Mary said they were serious about each and some planning for the future may be forthcoming. The Petersens asked if they would only consider finishing their degrees first. There was no question that they would. That seemed to satisfy the Petersens.

Saturday morning, as breakfast was ending, an insistent knock on the door annoyed Werther. Wolfgang was on his way to a friend's house and as he made his exit, he almost slammed into cousin Joanie who was standing there in baggy jeans, a military jacket and carrying an overstuffed backpack. Wolfgang announced that Joanie 'is here' and left. Werther's heart sank.

Joan Kaufman was Elsie's older brother's girl. The Kaufmans lived in East Germany so there had been relatively little contact with them. Periodically the Kaufmans would get visit passes to see their kin in West Germany but, all in all, there was not much closeness possible. Today Joanie had a patch over her left eye. Joanie was always in the thick of the resistance to the Communist government. She was not really violent or reckless and so did not get executed or sent to a Gulag but she had been jailed several times and was on the Stasi list of rabble-rousers. Werther's position as a diplomat depended on being "diplomatic" and not associated with protesters and troublemakers. Trouble seemed to follow Joanie wherever she went. Werther was not amused by the visit.

"We may finally be winning, Aunt Elsie," she announced. She was in the area to attend a meeting in East Berlin and, with the end of the Wall, came by to say "Hello."

The patch over Joanie's eye was of concern to Elsie who tended to worry about everything. "What in the world happened to your eye, dear?" Elsie asked in German. Elsie did not realize the injury was permanent. "Just a battle scar, Aunt Elsie. But I am still fighting the good fight." Alan was introduced and there were a few obligatory hugs and handshakes and as quickly as she appeared, she was gone.

The week was over much too soon. Elsie dreaded the last good-byes before Alan and Mary boarded the plane. The trip back to New York was pleasant enough except for an unfortunate flat tire on the way to the airport in Berlin. Unload the luggage, change the tire, reload the luggage. They still had plenty of time to catch the plane. They arrived back in Manhattan and Alan realized he liked his Volkswagen that he kept at his parents' home even more after the German experience.

25. WHY US?

After they arrived back in New York, Mary was getting into the holiday spirit. Being Jewish meant that Alan had never had a Christmas tree growing up but Tannenbaum was a large part of Mary's upbringing especially decorating the tree. There was never a lack of Hanukkah presents, and Alan did attend a lot of Christmas parties. His folks were big on attending holiday gatherings and they had many Gentile friends. They just never had a Christmas tree. Mary wanted one and he agreed to it. Even the Silvermans didn't seem to mind. The more Mary wormed her way into their hearts, the more lenient they became with Alan's day-to-day decisions.

It was Saturday and Mary talked Alan into buying the tree. They decided to walk around Second Avenue until they found a place with less than florist shop prices. Mary took her time in selecting the perfect Christmas tree. Alan worried how to get it back to the apartment but the tree lot guys bundled it up so the two of them could carry it on their shoulders. This was a new experience for both of them. Mary ran up to open the front door while Alan stood at the foot of the steep stair with the tree. "You didn't lock up again, Mr. Trust-Everyone Silverman."

"I'm sure I did, sweetie," he answered, slightly exasperated as he struggled to get the tree up to the second floor walk-up. He was sort of glad that Jews didn't like to drag big dead trees into their houses for the holidays.

They both wrestled it into the small apartment and it quickly sank in that an uninvited person or persons had done a number on the place... Books, pillows, chairs. Things were scattered everywhere.

"What the hell? Don't move...I'll check the other rooms!" Alan quickly looked around the small apartment and in the closets. "No one is here, but something's not right."

Mary was always adamant about leaving everything in order. "What happened? And who would break in just to screw things up?" Alan had a puzzled look on his face. Mary panicked as she picked up a small, framed photo from the floor. She felt so 'violated' that her personal things might have been rummaged through by a stranger. It used to make her furious when her brother Wolfie would go through her belongings, but this was someone she probably didn't know. She had heard about break-ins in the city, but it didn't look like anything was taken. Someone had picked the lock.

"I'm scared, Alan." She looked at the chair that was dumped upside down and, putting her hand over her quivering chin, she started crying. Alan pulled her close to him, kissed her forehead and tried to comfort her. He felt funny too...damned funny. "I don't think we are in any danger, but I don't quite get it..."

"Is anything missing? Jewelry? Stereo? Records? Drafting stuff? We really don't have much worth stealing and they didn't bother to take the little prayer rug which is the only thing we have of any value."

Alan wiped the sweat collecting on his glasses while Mary cautiously walked into the bedroom. "I'm not sure that nothing was taken, but it really looks like someone was searching for something."

Mary noticed papers scattered on their bed. "What are our passports doing out? You weren't looking at them, were you?"

"Not since we got back from Berlin. They were in the dresser drawer."

Alan was still trying to make some sense of it. "Maybe some frat house had a pledge rally with a scavenger hunt. You know, find a yellow Number 4 pencil or something. At my prep school I once had to come up with a "chicken asshole on a stick" at two in the morning. Frat brother or not, I still wish Jerry Bartley pounds of grief for that assignment. Of course, this is New York. That wouldn't be an explanation."

Mary tried to smile, but was not reassured. "More like a random break-in for drug money," she offered, "but that freaks me."

"Druggies are not usually this neat," Alan responded. "Very weird."

They thought about calling the cops but if nothing were stolen, the cops wouldn't do anything…maybe file a "break-in" report but how would that help?

They straightened up the apartment and set up the Christmas tree. The stand holding the tree was a bit flimsy. It still did the job. The two strands of lights they bought were obviously not enough. Mary wearily looked at the tree and realized this little break-in episode had dumped a wet blanket on her holiday spirit. What could they have been looking for? Alan had mentioned that he was hungry on the way home but she had lost her appetite. Maybe something to eat might settle them down and they could think. Mary prepared her German potato pancakes and Alan pulled out a couple of forks from the drawer and applesauce from the fridge. Alan commented that the Latkes tasted so much like the ones his mother makes. He always said that. She said "No, these are Kartoffelpuffer when I make them." She always said that. Alan ate, she nibbled, and they sat quietly.

The phone rang. It was Alan's father in Larchmont. In a shaky voice, he told Alan that someone had broken into the house. They were not absolutely sure if anything was taken or not. The police were still there. The front entry door had been pried open, the Mezuzah was on the floor and some personal papers including insurance policies and passports were strewn about. He said mom was horrified. The burglars entered through the front instead of the garage and Janet found the entry door wide open. So far, it looked like everything was still there, just messed up. They were asking "Why?"

This was double-weird.

26. WHO HAS THE BOTTLE?

Ernst Wollweber went over to the monitoring station. The archive was there. He shoved the cassette into the player and started it. Interviews with Kohl in Poland this historic day, interviews with Honecker then Krenz, the new East German Chancellor. Finally the American. The session was less than a minute long but there in the background was the very ruin where he had spent the day. "…a bottle and a rock," the interviewee said. The bottle appeared to be a wine bottle. The rock appeared to be a rock. The American's name was Alan Silverman. Now it got a little sticky.

Ernst Wollweber was not exactly welcome at the American Embassy or the Bonn government's customs operation. While not really a famous spy, he was known by enough people that someone in the office would probably recognize him and freeze him out. How could he find this Silverman character? Maybe Wally from Cologne would be able to nose around without arousing suspicion. He made a video copy of the interview and left for Wally's hotel.

Wally was not in his room. Ernst decided to check in the bar. Sure enough, Wally was there at the bar nursing a beer. Ernst walked over and rested his arm on his shoulder.

"So where all did the limo go? Do we know any more or is it yet another dead end?" Wally was not hopeful at this point.

"Finish your beer and let's go somewhere more private than this. I think I have a good chance of finding the missing document." Ernst was almost whispering yet had an urgency in his voice. Wally paid his tab and they went up to his room.

Ernst recounted the day's activity as Wally grew ever more incredulous. Could this blowhard and spy wannabe have actually discovered the whereabouts of the missing birth record? Ernst loaded the cassette of the news piece in the room's VCR and started the playback. After the piece was over Ernst asked, "Do you think you can trace down this Alan Silverman person? He seems to be American. Since we have not heard anything about the birth record it seems likely that they do not know it is in the bottle. If, that is, the bottle is really the bottle."

"It is really a strong coincidence if it isn't the bottle. If he took it back to America then the search is likely to require a much larger commitment than I can muster. Let me see if Carrie and the party want to pursue it further. In the meantime I will see if I can identify this Alan Silverman person." Wally was disappointed that this simple proof about the documents was getting so complicated.

****

Luther Glocke and his wife were chatting about the day's activities over schnapps that evening. Annie Glocke said that she remembered a news item about an American getting souvenirs at the Wall and she thought it strange that he would pick up an old bottle. It seemed to be in the Kreuzberg-Mitte part of the Wall. Luther pressed her to remember more but all she knew was that it was probably on the day the Wall came down in that neighborhood and on the evening news.

The next morning Luther called Andy and related the story on the unlikely basis that it just might be about the missing bottle. Andy was intrigued and told Larissa that she would have to spend another day on her own in Berlin.

There were three local news organizations and a few independents that did these sorts of interviews and tried to sell them to the media. It should not be too hard to find the footage. Andy started calling them all and asking about the story. Being pretty well known in the PR business had its perks. All of the newsmakers were willing to talk to Karl Schneider's PR guy. Soon he found the right group and asked for a copy of the piece. The station manager retrieved it from the archive and asked his assistant, Klaus, to make a copy for Andy. Klaus Meister watched the screen as he made a copy. Why would Karl Schneider's organization be interested in Alan

146

Silverman? Or a rock? Or a bottle? Klaus put the cassette in a case and delivered it to Andy.

Andy took the tape back to his apartment. He called Luther to thank him for his help and that of Annie's, his wife. He put the tape into the VCR and started it. It ran about ten minutes. Alan Silverman was the young man's name. He and Larissa watched it again and again and again. Wait! There at the opening, before the tape's punch marker, in the distance, was an East German cop writing what looked to be a summons to the American. Then the cop seemed to be writing one to the girl. The question about the GDR police made sense now. This part of the tape before the punch mark was probably never broadcast. Only the last couple of minutes with the interview itself ever made it on the air. The timestamp on the video was 89.11.09.04:13:11.22. The next morning Andy went to the GDR police station in Mitte.

Could he "review the summons list for November 9?" he asked the clerk on duty. "8 Ostmarks," the clerk replied. The East German currency was almost worthless at this point. "That is 2 Deutsche Mark," Andy offered. "3 Deutsche Mark," the clerk responded. "Fine," said Andy, only slightly offended at the rip-off. The clerk took the bills, opened the gate, and allowed him to thumb through the summons for November 9. He had no trouble finding the summons and copied the names down. Alan Silverman, 12280 Boston Post Road, Larchmont, NY, USA and Mary Petersen, #11 Rattenhaus Strasse, Kreuzberg, Berlin. "Loitering in the forbidden zone" was the infraction. He returned to the company apartment.

A little research on "Petersen" and "Rattenhaus Strasse" turned up "Petersen, Werther, Siemens Corporate, Special Diplomatic Priv." Apparently, Mary was his wife or daughter. Andy knew that formality was in order so he called the Siemens Headquarters to arrange for an introduction "for the purpose of promoting friendly exchanges with the Parliamentary Offices." Since Petersen's duties happened to be exactly in that line, Siemens would have him call at his next free time.

Andy called the Larchmont, New York information operator and asked for information on Silverman on Boston Post Road. The operator replied that the number was unlisted. An extra click on the phone line went unnoticed. Unlisted or not, it seemed that Alan Silverman probably was back in Larchmont. Andy called his office in Cologne and spent the rest of the day dealing with the past several days' activities. Had he only been gone three days? Larissa came in, obviously from shopping, about 6:00 PM with lots of boxes. Boy, could that girl spend.

Outside on the pole was Wollweber, complete with lineman's uniform and a Telco truck below. He had missed the Petersen call but caught the Silverman one. He left a miniature tape recorder on the phone tap, climbed down the pole, and drove away. Smiling.

Becker and Associates subscribed to a worldwide media monitoring service. He called the local office and asked for a search on "Silverman," "bottle," and "certificate" in the USA. Searches usually took several days. Since no scandalous reports had made it to Berlin, he was pretty sure that the bottle, if, indeed, it was the bottle in question, had not been opened, or, if it had, the contents were unreadable or not appreciated by those in attendance. Still, he would like to be sure….

December 7—

Werther Petersen returned the call the next morning. When Andy started right out with a question about Mary, Werther became a bit guarded in his responses. He suggested that they meet for lunch. Werther did not trust phones, taxis, theaters, or any place where eavesdropping was easily accomplished. He sensed that a sensitive matter might be involved and his years as a diplomat took over. They met at a bar in Tiergarten.

Werther was originally apprehensive but Andy's outgoing way and sincere demeanor soon led to at least a little trust. He eventually confirmed that the girl on the news that night was indeed his daughter and the young man was his daughter's friend and that they were studying architecture at Cooper Union in New York City and were there now.

Did he know the whereabouts of the souvenir bottle? Alan took it back to America perhaps as a gift for his mother. Would he feel comfortable to call and inquire?

He telephoned Mary on Sunday afternoons when rates were low. No use wasting money, you know. He said he would ask. Could Andy be more forthcoming with the reason for the sudden interest in the bottle? The bottle might contain a document mentioning the Schneiders from the 1900s and they were anxious to possess it.

Werther Petersen was doubtful that the ancient bottle buried for so long could be of interest to anybody. That it contained a document was even more ridiculous.

It was Thursday. The election was just over 8 weeks away. Andy and Larissa decided to go back to Cologne.

Andy had just arrived at his office on Friday morning when he got a call from his security firm in Berlin. A phone tap had been discovered on the Becker Associates' apartment during their monthly sweep. It was Stasi issue and had a fresh tape with no calls. Probably at least the last week or so of his calls had been compromised.

"Stasi! What in the world would they be looking at me for?" Andy was alarmed at the possibility of being a target since the Communist organization was notorious for gathering information on the innocent individuals and causing extensive grief entirely by accident. Andy always taped his own calls so he spent the next few hours reviewing his conversations. That is when he discovered the click in the call to Larchmont. He sent the tape to the local branch of the security company. By analyzing the signaling tones and other characteristics they confirmed that these clicks probably represented the original attachment of the tap and that previous conversations were therefore secure. "I certainly hope so!" he sighed. He had the security sweeps moved to weekly at all of his locations as well as those involved in the campaign of Karl Schneider.

Wollweber was just getting in the truck after changing the tape on the phone tap on the Becker apartment when he saw the security team show up. At least he had one full day of transactions. Disappointingly, the only call on Wollweber's tape was the one from Werther Petersen setting up the lunch date. The only intelligence he got from the tape was the two names "Werther Petersen" and "Mary." He had no way to connect them with the caper. Still, he dutifully added the names to his growing file.

Ernst was not an "international" guy so he started asking around for a contact in the Eastern US. After several inquiries he got a name. He called Boris Trotsky who was a part-time agent in the New York area. He went by the name Boris Trotter since Trotsky tended to raise flags among the locals. With the liberalization of the Soviet Union there was not too much real espionage going on and Boris wanted a road trip. Could he find Alan Silverman who was in Berlin last month and lived on Boston Post Road in Larchmont, New York? "No problem, Comrade. What has he done to us?" Boris was bored and anxious for a chore.

"Well, I think that, when he was in Berlin, he found this wine bottle in that is a very important document to my Client. I don't think he knows that the document is inside. I wish I had more. The bottle was probably from about 1910. It is not valuable in itself but only in its contents. It is just a liter or less and dark glass." Ernst was trying not to sound too desperate.

"Is this a big budget task or are we talking just expenses and a little per diem?" Boris got right to the point about money.

"I really haven't got a budget yet for an operation over there. I think that my client will be fair. Give me a range." Ernst was hedging a bit.

"If it is as simple as it sounds then it's three hundred a day plus a few hundred for travel. I think three days...twelve or fifteen hundred dollars US, cash, of course, and no guarantees. An extra thousand if I find the bottle for you. If this Silverman is a player or has some security, then it will probably be more." Boris sounded confident.

"I'll talk to my client and let you know in the morning your time. Can you be reached at this number?" "Always."

Ernst called Wally. Before Wally could say that he had not had any success in finding the elusive Alan Silverman, Ernst said, "Alan Silverman is an American and lives in Larchmont, New York, wherever that is. I found a guy that can check him out but I will need some cash. I will be over in twenty minutes." When he arrived they called Carrie back in Cologne. Carrie listened to the various events and actions. "Either we have something or we have an amazing set of coincidences. I'll wire Ernst some cash. Ernst, see what this Trotsky fellow can find out. We can't spend a huge amount on this but we can gamble a small deposit."

With the commitment from Carrie, Ernst went ahead and called Boris and wired him the cash.

There was nothing more than could be done at the moment except wait.

27. MISSIONS TO AMERICA

Alan Silverman and the bottle were in America. Andy needed a favor in the U.S.A. and, since a local diplomat was involved, it needed to be discreet. Maybe some believable cover story could be invented to allow recovery of the bottle as some kind of favor. Maybe an appeal to Alan's patriotism or sense of duty or honesty or something. Karl actually knew Reagan. Perhaps Karl had a contact or other way to ask this favor but Karl was not aware of the situation. In fact, it was pretty clear that Karl had no idea of his Hitlerian ties. August was almost incoherent and Johann didn't know. He thumbed idly through the stack of papers in his inbox. A piece with the American Presidential Seal as a letterhead caught his eye. It was a copy of an invitation from Reagan to Schneider to the Rose Bowl football game on New Year's Day in California. George H. W. Bush was now the American President but Reagan was still a sort of "President Emeritus" and influential in American politics. Andy called Schneider's secretary to see if he had accepted. "Yes," she said, then volunteered the background.

At Karl's first meeting with then President Reagan Karl had mentioned that he was at Michigan State for two years during his graduate studies. The Rose Bowl was between the University of Southern California and Michigan this year and perhaps Karl would like to see the show. Karl was astounded that Reagan remembered the brief mention of his Alma Mater.

Could Andy go along and help smooth the trip? "Sure," she said and gave him the flight information. Reagan was borrowing *Air Force*

One for the occasion and room was reserved on the flight from Washington to Los Angeles for Karl and three security people. Karl would probably take only one so there was room for Karl's wife, Sonja, and Andy. "By the way, President Ford will also be in the box since was a football star at Michigan in the 30's." The Reagan - Ford rivalry from the 1980 campaign was apparently no longer an issue. Andy was not sure exactly who might help him find the bottle in America, but he was pretty confident that he could find a way. The PR chores for the campaign were not receiving adequate attention, so he spent the next few days catching up. He dreaded telling Larissa that she was not invited.

He called Werther Petersen on Monday morning and inquired of the whereabouts of the bottle. Herr Petersen had forgotten to ask in his telephone conversation the previous day.

Boris Trotsky reported to Ernst Wollweber also on the Monday. He had found Alan Silverman, Sr., a lawyer, in Larchmont but he had no Berlin stamps in his passport. A discreet search did not locate the bottle if it was in his house. Silverman did, however, have a son, Alan Silverman, Jr. who was a college student in New York City. The son had been to Berlin in the proper time frame but, again, a discreet search did not reveal the bottle. He was over budget by about $550.00 US. Alan Silverman, Jr., was apparently living with a German girl named Mary Petersen from Berlin. Her address on the passport was 11 Rattenhous Strasse, Kreuzberg.

Wollweber was getting closer. He now had an address in Berlin for the Petersen family and some information on the elusive Alan Silverman.

He would get more money for Boris. Could Silverman's apartment be searched more thoroughly, and maybe his car or locker. Did Mary have an apartment also?

Another $1,500.00 US would be needed but there were no guarantees. Wollweber called Carrie and got the cash but she said that this was the end unless something concrete was discovered.

28. WHERE DID THE BOTTLE GO?

December 15—

On Thursday, a week after the mysterious apartment break-in, Alan's father called to say that the Volkswagen in Larchmont was ransacked. This time no attempt to be discreet was made and belongings were strewn about driveway as well as on the floorboard and seats. Alan's Mont Blanc pen was still in the pocket on the sun visor. Who would leave such an obvious treasure? Only one window was broken. It did not seem the work of vandals. Alan was starting to get pissed. Who was tormenting him? Was it personal?

Alan wanted to go to the police immediately to see if there was a connection between the intrusions at their apartment and in Larchmont. They decided to wait until morning.

When Alan talked to his father on Saturday, he got a very ho-hum response. Doctors seem to ignore their own family's symptoms and the shoemaker's children go barefoot. Alan, Sr., the lawyer, did not think that there was an obvious connection between the vandalisms. Alan, Jr., and Mary were frustrated. They decided not to raise flags at this time, though.

Wollweber hurriedly installed a phone tap on the Petersen line. He also noticed the really impressive security in place at their home. He would need some serious equipment to break in here without setting off alarms.

When the Petersens called Sunday morning Mary answered as usual. After the opening pleasantries, Werther asked about the bottle.

Mary was surprised that he was concerned or even remembered. "I don't know where it is. We had it when we left home there, but it was not in the carry-on bag when we arrived here. I really don't know if it fell out on one of the planes since we had to change planes twice or it was stolen while we slept or what, but all I know is that we don't have it. Alan was so disappointed that we did not get back here with it."

The conversation then wandered to the weather in Berlin and New York and Mary's grades and did she have enough money and clothes and the other things discussed between parents and kids off at school. Alan was still asleep. The vandalism was not mentioned. The three Berlin Petersens were going to celebrate Christmas in Konstance at their timeshare and were leaving in the morning.

Wollweber intercepted the call to Mary. So the bottle was lost. It was the end of the road. He first decided to retrieve the phone tap and inform Wally Raudebusch. Then the Stasi paranoia set in. What if Petersen knew of or, at least, suspected the phone tap? What if the conversation with Mary was purposeful misdirection? What if Petersen still had the bottle? What if Petersen just thought it was a souvenir that was lost and knew nothing of the story? He decided to leave the tap in place until he confirmed that the Petersens had left for Konstance.

****

It was Monday December 18th. Andy called the Petersen home to inquire about the bottle, but got no answer. Siemens only knew that Werther was on vacation and would not be back until January 1. Could anyone else help? It appeared that nothing would happen until after New Year's Day.

29. THE BOTTLE REAPPEARS

Werther and Wolfgang were up early getting ready for the drive to Konstance. They did not notice Wollweber watching from behind the next house. Before loading the car they did the usual checking of the water and oil levels and spare inflation. Oops. There in that little well between the fender and the floor of the trunk was the missing bottle. During the tire change on the way to take Mary and Alan to the airport it must have fallen out of the bag it was in and dropped into the well. Being black, and in a dark hole, it had gone unnoticed for the last few weeks. Wolfgang retrieved it and held it up to show his dad. Wollweber listened and watched as they took it inside.

Although it was freezing, Wollweber's brow began to sweat and his slicked black hair began to feel like a frozen helmet. He was half right. The bottle had been lost, but now Petersen had it. So close and yet so far. The neighborhood was awaking and for Wollweber the risk was too great to hang around much longer. He got in his car and decided to circle the block a couple of times before leaving the area. His hands were shaking, but not from the cold.

Werther decided that it would be a lovely extra Christmas present for Alan if he sent the bottle on. They wrapped it carefully and packed it for mailing. They stuffed the suitcases into the car and tied the skis on top and left 11 Rattenhaus. There was a mob at the Post Office in Kreuzberg so they decided to just mail it from Konstance. It probably wouldn't make it to New York by Christmas anyway.

Wollweber saw the car being loaded and figured that the trip to Konstance mentioned in the call to Mary was real. Petersen probably did not know of the old bottle's importance and surely would not take it on the vacation.

On December 20, the United States invaded Panama. Now there was a fair fight. President Bush was under pressure to stop Manuel Noriega's drug and money laundering activities and secure the Panama Canal for international ship traffic. When Noriega overturned the Panamanian election in which he was defeated it was the last straw. Andy hoped that the planned Rose Bowl trip would not be affected. The international take was pretty ho-hum about the invasion.

The day after Christmas, Andy told Larissa about his upcoming trip to America as the guest of President Reagan. She wanted to go. She really wanted to go. Andy had trouble convincing her that the plans could not be changed at this late date and it was to be strictly business and boring. Larissa called Sonja. Sonja was excited about going, but she knew that girlfriends going along on politically important trips was just not appropriate. Wives, but not girlfriends. Larissa let her displeasure be known, grabbed a few of her belongings from the apartment and went back to Paris. They would work it out after Andy returned, she said. Andy had seen this drama before and was pretty sure they would not work it out.

On December 28th, the Rose Bowl invitees left for Washington DC. Karl Schneider and Sonja, Andy Becker, and Rudolph Klimpt, the security guard. Klimpt was a big guy with a bald head and a patch over his left eye. His American .45 was a noticeable bulge in his shoulder holster. He led the way into and out of everything with such fanfare that the group being "secured" could not help but smile and go along. Karl would have preferred a more discreet agent but the decision was made in Bonn, not Cologne. Klimpt constantly stared and scanned their surroundings. He did not even seem to blink. Ever. The other passengers on the government plane were used to security but even they were a little spooked by this guy. Andy just hoped that Reagan's Secret Service detail could work with him. The flight to DC was uneventful.

They relaxed and napped for a day in Washington to become accustomed to the time change. Andy tried to call Larissa, but she was not answering. On Saturday, they boarded Air Force One for the trip to Pasadena. President and Mrs. Reagan and Karl and Sonja were in the drawing room. Andy found himself in the lounge with the press corps, the Secret Service, and Klimpt. It turned out that Klimpt and the Secret Service detail were already acquainted in that on several diplomatic visits to Bonn, Klimpt was head of the host security detail. They all avoided the press corps.

The press corps, however, was anxious to talk to Andy as he was the only source of any information available to them on the flight. Who was this Schneider person? What made him special to President Reagan? Was his wife really Miss Sweden? Andy was trying valiantly to keep the answers general and conceal both his own mission and that of the great Rose Bowl visit. The Rose Bowl was not a published event on the Reagans' calendar and it would be safer for everyone if his visit was unannounced. Finally, convinced that no juicy tidbits would be forthcoming, the press corps left Andy alone and started talking shop with each other.

Andy went over to the Secret Service end of the room to escape the questions. Klimpt was talking to another cop who had been in the Postal Police before transferring to the Secret Service.

They were trading war stories and Andy listened idly. It seemed that Klimpt was not so strange, after all. Or, maybe, they were all a little strange. Andy had never really thought about intrigue and skullduggery in the Post Office, but some of the stories had real adventure and serious consequences. Klimpt had evidently had some covert assignments in Hungary and other Soviet Bloc areas. Andy tried for the third time calling Larissa, but her answering machine took the messages and she was not returning his calls.

After their arrival at LAX the "girls," Nancy, Sonja, and Michele, the appropriate member of the security detail, went to the Reagan's Bel Air residence. Everyone else had reservations at the Pasadena Hilton. It was to be a guy thing. On the way to the hotel, Reagan insisted that Karl show everyone the sketch Karl had made of Nancy and Sonja during the plane ride. It was a simple pencil drawing on the back of some *Air Force One* stationery available on the plane. It was a very good likeness. Andy and the rest were impressed. Reagan's staff person then outlined the itinerary for joining President Ford later that evening, the parade and then the game. A room had been reserved for dinner.

Dinner was in the Southwest Mexican style with enchiladas, fajitas, frijoles, and Dos Equis. Andy and Karl enjoyed it enthusiastically. Conversation was still about the Panama thing and both Ford and Reagan allowed that they were resigned that the UN and Europe in general would not be steadfast in championing human rights and democracy around the world. Karl offered that Germany could probably be convinced to support the US, especially in the collapsing Soviet bloc. Andy, knowing that the present government was not so inclined, jumped in and tried to steer the conversation towards the festivities of the next few days. Karl definitely needed PR guidance.

After dinner, Andy followed Karl back to his room. Karl was still talking about Germany's obligation to support the US policies. Andy cut him off.

"Karl, I think that I know how you feel. But you must not inject your own philosophy and diplomatic choices into conversations with officials or ex-Presidents of other countries. If all goes well and you formally become the elected junior representative from Cologne, you must only espouse the official line in these situations. The time may come later when you will be able to influence and even define Germany's role in the world. If you are careless in what you say publicly now, I assure you that that time will never come. We now are part of the Kohl administration and it is essential that the world see Germany as having a consistent, unified approach to international situations. The reason we have those Tuesday morning briefings is to make sure that we all know the official policy. When a reporter asks a question that has not been covered, it is easy to conjure up an answer, but you just must not. Put them off. It is even a little more complicated on an evening like this when the discussion is more informal. You must get used to the fact that the only time for brainstorming or offering new thoughts is within the Bundestag or Party meetings."

Karl's initial response was obviously anger at the chastisement, but he quickly recovered and tried to understand the wisdom of Andy's words. He would have to learn to play the game. Karl had never had to hold his tongue before. He was a Schneider, by God. Maybe he should not enter politics so far down on the food chain.

The parade route was only a short block north of the hotel. The bands and hoop-la came by starting at about 8:30 AM. There was no sleeping so Andy dressed and went out to see the show. Frank Sinatra was the Grand Marshall and the "Granddaddy of all Parades" was really impressive. After about a half an hour he walked back to the hotel. A note in his box revealed that the rest of the party was in Reagan's penthouse room with a pretty good view of the festivities and a breakfast spread. He went up and joined the group. Reagan was entertaining with stories of the movie business in the 50s and 60s and Sinatra and the "rat pack." It seemed that he had an endless supply of really fascinating tales. Andy was relieved that the conversation was not political and tempting for Karl to offer his more aggressive agenda.

The game didn't start until a little after 2:00 PM, but the plan was to arrive before the crowd and settle in before it got too crazy. They boarded the limo at 11:30 as the parade was winding down. It was less than a mile to the stadium so, even with the parade traffic, they arrived in about 15 minutes. Lunch was a light but delicious sushi spread with a nice California Chardonnay. Boy, the food was good on this trip. The game started.

Reagan, having been California's Governor, was a USC fan and Ford, of course, was for Michigan. Both seemed surprised at the fervor of the other in supporting his team.

The first quarter had no score. Then the USC Trojans scored a touchdown early in the second quarter. Reagan was smiles and confident. Ford had a furrowed brow. Then the Wolverines got a field goal. Ford became more confident. Then USC got a field goal. Ford remained confident. The half ended and Reagan was beaming. No one seemed interested in the half time show.

In the third quarter, Michigan tied the score. Ford was smiling broadly. Then in the fourth quarter, normally conservative Michigan coach Bo Schembechler called for a fake punt. It worked and Michigan gained about 30 yards, only to have a holding penalty wipe out the gain. Schembechler was furious. Ford was furious. Reagan tried not to gloat.

Michigan had to punt and USC scored, winning the game 17 to10. Reagan still kept trying not to rub it in. Ford was downtrodden for a few minutes, but then the relative insignificance of football sank in and the game was put behind them. Karl and Andy had expected the passion of European Soccer fans and the two former presidents' quickly waning interest in the game surprised the European guests.

They joined the girls for dinner in Bel Air. Reagan and Ford spent the night there and the limo took Karl, Sonja and Andy and the security detail back to the hotel.

The next morning Andy called his office to check in. He asked if Larissa had called but she had not. Then he called Werther Petersen, who was back from his Christmas vacation. He told him of the phone tap in Berlin and that he would be back in Berlin later in the week. No mention was made of the bottle, Mary, or the quest in general.

Back in Berlin Werther immediately had a sweep team come over and they found Wollweber's device and confirmed it as Stasi issue. Werther was very worried about this turn of events. His discrete inquiries both in Bonn and East Berlin turned up nothing. Whoever planted the bugs must have been from some rogue operation that could have been organized crime, terrorism, or political intrigue. There was no way to tell except that Andy was probably involved and he was more likely involved in a political caper. But if Werther himself was the prime target then it might be a move against Siemens by some Middle East group. He requested and received a 24-hour security detail.

Tuesday afternoon, the day after the game, the group was invited to the Reagan ranch for barbeque and skeet shooting. Andy did not participate, but Karl only missed one out of 50. Everyone again was impressed. On Wednesday evening the flight home was direct from LAX to Bonn. They arrived in Bonn at mid-morning on Thursday. Karl and Sonja went home to Cologne. Andy went to Berlin.

30. NEED TO KNOW

January 4—

To put it mildly, Werther Petersen was upset. Andy had to hold the receiver away from his ear for several minutes and hope that no phone taps were still in place. What was going on? Who was bugging his phone? Was Mary or Alan in trouble? What the hell was in the bottle? Was Siemens involved? Were they in danger? Why did the embassies and authorities know nothing? Who was this upstart Karl Schneider? He finally paused to take a breath.

Andy had tried to keep the affair confidential. Although Werther had some really powerful connections, he had a reputation for being honest, trustworthy, and very knowledgeable in politics and affairs of State. Andy decided that the best plan was to bring him into the fray. He basically disclosed the facts as he knew them, so far. Werther was silent for a time.

"Is this guy Karl Schneider really patriotic and good for the Party?" Andy answered that he had always been an upstanding citizen and his short term in the Parliament was impressive. He also, apparently, did not know of his own origin. "How in the world can you keep this from him, especially if the rumor is confirmed? What effect will it have on him mentally? Is he stable enough to 'move on' and let the matter lie? Or will he attack Poland again?" Andy replied that he had just spent a week with him and U.S. Presidents Reagan and Ford and all indications were that he was balanced and smart, if a little inexperienced in matters of State. He was successful and very popular in Cologne.

Werther was still wary, but moved on. "About the bottle. It is not in America, or, at least, Mary and Alan do not have it yet. My son and I found it in the trunk of our car. It probably fell out of the carry-on that Mary and Alan were taking back to America and went unnoticed until our trip to Konstance. We mailed it on about the 28th of December to Alan's address in New York. We didn't know of this international machination or, at least, political intrigue or we would have probably destroyed it or given it to you. I am not sure which. I know that it is not your fault, but we really would prefer not to be involved in this kind of thing. My position at Siemens is sensitive to rumors and scandal and this smacks of both. Have you found out who might be spying on us? I guess that the Socialists are behind it. You would think that they could be a little more forthright in their approach. What should I tell Mary?"

Andy relaxed a little, realizing that Werther was in control again.

"Well, I am not sure how much we ought to tell your daughter. I don't think that the Social Democrats are willing or able to pursue this bottle to America, although I guess that there is an outside possibility. I think that I have a contact in the American Postal system that could intercept the package. If that doesn't work, maybe you could tell Mary that Alan's spot on the news resulted in a request to return the bottle. Maybe we could arrange for a "reward" or something. Students can always use some extra cash."

The idea of deceiving Mary and Alan was really distasteful to Werther. He trusted Mary and, to a significant extent, Alan. He pushed for another solution. "This sort of thing has a very short lifetime. If your contact can intercept the package then the problem disappears. If you cannot snatch it, I will tell them as little as possible and ask them to send it back to me and to refrain from speaking of it until after the elections. I am sure that if Alan gets the package, he will return it. Alan had thought about giving the old bottle to his mother for a souvenir, but she would probably not appreciate it so long after his return from Berlin, at any rate."

Andy knew that this was about as good an outcome as he could expect. He hoped that the story would not be dispersed any further. But he still needed help and at least one other person had to be told. He went back to his apartment and called Rudolph Klimpt.

As he started to relate the story, Klimpt stopped him. "I really do not want to know why you want the damned bottle. Have you never heard of "need to know?" The more you tell me the more I have to be careful the rest of my life about yet another situation. I will see if Artie can intercept the package."

"A wine bottle from Konstance to New York City. That should be an easy enough trace. You haven't mailed any decoy bottles, have you?"

"Decoys?" Andy was taken aback.

"If no one in the opposition has seen the bottle up close and its description is not too extensive then perhaps you could leave a few dummies around and hope that they find one and conclude that there is nothing there."

Andy marveled at the turn of events. Werther wanted to know everything. Klimpt wanted to know nothing. The decoy idea seemed to be a good one. Werther had actually held the "vessel" in his hands so maybe he could assist in obtaining/defining/creating a decoy or two. Both Andy and Werther seemed to be under some intermittent surveillance so they would have to be careful in obtaining the decoy bottles. He called Werther and arranged to meet, this time at the airport as Werther was leaving again for Iran. Andy was waiting for him in the VIP lounge.

January 5—

The lounge was almost deserted so they felt reasonably secure. "Is a decoy bottle or two something we should consider? If so, could you describe the bottle?" Andy wanted to feel out Petersen about the best way to mislead the opposition and protect the Petersens and Alan. Werther thought for a moment or two and nodded. "It might not be very hard to throw them off a bit. As I remember, the bottle was a typical hand-blown wine bottle from the early part of the century. The glass was very dark with a slight reddish hue and opaque. It had a yellowed, hand-written label that was not familiar to me. The phrase "Nr. 10" was prominent but I don't remember any thing else. It was sealed with a wine-colored wax seal that looked original. I wish that I could be of more help. I had a box that some Cardinal Mendoza came in that was the right size so I packed it in that and sent it on."

Andy nodded. "You have helped a lot. That is a lot more than can be seen in the news footage. I will see if one of my staff can find something similar. We can find some old document from that era and crumble it and put it in the bottle. Where should we leave the decoys?"

"Well, since you are looking for it and would doubtless open and investigate it if you found it, I don't think it makes sense to leave one around your locations. I am not sure how much they think I know, but probably it should not be more obvious than the place it was lost in my car, and, since we just took a road trip, not back in my car. I think the most appropriate place would be in New York. Any reasonable person would think that Alan and Mary took it there. Is there any way to just substitute the decoy for the real thing?" Werther was trying to evaluate the various options.

"It would be better if the opposition could find the bottle without having to approach Alan or Mary. Perhaps two decoys are called for. One, which we can somehow throw at their feet and the other to stop the hunt if they nose around Alan and Mary's surrounds and find it. You don't suppose that they will search St. Sophie's again, do you?" Andy was also trying to plan.

"I don't think so. But that architect, his address is now connected with the church. Has he been bugged or harassed? Does he know to be careful? Does he know much of what is happening?" Werther did not want any surprises."

"Glocke was really not told any of the Nazi stuff. But you know, I hadn't even thought of it. I think that he would have contacted my office or the Schneider organization if he had discovered that he was under surveillance. But, again, he might not have been vigilant enough for this kind of thing. I will try to discretely see if they are after him. But there is the announcement that your flight is boarding. We will talk when you get back."

Werther decided to arrange a code for further communications. "If I need to talk to you before I get back I will call as Herr Myron and leave a message for Herr Goldberg at your office. This card has my phone number in Tehran. I will be back Wednesday the 10th in the evening."

Andy stopped at a pay phone in the VIP lounge, tried Larissa again, and called to ask Klimpt if he could arrange the decoy swap. He caught the evening train back to Cologne. Larissa must really be pissed and he didn't know how to make it up to her. He had more than his share to take care of right now and just didn't have time to make amends.

31. ANOTHER PARTY HEARD FROM

Klaus Meister, who had made a copy of the Alan and Mary tape for the station manager when Andy requested it, was helping to organize a Nazi recruiting rally for his 'Alternative Front' in East Berlin. He lived in West Berlin and really had not thought of Andy and the videotape of the American and the bottle since the day the copy was made.

Ernst Meister, Klaus' grandfather had been in the SS and was still bitter about the loss of the War. He kept Hitler's picture on the wall in his study. Klaus and his brother, Harald, spent many hours listening to his tales when they were young. When the neo-Nazis became especially active about kicking out the Soviets and reuniting the country the brothers were not repulsed with their allusions to Hitler and the Reich. They both joined the movement while they were attending Trade School in Cologne.

Klaus and Harald were both big guys. They were body builders and their physiques showed it. They had large features and shaved their heads and had matching Totenkopf or Skull and Bones tattoos on their right shoulders.

Klaus moved to West Berlin then joined the Alternative Front, one of the more restrained and intellectual skinhead groups. He soon was its leader. Harald stayed in Cologne and went to work for Philips. Klaus called his brother Cologne to ask if Harald make the Neo-Nazi bash this weekend in Berlin.

Harald Meister answered the phone and assured Klaus that he would be there. By the way, had Klaus heard the rumors about Karl

Schneider, that he was Der Führer's grandson? Harald had been at the table and overheard when nerdy little Christoph told Peter Warren about the microdots. Being a good Nazi, he rifled through Christoph's desk the first chance he had and found and copied the papers. A birth certificate was in St. Stephen's Church in Berlin.

"Can you FAX me the papers, Harald?" Klaus was intrigued by the rumor. When the FAX arrived he studied both cover letters and the decoded microdots.

Then it clicked for Klaus. Karl Schneider's PR guy. The tape. The bottle. Becker's secretive manner. Could it be that Der Führer lives? The search for the bottle was just about to become a three-way race.

Klaus retrieved the videotape. He verified the timestamp and location from the location log book for the day. He also noticed the GDR police writing the summons. He traced down the summons and got the names of Alan and Mary. Alan lived in New York and Mary around the corner from the church in Berlin.

The real advantage to a zealot organization is that there are hundreds of zealots who will work for free. He posted a round-the-clock watch on the Petersen house. He contacted the organization in the US and asked that they discretely watch Alan if they could find him.

Werther called home on Friday. Elsie answered and, as usual, was relieved to find him safe and sound. They chatted for a while then Elsie said, "You know the bench across the street where people wait for the bus? It is usually vacant but all last night and all day today there has been a young person sitting there. Not always the same person, but always someone. Could they be surveying traffic or something or do you think they might be waiting for me to leave so they can rob us? They don't look old enough to be city workers."

Werther tried not to show any alarm. He told Elsie that he would check with the city and then make sure that no one was up to any mischief. He then assured Elsie that he would call again in the morning and that she should be on guard a little and warn Wolfie to be vigilant also. Lock all the doors.

This was really odd. It had seemed that a pretty sophisticated surveillance of the Petersens had been underway and this was very amateurish. How many players were in this game?

Werther called his Siemens security administrator and asked that they check out the watchers and make sure that they were harmless or also watched. An operative was dispatched immediately.

On Saturday the information came back that the watchers seemed to frequent a NeoNazi club up in Wedding. It seemed highly likely to Werther that there had been a leak and the water was getting very muddy. He left the word at Andy's office for Herr Goldberg. Andy would call him in Tehran from a secure telephone.

Joanie Kaufman was having coffee at the Steel Heel North of Berlin. They were all watching the news on TV about the "East German Problem." One of the girls in the group bragged about "at least doing something about it." Joanie shot back, "Right Lulu. You're going to save the system." The rest of the group laughed. Lulu was very smug. "I'm part of a surveillance team down in Kreuzberg. I have the 2-to-5 shift in the afternoon. We're gathering information on this Petersen guy."

Joanie's ears perked up. Her aunt and uncle? "So what are these Petersen people up to? I hope not murdering innocent children of Capitalists." There was more laughter.

Lulu seemed satisfied that she was making her case. "I'm not sure what they've done but somewhere around them is an old wine bottle that they are trying hide from the world. Who knows what it contains. Germ Warfare or maybe just a plan to take over the world. Klaus just wants us to watch for it."

"So, have you seen the terrible bottle from Hell?" Joanie was trying to flesh out the story.

"All I have seen is the son coming home from school every day. I think his name is Wolfgang. Boring but necessary." Lulu was still trying to maintain the importance of her contribution.

Joanie was troubled by the new information and unsure whether the Petersens were in any danger. It sounded like just watching but some of the Nazi groups were ruthless. She went down to Kreuzberg the next afternoon.

Sure enough, Lulu was across the street watching. Joanie slipped around back and knocked on the door. Wolfgang answered the door. He evidently was home alone. "Hi Joanie. Why the back door?"

"You know me, cousin. Always unpredictable. Is Elsie home?" Joanie did not want to appear anxious.

"She won't be home until about 6:00 PM. Could I get you a Coke or something?" Wolfgang was getting to be a little gentleman.

"I only have a few minutes. Do you know anything about a mysterious wine bottle?"

"How did you know about it? Alan stole it from the wall then lost it in the trunk of our car. We mailed it to him last week." Wolfgang was not aware of the controversy surrounding the bottle.

This was a complete mystery to Joanie. Why would Klaus Meister be interested in a piece of trash from the rubble of the wall. "OK Wolfie. I just overheard a conversation in a coffee house. Maybe they were talking about someone else. Say hello to your folks for me."

She bade him farewell and she left. Wolfgang was finishing his Messerschmitt and forgot about the visit.

Andy was up early Saturday morning. Four old wine bottles were procured along with some pre-war birth certificates and an only half-used sketchbook from the era to use for the labels. He also picked up a two bottles of gift boxed Cardinal Mendoza. He might as well be thorough in the packing. Lastly, in a final effort to be genuine, Andy called and asked his parish priest if the phrase "Nr.10" in reference to a wine bottle meant anything ecclesiastical.

"Well, yes and no." the priest replied. "If a rector is really formal he will usually choose Palwin Nr.10 for the Sacramental wine. Palwin is the mark of the Palestine Wine Company in Palestine... where else? Their "Nr.10" is sort of the gold standard for communion wine. Why do you ask?"

Andy demurred on the answer and thanked the priest. He seemed to have stumbled onto another small piece to the mosaic. He went to the library to research wine labels and, finding that Palwin's labels were usually hand printed in that era, made an attempt to duplicate the writing with a hastily obtained calligraphy set. A little hide glue was used to attach the label. A birth certificate in each bottle, a rolled up sketchbook page in place of a cork and a dark red wax seal finished the job. They looked pretty good. He put two of them in the Mendoza gift boxes like Werther had described and addressed them to Alan properly and added local postage and customs forms.

Andy's secretary had only been told that calls for "Herr Goldberg" should go to Andy. She thought nothing of it. Andy got the message at about noon on Saturday, January 6. Although he didn't think that he was under surveillance he took one of the decoy bottles and drove to the outskirts of Cologne where he used the phone at a roadside tavern. The conversation was brief.

The involvement of the Nazis in the bottle caper was really not what Andy wanted to hear. The Social Democrats were, at least, civilized and reasonable. The Skinheads were unpredictable and irresponsible to the extreme. They also were loosely organized worldwide. The clash between the Skinheads and the village of Skokie, Illinois, in 1977 and 1978 was still in his memory. Skokie was a suburb of Chicago with a population of about 60,000, most of whom were Jewish. The Skinheads wanted to hold a parade there. Although with the help of the American Civil Liberties Union they won their court case that the 'Swastika' was not 'deliberate provocation' to display, the court held that the Nazi Uniform and printed materials which were not part of the case might be. The parade was held in Chicago's Marquette Park as a compromise.

The Nazis surely had the resources and if they were trying it would probably not be long before they found Alan and Mary. They were obviously not going to find her in Berlin but they could talk to neighborhood shopkeepers and probably find that she was in America. Replacing the real target with a decoy became much more urgent. Werther would not be back in Berlin until the 10th.

Andy drove on to Berlin. He stopped at Tegel Airport and deposited the decoy bottle in a luggage locker there. Then back to Cologne where he wrote a note seemingly from Alan explaining that he did not want to risk US Customs confiscating the bottle, especially since Werther could forward it with a diplomatic cover sheet. He put the locker key and the note in and envelope addressed to Werther. If Werther was under any surveillance it would surely include his mailbox. He would warn Werther of his actions.

Andy called Klimpt again for Artie's address. Then his secretary sent the two packaged decoy bottles and the letter with the locker key DHL overnight to Artie in the U.S. Artie was to try to make the decoy swap and also mail the letter DHL back to Werther. Andy took the actual Cardinal Mendoza and the other decoy bottle home.

On Sunday morning he called the Luther Glockes and invited them to dinner and it was back to Berlin. Dinner was pleasant and Andy's gentle probing convinced him that Luther's family was not at risk in the affair. On Monday morning, he returned to Cologne. On Tuesday, he heard from Klimpt that the bottle swap had been successful. He would bring Werther up-to-date in the morning. Maybe by that time the real bottle would arrive and he could see if all this was worthwhile.

32. DECOYS AND DECEPTION

Klaus Meister had wasted no time in following up on the rumor. It took little time for his society members to discover that the Petersen family was very predictable. Dad traveled a lot, Mom worked from 9 to 2 at a school, Wolfgang went to high school, and Mary was in the US, probably with Alan.

The US branch had also found the Silverman home in Larchmont and discovered that Alan attended school in New York City. It was short work to find his apartment in the East Village. The instruction for all the watchers was to be discreet but try to find the bottle. Klaus did not reveal the bottle's possible secret. His organization was based on unswerving loyalty and discipline so he was sure that the bottle, if found, would arrive intact and unopened.

On Tuesday afternoon, Klaus was told of the bottle in the airport locker. The letter about the bottle had been intercepted and the key found. He had the locker key personally delivered to him at the station. Tuesday evening, he heard from the US branch. They had intercepted a package to Alan that was the right size. When they opened it they found the bottle. Oh, great. Bottles everywhere. The US branch would air-express the bottle to him.

He went to the airport after work and, sure enough, the locker held an old wine bottle. He hastily put the bottle in his backpack and spent a minute or two seeing if anyone was watching. The airport was almost deserted and nothing suspicious seemed afoot. He put some more coins in the locker register, kept the key, and went home.

He had purchased surgical gloves to slip on as a precaution but his hands were shaking as he carefully opened the bottle and extracted the yellowed document inside. It was a birth certificate. But it was for one Matilda Kohl who was born in Berlin in 1912. Klaus was at once furious and confused. He made a photocopy of the certificate and took pictures of the bottle then re-sealed the bottle, using a hair dryer to soften and fuse the wax.

Wednesday morning, Klaus replaced the bottle in the same locker, resealed the key in the stolen envelope, and had the envelope replaced in the Petersen's mailbox, only a day late.

On Thursday, Klaus received the bottle from the US branch. In a repeat of the night before, he opened the bottle when he got home. Another birth certificate. This time the subject's name was Dieter Dietrich and the date was 1909. Then it dawned on him. DECOYS!. He had managed to retrieve two of them and, luckily, replaced one. Any group that would go to this trouble to hide something must really have something to hide. And only having one decoy disappear would probably convince them that the scam had worked.

The microdot message claimed that Schneider did not know of his heritage. Could that still be true? Karl Schneider's campaign was about to get some underground support. They couldn't be too obvious in their support but they could certainly trash the opponent.

33. EVERYBODY TAKE A BOTTLE

Before Andy could call the Petersen home on Wednesday evening, Werther called him. He had just opened the letter with the key to the airport locker and was alarmed, to say the least. Andy assured him that this was part of the decoy placement plot and, since he had the letter, he was probably not being closely watched. Werther was not convinced. "The timers on those lockers are only good for a week. I'll pick up the decoy in the morning so no surprises will result." Werther was obviously annoyed.

On Thursday morning, Werther drove to the airport to retrieve the decoy bottle. Wollweber was following him. He retrieved the package and threw it on the back seat of the car. Since the American decoy was still in play, this one was not critical any more. He stopped on the way home to pick up a short list of groceries. He didn't lock the doors. Wollweber made his move and stole the package. When Werther arrived home, the package was no longer on his mind and he just took the groceries inside. The second decoy bottle was gone unnoticed and without a trace.

The intercepted "real" bottle would arrive on Thursday according to Klimpt. Klimpt had it addressed to his apartment in case Andy or Werther were under watch. He called Andy on Thursday afternoon and they arranged to meet on Friday morning in the western outskirts of Berlin.

Andy called Werther and asked him to be at his Berlin apartment at about 10:00 AM to identify the package and investigate the contents. Tomorrow would be the day.

Andy left Cologne before dawn to get to Berlin in time to meet Klimpt. Almost no words were exchanged, but Andy finally had a package that contained the elusive bottle. He headed for the Becker Associates' apartment. Werther was waiting in the lobby. They went up to the apartment.

Andy opened the outer package to reveal a wrapped box addressed to Alan Silverman. Werther nodded and identified it as the box he had mailed just before New Year's Day. He carefully unwrapped the Cardinal Mendoza box and opened it to reveal the bottle wrapped in tissue paper. "It is exactly as I remember packing it," Werther volunteered. Andy cut through the wax seal to reveal the sealing cork. The cork was removed and, with a small flashlight, they discovered a rolled document inside. Andy went to the bathroom and came back with some long tweezers to use to extract the document. He grabbed a corner through the neck of the bottle but it crumbled off when he tried to pull it out.

"I don't think we can get it without destroying it," Andy surmised. "Even if we did, it might disintegrate when we try to open it. I am afraid we need some professional help and I really don't know any facility we can trust."

"Elsie has a little craft tool that cuts the bottom out of wine bottles. She used to make decorative windows and tabletops out of them. I'll go see if I can find it and be back in an hour." Werther donned his coat and left. Andy called down and ordered some sandwiches for lunch. He checked in with the Cologne office, put on a Mozart tape, picked out a bottle of Riesling, and contemplated the wine bottle that started it all.

Werther returned shortly after noon with the gadget. They decided to delay the surgery until after lunch.

The directions for cutting the bottle were clear and they clamped the device to the bottle and ran the scriber around the bottom as directed. They cocked the spring-loaded hammer-thing and pulled the trigger. Clunk! Nothing happened. They cocked the hammer to a higher tension setting and pulled the trigger again. Crash! The bottle shattered into tiny shards all over the table leaving an unscathed rolled document. It was doubtful that any information could have been recovered from an intact bottle but there was no way now.

The document was obviously too dry and crisp to be unrolled. Werther had come equipped with a spray bottle with a glycerin and water solution recommended by Elsie. They sprayed the outer layer of the scroll lightly and let it soak in. Slowly, the outer, moistened layer, relaxed slightly. Over the course of about two hours, they straightened the paper. Sure enough, it was a certificate of the birth of one KARL BERGMAN HITTLER. Both Andy and Werther gasped. Suddenly Andy was very aware of his lack of a plan of what to do with the apparent proof of Karl's heritage. Werther was very aware of the consequences of possession of this important state document. Did Karl have claim to Hitler's estate, if any? *Mein Kampf* was still selling briskly. Did the State have any claim on the Schneider empire? All of Hitler's property and fortune that they could find was confiscated by the victors after the war. Surely a statute of limitations had expired in these matters but War Crimes had a life of their own.

Andy poured two tall glasses of the chilled Riesling and motioned toward the conference area in the front room of the apartment. They sat quietly for a while contemplating the gravity of the situation. Andy spoke first.

"The election is about five weeks off. If this gets out before the election, there will be nothing else in the news. If we wait until after the election, the party will be accused of hiding important information. The only safe course seems to be to just sit on this for a year or so."

Werther was frowning. "I think we need to get some legal advice. And, we need to consider who all might have other evidence that could force our hand. This fellow Raudebusch. What all does he know, and who has he told?"

The phone rang. It was Elsie with more complications. Joanie had called and was cryptic about some Skinheads and a bottle and them watching our house. She told me, "Don't leave the bottle where they can see it." What the Hell does that mean? Then Alan called from America to wish Wolfie a happy birthday. When she mentioned the bottle, he said that he still had not received it. Elsie told him that it was found in the boot of the Mercedes and she also told him of the strange goings-on and wiretaps and strangers at the bus stop across the street. Were those the Skinheads Joanie was talking about? Alan then told her of the break-ins of his apartment, the VW, and the Larchmont home of his parents. "What was going on?" Elsie's hands started to shake. She wanted to know.

Werther told her not to worry but it didn't work.

"OK, Andy. I think one of our adversaries intercepted the decoy in America. You have to tell me what all evidence you have seen or heard about and we have to find out who all might know and exactly what they do know. This is not looking like a thing we can hide for a year. I have some favors I can call in to keep this in the box but I really have to know as much as I can." Werther was serious.

Andy started at the beginning. The lost letter in the Post Office. The Himmler collection, Walter Raudebusch, curator. His son Eric. The microdots. Christoph, the Philips engineer who decoded the microdots, and Peter Warren, who came to see him with the copies of the letters and the microdot enlargements. The knowledge that Raudebusch went to the old Schneider facility and found the addresses in Berlin in 1908. Andy paused for a minute, then continued.

Luther Glocke. Probably knew nothing. The priest at St. Michael's. Probably knew nothing. By the way, here is the note referencing the bottle that was in the with the birth records at St. Sophie's. "I don't think anyone but me ever saw it." The station manager and clerk who retrieved the interview with Alan and Mary. The summons at the East German Police station. "By the way, here is the VCR of the interview. And you have been involved since the day I got the tape."

Werther added. The wiretaps. The decoys. The burglaries in New York in December. They almost had to be at Raudebusch's hand but how could he pull that kind of caper all the way in the US? The Skinheads. Their first involvement seemed to be in January. Where did they come from? They are more likely to be active in New York and get the decoy there. If the Social Democrats, however, had an American operative in December, then can we be sure that the Skinheads are the ones who intercepted the decoy bottle?

They started constructing a matrix of the players and assigning them threat levels. By the late afternoon, they were beginning to think that they had to bring the Kohl government into confidence. They were also amazed that the media still did not have it.

That evening Werther told Elsie as little as he could about the affair and that it seemed to be mainly Andy's and Karl's problem. If the Skinheads had the bottle from America it was probably over for the Petersens.

****

Back in the Social Democrat quarters in Cologne, Ernst Wollweber, Carrie Schmidt, and Wally Raudebusch opened the bottle that Wollweber had taken from Werther Petersen's car. The wax seal was peeled off and the wad of paper that served as a cork removed. They could see the document inside and they carefully pulled at it. After several attempts not to damage it, they decided to use the wire coat hanger method. Like they expected, it was a birth certificate. Like they expected, it was sealed in an old sacramental wine bottle. They did not expect the record of the birth of one Matilda Kohl.

INTERMEZZO
THE FALL OF THE BEAR

34. THE EAST GERMAN CONDITION

In September 1989, the East German border with Hungary was opened. Soon about a thousand East Germans each day were fleeing to Hungary and beyond, asking the West German Embassies in Budapest and Warsaw and Prague for asylum. This was covered extensively by West German Television and watched by East Germans.

Joanie Kaufman, Elsie Petersen's cousin and the thorn in Werther's side, and her family lived in Leipzig, which was in East Germany. While Joanie's birth family lived in Leipzig, it was unclear where Joanie herself lived. She had joined a commune during her last year in high school much to her parents' dismay, refused to get any higher education and it was never clear if she ever married one or any of the guys she was living with. The roof anyone ever saw over her head was a tent tossed anywhere there was political action. Wherever there was controversy, there was Joanie.

In September 1989, an International Trade Fair was held in Leipzig that attracted reporters from around the world. Many citizens, including Joanie, were still enraged about the elections of the preceding May that were widely believed to be rigged. A demonstration was organized to take advantage of the foreign press in Leipzig. Joanie was in the thick of it. The demonstration was forcibly broken up with some brutality by the local police and Stasi. Joanie was arrested but released.

The following month the East German government planned a celebration on October 7, the fortieth anniversary of the accession of Soviet rule. Gorbachev, Honecker and many other dignitaries were to be in East Berlin. Joan Kaufman went to Berlin with a contingent from Leipzig to petition for more freedom and jobs and less interference with daily life, Most East Berliners were hopeful that 'Glasnost' would spread and improve their lot and allow families separated by "The Wall" to be reunited. Joanie was pretty sure that, like other anniversaries, the celebration would be only more of the Honecker line: Hymns of praise and hollow phrases lauding the East German government that was so wonderful that citizens were leaving in droves to escape the deprivation. The police and Stasi had been warned that 'dissidents and enemies of the State" would probably try "counter-revolutionary" actions. Their years of indoctrination kept them from seeing the real change that was in progress. When Joanie and thousands of other East Berliners gathered in the first large East Berlin demonstrations since the 1950s, it was a challenge they were not up to. Again they put down the demonstrations with brutality. More than one thousand citizens were arrested and many were beaten, tortured, and humiliated. Joanie had lost her left eye in that free-for-all.

On October 9th, a small prayer service for peace, which was a normal Monday morning affair in Leipzig, turned into a demonstration by seventy thousand citizens. Joanie was still in the hospital in East Berlin. The East German army was mobilized and police and Stasi assembled, but local politicians intervened. For the first time since 1949, a protest assembly was not forcibly dispersed. Change had started in East Germany. Honecker resigned protesting the weakness of the action in Leipzig. He predicted that the 'Wall' would last another hundred years. Egon Krenz was appointed to be the new Chancellor of East Germany. One month later, the Wall came down.

Most other Communist states that were throwing off the Soviet yoke had been changing for decades. Hungary and Poland had considerable private enterprise and property rights but East Germany was still solidly under Soviet control and had no experience with either the positive or the negative parts of Freedom and Capitalism.

West Berlin was technically an occupied city with much of the policing and public works controlled by the military from the US, England, and France. Although West Germany's gun laws, while more restrictive than some states in America, were among the most liberal in Europe, gun ownership in West Berlin and all of East Germany was severely restricted. With unification in the wind and the absence of the checkpoints between East and West, the gun market exploded. Joanie and her associates were aware that one of the tenets of Soviet control was that the populace was to be kept unarmed. Joan Kaufman came back to Leipzig with two pistols and several hundred rounds of ammunition. Little did she realize how easy it would be to just wait a few weeks and buy serious weaponry right in Leipzig.

The East German Army had no real mission any more and its weapons and other equipment soon appeared on the black market. A previously disarmed citizenry now had access to automatic weapons and grenades. The new "freedom" also was ill-defined without the historical background of a Rule of Law. A kind of "anything goes" anarchy described the philosophy of many East Germans. The Golden Rule, "He who has the gold, makes the rules," was soon joined by the corollary "He who has the guns can get the gold." The "worker's paradise" was soon the "robber's paradise." At first there was not a lot worth stealing in the Eastern sector. The East German cars Trabant and Wartburg were not high on the desired list but soon the BMWs and Mercedes Benzs were appearing.

During the Soviet days, bank robbery was rare in East Germany and banks had none of the protective devices taken for granted in the West; they resembled mere shops with counters. There had been little incentive in the past to steal relatively worthless Eastern Ostmarks, especially in a communist state one could not leave. With rigidly controlled prices and limited opportunities to spend extra money, it was just not worth the risk. But now, Western goods were in the stores, travel to the West was easy, and Deutschmark could be spent anywhere. Banks became easy prey.

An effort was made to absorb the East German police into the West German police organization but it was only marginally successful. The nature of crime, especially the crimes investigated by the East German police before the Wall fell was drastically different than the "Western" version. They almost never had armed assailants to apprehend. Robbery was rare and most police action was related to bar brawls and domestic violence. The Stasi were in charge of "crimes against the state" that was most of the crime in the Soviet system. Public criticism of the government or distributing leaflets condemning this or that government action were the serious crimes. Citizens were given rewards for reporting such incidents and, often, the report was a complete fabrication. The Stasi sometimes requested the assistance of the police in prosecuting these offences. Essentially the administrative law and regulations protecting the State's interest took the place of the Rule of Law so central in the West. Without the permanence of the Rule of Law, every response had to be sent up the chain of command to get a ruling as to what to do next. Dealing with the racist violence toward East Germany's African and Asian guest workers quickly became unmanageable. The East German police cars were no match for the Audis and other high performance Western cars available to the criminals. It soon became obvious that the organization had to be rebuilt from the ground up. The high-performance Western cars had another effect. The roads and highways in the Eastern sector were not designed for the heavier, faster machines. Traffic accidents caused by the bad roads and fatalities caused by the relative fragility of the Eastern cars blossomed.

Drugs started appearing but, fortunately, not in the quantities predicted. East Germany's Skinhead sub-culture became more active. The Neo-Nazis from the West found their disheartened and disillusioned and unemployed sympathizers in the Eastern sector to be fertile ground for expanding the movement. But the East German members had an agenda that was born of the Communist repression instead of the Western condition. Their goal was to create an "Ideal" civilization. Their main tenets were to deny the Holocaust fervently and not lionize Hitler, especially his last years. The Nazi trappings were more a sign of rebellion against the government than a desire to reproduce the Reich as it really was. Their racist attitude was mostly directed at the alien workers imported by the GDR. These individuals were allowed to keep their passports and generally had more freedoms to come and go than the natural citizens. That they were largely African and Asian made the envy and hate more pointed.

It was in this tapestry, but not necessarily because of this tapestry, that Klaus Meister became convinced that the rumor of Karl Schneider's heritage was true and that Schneider could be coaxed, perhaps drafted or impressed into leading the Fatherland back to its destiny. The microdot said that Karl's father never knew of his heritage. Perhaps Karl II did not know either.

Michael Kühnen and Ewald Althans and other Neo-Nazi leaders, at the time, were obsessed with confrontation and in-your-face type activities, but Klaus and Ingo Hasselback, who later left the movement entirely, were convinced that they could work within the system. Klaus wanted to found a political party, a "Fraktion," and have seats in the Bundestag. If the "Greens" could do it, and they had done it in 1983, then a real philosophy could surely do it. Karl Schneider would be someone that the Hitler lovers could rally around. But he could also be sanitized and supported without the Swastika and the funny mustache. Klaus started following Schneider's campaign closely.

PART II: THE EFFECTS OF HERITAGE

35. HANSEL DERRICK

Karl Schneider had been a Member of the Bundestag (MdB) since early 1988. Though "change was in the wind" about the reunification of Germany, nothing significant had happened in West Germany up to the time he was nominated to run by the Christian Democrats. He looked forward to a popularity contest and his incumbency and general name recognition seemed to make his candidacy almost a shoo-in. Now, in mid-cycle, the Wall came down, the GDR collapsed, and suddenly the Kohl administration had to rein in the confusion and anarchy that was East Germany and East Berlin. The road to success in this effort was far from clear. Every day seemed to spawn a new crisis with no historical precedent to guide the country towards a solution. With each misstep the opposition and the press criticized loud and long. The Party positions, as defined by the Kohl and the Party Hierarchy were seldom, in Karl's mind, on target. The opposition's position was often much worse but neither made much sense. The problem was that Kohl's approach was the one being implemented and it proved to be less than optimum and left plenty of room for criticism.

Karl's speeches continued to come from the Party and they seemed to ignore the subjects that interested his audiences. Cologne residents really weren't too into the policies of NATO and the intricacies of joining the European Union. Things that had been hot-button in the Fall were completely off the chart now. The Eastern

Sector needed security in the form of a new police force and billions in infrastructure investment. Unemployment was soaring since the state-run factories were no more. Quasi-government functions like water and power were suffering. If Bonn wanted to fix all of this it had to get the resources somewhere and that included getting a lot of it from the residents of Cologne. They wanted to know how Germany was to embrace its long-lost province without perishing in the process.

Karl's requests that he be allowed to address some of the unification problems were denied. The only thing he could do was deny that the Socialists had a better plan and plead for patience for the Kohl plan. His natural instinct for leadership was effectively squashed. He was miserable. Sonja understood. His close friends understood. But no one yet understood the accelerating consequences and avalanche of change that the collapse of the Soviet Union was causing.

On New Year's Day 1990, *Der Spiegel* published the "When the Ice Breaks Up" issue celebrating the collapse of Communism in Europe. *Time* magazine named Mikhail Gorbachev as the "Man of the Decade." The description of the beautiful things to come, as intellectual as it was, gave no hint of the tortuous path which most of the previously Communist countries would have to navigate. It did, however list a few real fears:

"The new freedoms give rise to new fears: the physical fear of responsibility; political fears of a "Fourth German Reich" that could again wreak havoc in Europe; and fear of a terrible "General Winter," that could finish off destitute Russia or give it its own "Napoleon."

The issue resulted in a storm of letters to the editor. The one that caught Klaus' eye was from one Hansel Derrick.

"To the Editor:

The confusion and anarchy in the formerly Eastern sector of this great country must be confined lest it corrupt all that we hold dear. This will take at least the following steps:

1. Sale of the State-Owned production facilities to our successful companies here. Sale would be to the highest bidder and include tax incentives and other advantages. Capital improvement of these facilities would also be similarly encouraged. Revenue from the sale of the State-Owned property could partially offset the cost of the re-unification.

2.   Re-education of the citizens with that knowledge that we have grown up with but they have never experienced. This includes, but is not limited to, Civil Law and Contracts, Federal Agencies and their licensing and standards requirements, Tax responsibilities and record keeping, governmental structure and voting, and the criminal justice system and the Rule of Law. We must require that every adult attend a ten-week course in these subjects and institute their inclusion in the education system there.

3.   A Census of the citizenry with voluntary educational information so that the talent that is there can be identified and properly utilized. Documentation in the form of ID cards and/or driver's licenses and/or Passports should be universal.

4.   A social welfare system that keeps families fed and sheltered until the re-organization and conversion to Capitalism is complete.

5.   A military occupation of the areas to enforce order and facilitate the implementation of the above while maintaining public safety and law enforcement.

This is by no means a complete plan but it is certainly more likely to succeed than anything our two major parties are offering.

Hansel Derrick"

Klaus smiled. Temporary Fascism was better than no Fascism at all.

There were even more letters in reply to Hansel Derrick than about the original piece. Many recommended that he run for office. Few found his solutions too heavy-handed for the situation that seemed in a dangerous tailspin.

On January 17, Karl Schneider was invited to speak at a meeting of the Catholic Knights of Malta in Cologne. After his uninspired dissertation about the consequences of joining the EU and very mild applause there followed a question and answer session.

The first question was "Did you see the Hansel Derrick letter to *Der Spiegel* and, if so, what did you think of it?"

Karl could not suppress a smile.

"I think we need to keep an open mind on how to manage the transition of our Eastern provinces to the system that we have built and enjoyed for the last 40 years. The present plan is an excellent one but I am sure that it will need to be refined and honed over the coming months and years. There was resistance to the US Marshall Plan back at the end of the War. Some felt that it was too much and others that it was too little and others that it was the wrong approach completely. But, as it matured and ended up, we have what we have today. I am not sure that there could not have been a better plan but, considering the problem of planning a future that is so significantly unknown, I think that it was a good plan. Our plan also will evolve and be successful."

"May we take that as a 'Yes,' Minister?"

"Yes." Karl smiled again.

"Your opponent's wife is Chinese and there are rumors about her support of the Communist regime there. Would you care to comment?"

"Frau Mosel is not running for office; Gerhard is. My wife, Sonja, is well known to have Socialist leanings. I do not think that is relevant to my campaign either. Thank you all."

The meeting organizer took the cue. "Thank you for speaking to us Minister, and thank you all for coming today. I hope the topics covered will help you make a good decision on Election Day and that Professor Mosel will accept the invitation that we have offered him."

Only a few seconds of the speech were on TV than night but the short question and answer session was shown in its entirety. Also, a short item about the inability to locate the outspoken Hansel Derrick was presented.

That night "Communist Pig" was spray-painted on Gerhard Mosel's car windshield. Both he and his wife were rattled. Security was not commonly in place for candidates like Schneider and Mosel so there were no witnesses to the vandalism.

Andy Becker read the report on the vandalism of the Mosel automobile and decided to add Karl and his family to the security request already around him and the Petersens.

Klaus Meister called his brother Harald when he heard of the Mosel incident. Sure enough, some of the Skinheads in Cologne were the culprits. Harald had done some digging and found that Soo Li Mosel had been actively radical in her youth in support of Communism, Chinese style, as it was exported throughout Southeast Asia. A couple of his more aggressive associates had sprayed the car. Harald also discovered Gerhard's Jewish roots. "Tread lightly on that issue, Harald," was Klaus' advice.

They discussed the evidence, so far, that Karl was the grandson and tried to plan exactly how far they could go in furthering his election in February. They concluded that a reasonable amount of intimidation of Mosel was probably not traceable back to them as long as there was no extra security watching the Mosel residence. They would not want enough intimidation to elicit sympathy for the Socialist cause, though. They also agreed that their belief about Karl's heritage should be kept from the public at all costs.

Discussion then turned to Hansel Derrick. Rumor was that he was from Cologne, at least it seems that the letter was postmarked from there. Harald had not seen the letter in *Der Spiegel* and never heard of him but would ask around.

The second Derrick letter was printed on January 22.

"To the Editor:

I do appreciate the support of your readers in suggesting that I become a candidate for office but it seems that our system makes it hard for a single voice to lead. The present parties have allied themselves out of tradition and the leadership of professional bureaucrats. These professionals are convinced that they themselves are the best and brightest the country has even though, for the most part, they have never dwelt among the greater populace and have only the most meager understanding of what the constituency wants for peace of mind and security. Probably a new party is required. Building the five percent base required by our constitution is not a task for the meek. For various reasons I am not a viable candidate for the chore. But be patient! One comes after me."

Klaus Meister was the first to place a classified ad. "Hansel, I have a significant organization and would like to help. Reply to Klaus at *Der Spiegel* Box 2271." By the January 29 issue there were two pages of similar ads. The German government had tried several times to intimidate *Der Spiegel* and been severely reprimanded by the courts. They left this incident alone.

Klaus received 29 responses to his ad. Twenty-eight of them were either requests for money or advertising offers or other obvious scams. One caught his eye.

"Klaus,

For the immediate future I need to remain anonymous so I need an agent to begin the task of creating a new political party. You were the first respondent to my letter printed on January 22. You claim to have an organization that could be the seed for such an undertaking. I wish that I had some way to authenticate that I am the one that you know as Hansel Derrick but for now I can only hope that you just believe me.

The new party should be called the National Democratic Union because the Nation comes first and only through a strong Nation is there peace, security, and order. If you can, please do the Incorporation and obtain a Post Office address for the new organization. If you publish notes in the Der Spiegel *classifieds addressed to "Hansel" and signed "ND" then I will respond to them at the new PO Box. Depending on the momentum we can generate I should be able to go public in the summer. Hopefully, we can meet before then.*

Hansel Derrick.

Klaus opened a Post Office Box account and had the papers drawn up and filed incorporating the "National Democratic Union" on February 5. As soon as the certificates were received back he would open a bank account.

Harald Meister called Klaus that evening. He related another strange thing involving Christoph that had happened at lunch that day at Philips. The discussion around the table was the day's news, which was about the Karl Schneider *vs* Gerhard Mosel election and the letters from Hansel Derrick. After lunch as Harald and Christoph were walking back to their lab, Christoph, in his savant mode, offered, "Isn't it weird that Hansel Derrick is an anagram for Karl Schneider?"

"Anagram? What's that?" Harald was unfamiliar.

"They have exactly the same letters, re-arranged. Anagram." Christoph was surprised that the word was not understood. Anagrams were things of beauty. He did not notice the gasp the remark elicited from Harald.

Harald quickly recovered and answered calmly, "Weird things happen." Christoph let it drop.

Klaus didn't sleep a wink that night. The National Democratic Union would build into the Fourth Reich!

36. REVELATIONS

Election Day was set on February 25, a Sunday as was usual for German Elections

In the evening on February 9, the neighborhood around the University of Cologne was disturbed by police sirens and general commotion. A group of Skinheads was apprehended preparing to spray-paint Swastikas on the building housing the History Department. One of the hooligans in the group was quoted as saying "We don't need no more damn Jews in the Bundestag." As usual, it made all of the tabloids. Klaus was appalled.

Carrie Schmidt was alarmed. How did the Skinheads know or find out about Gerhard? Since he was not openly "Jewish," why would they care? The Karl Schneider rumor was still in the back of her mind.

Klaus called his brother. "Why don't you control your troops? I thought we were going to go light on the Jewish angle."

"They are not 'my' troops, brother. I am only a cog in the wheel here in Cologne. I certainly did not broadcast the information that Mosel's mother was Jewish but I may have mentioned it in passing to someone. Do you think that any real harm is done?"

"I hope not." Klaus was obviously irritated. "If Mosel's organization has heard the rumor then it might cause them to probe further. I hope there is no evidence out there that we don't know about."

Ernst Wollweber studied the reports of the Skinhead involvement with interest and the usual paranoia. This had the aroma of a huge conspiracy. Could the bottle have been a plant? Or a simple decoy? The label on the bottle didn't look like it had been stuck in a niche in the Wall for forty years. He called Carrie with his suspicions. In order to keep the story factual, Carrie asked him to write a narrative of the tale so far as it seemed to him. "Just keep the break-ins and wiretaps out of what you give me. We really can't afford that kind of publicity," she said.

Of course, the press wanted a comment from the Christian Democrats about the incident. The response, quite naturally, fell to Andy Becker. He submitted a brief press release on Saturday morning, February 10:

"Karl Schneider and the Christian Democratic Fraktion have no connection with the Nazis and their various clubs and organizations. There is no hint of anti-Semitic words or deeds in Minister Schneider's record. We deplore this kind of hate mongering and hope that the perpetrators will be punished to the full extent of the law. We will have no further comment on this issue."

Mosel was losing some of his enthusiasm with the intimidation tactics. It showed in his campaign appearances and his poll numbers. The numbers were not encouraging to begin with but they sagged even further. Perhaps if Carrie showed him the evidence she had so far, it would give him a reason to fight harder. She went to him with the documents and the tale about the bottle.

Gerhard Mosel was incredulous. Being a historian, he was familiar with the story of Stefanie in the Linz town square. He knew of the Vienna sojourn of young Hitler and his academy rejection. There were just enough facts to make the story true, however unlikely. He immediately wanted to challenge Schneider and "clear the air."

Carrie was more cautious. "Let me discreetly inquire before we go too far. The message said that Schneider's father did not know of his heritage. It is entirely possible that Karl II doesn't know. It does, however, seem that Becker, his PR guy, knows, or, at least, has heard the rumor. If the bottle we found was a plant, then Becker may have found the real thing or maybe the whole bottle episode is a red herring. I know Helmut Grainger pretty well. He runs the Christian Democrat show here in Cologne. Let me see what I can find out."

Carrie Schmidt and Helmut Grainger met at a coffee house on Sunday afternoon.

Helmut Grainger was an ordinary looking guy, just shy of 6' tall, and rather stocky in build. It was hard to tell his age but he probably was in his late 30's or early 40's. His already thinning light brown hair was on the verge of turning gray and he obviously used some sort of pomade that kept every hair in place. Carrie could not remember if she ever saw him without a suit and tie nor could she ever look at him without thinking "used car salesman." He had the "gift of gab" and always spoke carefully without sounding contrived.

Helmut got into politics to try to oust West German Chancellor Willy Brandt whom he called "the imposter" during the '70s. Willy Brandt's real name was Herbert Frahm and he was a Communist during Hitler's rise to power. He fled to Norway and assumed his new name to escape the SS. He came back, had his name legally changed, and, while strangely espousing a conservative policy, was elected Mayor of West Berlin. When Brandt became the Chancellor in 1969, he wanted all to accept Communism as a permanent feature of East Germany. The West should simply recognize the situation and live with it. Helmut thought he was the ultimate appeaser of the Soviets and he was outraged when Brandt won a Nobel Peace Prize for his efforts.

"What is all the intrigue about Carrie? Is your guy wanting to pull out of the race? It seems to be about over anyway. Karl is about fifteen points ahead in the polls." Helmut was smiling and confident.

"Take a deep breath, Helly. This stuff may knock your socks off. It is not quite enough to go public yet but the evidence is growing. Has Andy kept you up-to-date on his actions? He may actually have a smoking gun."

"Do you remember the incident of a lost letter to Himmler found in the renovation of a post office last fall? That letter led to these documents and a search of churches in Berlin and, eventually, to some students in America. The pertinent steps we took to get this far are described in the narrative. I really don't believe that you could know less than we do and I thought it was the right thing to do for us to be forthright with each other." Carrie paused.

Helmut was obviously taken by surprise. He had heard none of this. "This is all complete news to me." He looked over the documents for a few minutes. "I really have to check this out. Could I get back to you next week?"

"How about Tuesday?" Carrie figured that she held the trump cards in this hand. If Andy was keeping the whole thing from Helmut then they must be trying to bury it until after the election.

Helmut attempted to dismiss the issue. "Finish your coffee. Would you like a strudel? I am buying today."

"Do what you need to do, Helmut. I can't sit on this for very long. I really have to run. Thanks for the coffee." Carrie left in a hurry.

Helmut called Becker's office but there was no answer. He was furious. On Monday, February 12th, he called Becker at home at 6:00 AM. Andy finally returned his call just after 7:00.

Helmut Grainger answered with a gruff, "You're an asshole if you are hiding news from me. I'm as much a part of this campaign as you are."

Andy offered no apology. "Calm down, Helly. Yes, we have big problems. I have held off telling you anything until I had some proof. I haven't slept for several nights, I have eaten a half bottle of Rolaids, can't afford any more cigarettes, feel like shit and look like shit. Give me time to shower and I will meet you at my office at 8:30. We'll go over everything then." Andy called for the car to pick him up at 8:15. Larissa would have to wait.

Helmut promptly stormed into Andy's office at exactly 8:30, pushing past Anna who was just taking off her coat. He politely nodded to her, but said nothing. He almost tripped over the chair sitting on the opposite side of Andy's desk, abruptly threw down a few papers and demanded some answers. His face was blistered red. He walked back and slammed the door between the reception area and Andy's office, almost rupturing Anna's eardrum. Anna wondered what was going on.

"Since I am supposed to be managing this campaign, do you mind explaining exactly who this candidate is and what the hell is going on?" Helmut was not a happy man.

Andy had never seen Helmut so enraged. Then Andy saw the copies of the microdot messages spread before him. He just nodded sheepishly, but carefully examined the evidence Helmut had laid out. One of the papers shocked him unexpectedly. How in God's name did they get the wording on the note found in the church undercroft? No one but he and Werther had ever seen the note. And they had the "Matilda Kohl" bottle. That was the one put in the airport locker and now supposedly Werther had it. Could Werther be the leak? It really seemed unlikely, but it certainly was the simplest explanation. He turned his attention back to Helmut who looked like he was about to have a stroke or climb onto the desk and punch him or both.

"I really am at a loss, Helmut." It was obvious that Becker was shaken. "You would have been the first to know about this had your staff been willing to put the phone call from Peter Warren through to you. Since he could not get you on the line, he called me, and believe me, I had no idea that the Social Democrats could possibly have this much of the story." Andy cleared his throat. "This whole thing has been confusing from the beginning. I didn't want to say anything, not to you, not to anyone, until I had more proof. It looks like Karl Schneider might really be, biologically, Karl Hitler. Is that not a pisser? And why do you think I have been in Berlin and in America? I have been trying to get to the bottom of this. At first, I thought it was a nasty little rumor, but I have too much physical evidence in my possession now to pass it off as a tale."

Rubbing his forehead brusquely to assuage the migraine that had manifested itself in Andy's left eyebrow, Andy continued... "It seemed that Carrie was involved because this Raudebusch character is a local party organizer for them and he seemed to have the letters and the microdot communications. He also got the Berlin locations of Schneider's company in 1907. But I never saw him there, I swear, and, although we discovered some phone taps just before Christmas, it was not clear that the Socialists had the resources or the inclination to go that far. Then after New Year's, it seemed that the Skinheads started watching the Petersen house. Where the hell did they come from? About the same time, someone broke into the Petersen kid's place in New York, but nothing was taken. We made several decoy copies of the real bottle and one disappeared in New York. It seemed that only the Nazis, those son-of-a-bitch Skinheads, could be so brazen so far away. But now, another of the decoys turns up." Andy was genuinely confused. "Let me show you what I have that Carrie does not have."

Becker pushed his chair back, got up and held his lower back that ached from lack of sleep, and went over to one of his favorite photographs of himself taken with Margaret Thatcher. It was hanging on the wall behind his desk. He removed the picture and Helmut saw that it had cleverly hidden a small safe. Becker turned the knob to the right combination, opened the round iron door and pulled out some papers and obviously old documents. He walked back to the desk and one by one, carefully handed them to Helmut.

"First, here is the note from the church records I discovered in Berlin near the wall in Kreuzberg. The rector seems to have taken the birth record and hidden it in a bottle. I assume, at Stefanie's request. It really has not left my hands, so I am at a total loss to explain how Carrie's crew knew its contents." Becker handed it to Helmut.

"Now here is the biggie." Andy handed Helmut another slightly heavier discolored sheet. "This is the birth record from the bottle buried in the Wall." Helmut's eyes narrowed. There was complete and deafening silence in the office. "Yes, Helmut, it appears that Karl Schneider, Sr. was Adolf Hitler's biological son. Our Karl is Hitler's grandson, so what do you make of that?"

Andy cleared his throat again. Maybe he was coming down with a lousy cold. Stress and no sleep were taking their toll. "I really wrestled with what to do with this information. It is heavy duty and I know Karl well. If this comes out before the election, it will not only ruin his career but Germany would be the worse off for it. Maybe, if we could sit on this a year or two until he establishes a really positive image, then the telling of this story could be sympathetic enough that it probably wouldn't hurt him. But then, there are historical records and legal ramifications. I am truly certain that Karl does not know about this. In fact, I have other written documents from Stefanie herself. That was Karl's grandmother. She stated positively that neither Karl, "Manny" as she called him, nor his father, when he was alive, knew anything about her lover being Hitler. Johann Schneider adopted the boy immediately after birth and Karl Sr. never knew that Johann was not his real father. This is going to be tough but I think Karl is stable enough to handle it, but one never knows." Andy seemed to be rambling. "So, where do we go from here?"

"When the going gets tough, the tough go drinking." Helmut went over to Andy's liquor cabinet and poured each a stiff glass of brandy. "I, like you, don't even know where to look for the answers." For the first time, Helmut was without words. He was just beginning to grasp the magnitude of the problem. "I know that we should be forthright and transparent and immediately tell all to the Fraktion, but Lord, it seems a huge sacrifice, especially of Karl's career, when this is not a "sins of the father" civilization. I am going to have to sleep on this one. I am supposed to meet with Carrie for lunch tomorrow."

They tossed down their brandy before realizing that it was only morning and much too early for drinking. Helmut had to move on. They shook hands and looked at each other. "Until tomorrow. Thanks, Helly."

Andy looked for some aspirin in his drawer and called Werther. After a few casual exchanges, he asked, "Where did you put the bottle that I left at the airport? It seems to have turned up with the Social Democrats here in Cologne."

"I picked it up that next morning. I don't remember bringing it into the house. I guess that it should still be rolling around the back seat of my car." Werther was a little embarrassed. "Damn, I don't usually forget something like that, but, I guess, when the other bottle went missing I just didn't expect any more activity or importance in the bottle part of the game."

"Well, somehow they stole it. They also have the text of the priest's note from the records at St. Sophie's. That really spooks me. I don't think you even saw the note."

"I remember that you had the note, but I don't think I paid much attention to it." Werther sounded convincing. "Could there have been two copies in the file?"

"I don't think so." Then Andy remembered the wind blowing the note and the stranger. His German was with a slight Russian accent. He also seemed vaguely familiar, in retrospect. Oh, well. Done is done. If Werther were the leak the effect would have been much worse. Werther then said that he would look for the bottle and call back.

On Monday night, news came that Gerhard Mosel suffered a stroke right before he stepped onto the podium to deliver one of his final campaign addresses. He was rushed to the hospital but on the way, he slipped into a coma. This was not at all what the Social Democrats needed. Though doctors were hopeful that brain damage was minimal and he would recover in a few days, this tragedy could not have occurred at a worse time. Soo Li Mosel was adamant that Gerhard not be withdrawn from the race. Carrie reluctantly agreed. She cancelled her meeting with Helmut and confessed to him the severity of Mosel's condition. The press had only been told that he was "admitted for observation." Helmut promised to keep Carrie posted on his investigations. He never intended to keep this promise.

Mosel drifted into a deeper and deeper coma. All of the efforts on his behalf by the campaign workers were turned upside down. With Mosel's health problems, Carrie knew that the election was lost. Even if he won, he could not serve and Kohl would appoint another Christian Democrat. She and Helmut agreed that the issue was essentially moot.

Karl Schneider was elected to the Bundestag by a landslide. Since he was already a serving member, there was little change or even interruption noticed. Helmut and Andy asked for a private meeting early in March. They met on March 5 at Karl's office.

Karl was happy to see them and thought that the visit was congratulatory and social. When they asked his aide to leave and close the door, he became quiet and a little worried.

Andy spoke first. "Karl, what do you remember about your grandmother Stefanie." Karl was aggravated. "Stefanie, Stefanie, why is everybody so worried about Stefanie? Johann said that was all you could talk about. Stefanie was all a grandmother should be. Kind, loving, understanding, caring. Our family was always close. Stefanie and my mother, Emma, and August and his family, they all were wonderful. Johann manages the company better than anyone else could. What is it with Stefanie?"

Andy spoke again. "Well, it has come to light that Stefanie was pregnant before she met your grandfather Johann."

"I don't believe it. I barely remember my father, Karl, Sr., but there was never any doubt that he was Johann's. Karl and August were brothers. They were given the same education and had much of the same interests. My father was, it seems, a little more aggressive than August and that may have led to his early death, but no one has ever suggested that he was less than one hundred per cent Schneider."

"Just listen to Andy, Karl. We are all having a problem getting our minds around this new information." Helmut tried to calm Karl down a bit. Karl jumped up from his chair, then sat back down.

"Let's see what you have." Karl was not enthusiastic.

"OK." Andy continued. "You know that Cologne Wool Goods really took off when they got the contract for the SS uniforms."

"Yes, but it was all won in competitive bids. Somebody had to make them."

"It seems that August and Himmler were closer than had been thought. Some letters have come to light that indicate a cooperation which was not previously known."

"And this has 'what' to do with my grandmother Stefanie?"

"In the letters, they were communicating secretly using microdots, miniature photographs of documents. Some of those documents, written by August, speak of Stefanie. Specifically, Stefanie, on her deathbed, told August, your uncle, that she had had an affair with none other than the infamous Adolf Hitler in 1907, and your father was born in Berlin in 1908. Wait.... let me finish. She recorded his birth in Berlin in 1908. Believe it or not, here is that birth record." Andy handed it to Karl.

"You have no idea how convoluted the path was to retrieve it. Suffice it to say, we were trying more to disprove the heritage than to verify it. But the clues were pretty specific and known, at least in part, by the Social Democrats. So we had to follow them. It has been a bitch trying to get all the information that we now have to blend together.

Only four people counting yourself have seen this certificate since 1908. The fourth is Werther Petersen, a diplomat who works for Siemens whom I trust completely and helped me get this far. I am not sure how this could have been kept out of the press if Mosel had not suffered the stroke."

Karl stared at the ancient document. He couldn't believe what he was looking at... Could it be? He then shuffled through the other letters and copies of the microdots and the priest's note about the "innocent bastard," that Andy gave him. "Oh, my God! Oh, my God!" He settled back in his chair. "Are these documents real? And, should I resign?"

"Yes, the documents are real, without doubt. And you should not think about resigning. You are not guilty of any of Hitler's crimes. In fact, your service to Germany is a tribute to the democracy and stability and, yes, values that we all hold. It is just that this needs to be handled carefully to keep it under control and out of the more sensational media organs." Helmut tried to calm him. The look on Karl's face was that of a frightened child. He was pasty white. He knew he was doomed if this all got to the press.

"The Skinhead attacks on Mosel. Is there a chance that they know of this?" Karl was getting back in control and starting to think constructively. Karl's hands were still shaking as he held the documents.

"It seems that they know some of it. I have no idea how they would have stumbled on to this tale, but this is what I know."

Andy went through the series of events. Alan and Mary finding the bottle. The item on the nightly news. Losing the bottle. Finding St. Sophie's. The birth registry and note about the bottle. The GDR Police and Summons list in Mitte. The telephone taps.

"Telephone taps? That takes some serious resources." Karl was getting agitated. He could not believe all that he was hearing. His mouth hung open and all he did was shake his head back and forth.

"At first it seemed that the surveillance on me and Werther Petersen, who is the father of the girlfriend of the boy, Alan Silverman, who found the bottle, was the work of a professional of some stripe. I assume it was Carrie's doing. After it seemed that the bottle was lost, the professional monitoring of us seemed to have stopped, but then the Skinheads started watching Petersen's place. I have no idea how they heard about it."

"When the bottle was found by Petersen, he mailed it to Alan in America. He didn't know any of the story yet. It was held up in the Christmas mail rush. The Skinheads spooked Petersen so that I had to bring him into my confidence to try to retrieve the bottle. We made some decoy copies of the bottle and I had a contact in America intercept the real one and put a decoy in its place."

"The Skinheads probably found out about the kids going to school in New York and had their pals in the US start trying to find the bottle there. There are two of the decoy wine bottles missing. My best guess is that the Skinheads retrieved the one in America addressed to Alan Silverman. If they somehow discovered or deduced that the bottle was a decoy, then they would probably also conclude that the rumor was true and someone was trying to mislead. I really don't think that Carrie would be involved in anything as radical as an operation in America. The other decoy seems to have been stolen from Petersen's car after being in play for a while. Carrie ended up with this other decoy and she is has a lot of the story, but not this Birth Certificate." Andy shook his head as in apology for being the bearer of such disturbing information.

"Well, the Nazis surely haven't approached me. I really would not know how to respond if they did. Perhaps they don't know anything and the attacks were really just were against Mosel." Karl was still trying to digest what the evidence meant.

Helmut guided the discussion back to generalities. "The reason for this meeting was to make you aware of the apparent new discovery. We will be planning how to handle it gracefully but, in the interim, you need to be diligent in keeping us up-to-date on any contacts or events that might be related. Your duties in the Bundestag are all you need to worry about at this time."

"I will try. But this will take a while to come to terms with. Ask my aide to step in when you leave." Karl seemed calm enough considering the day so far.

Andy apologized for being the bearer of strange news. He and Helmut left.

Karl's aide came in. "Please get me a flight to Berlin, Dirk. I need to see my uncle." Karl wanted to see if August was well enough to shed some light on this and get it straight from the horse's mouth.

The Schneiders had always been a "stick together" family who could be counted on to help each other through troubles and, conversely, completely open and above-board with each other. That August would keep this infamous ancestry information secret was the worst part of the new revelations. Karl felt betrayed. He had always felt trusted in the family and trusted every member completely. He considered the little fling with Hannah Junkers as insignificant and unknown by anyone else. The betrayal by his uncle seemed to almost justify this and his recent compounding secrets. He should have felt badly about inventing Hansel Derrick and not telling anyone. Andy and Helmut obviously thought that he should not tell his cousin Johann or even his wife, Sonja, about the Hitlerian ancestry. But the guilt he might have felt a year ago for this secrecy was now completely absent.

August was not lucid at all when Karl got to the Schneider Compound northwest of Berlin. Karl tried to coax him back from his dementia. "So Himmler was your pal, uncle. Tell me about him."

August' eyes brightened slightly. "It was all done in room 209. They were really sharp. Heinrich loved them."

"Room 209 in Cologne?" Karl pushed a little harder.

"Of course in Cologne. That is where the trunk was delivered, too." The light in his eyes seemed to diminish slowly and soon August drifted off again. Heidi came into the room. "Does Room 209 mean anything to you?" Karl was hoping that someone remembered something.

"There is a key in August's study with a tag that says 209. I have always wondered what it was for, but father wouldn't say and no one had the courage to push the point."

"Could I borrow it? It might really answer some burning questions." Karl was almost pleading.

"He will never know now, Karl. Just tell me what you find if you find what door it opens." Heidi smiled and retrieved the key. Karl left for Cologne.

37. ROOM 209

"Hello Miranda. Is Spring finally upon us?" Karl greeted Miranda in his most sincere persona.

"Minister Schneider, congratulations on your election. I'm sure this has made the Schneider family very happy. It has been a long time since you came visiting. To what do we owe the honor today?" As usual, Miranda was happy to receive visitors.

Karl got immediately to the point. "What does 'room 209' mean to you?"

"There is a door on the second floor marked 209. I have always been told that it was a closet but the closets have shorter doors in this building. I have never seen it opened and have always just assumed that it was unused. The door is locked and the passkey set does not open it, not that I wanted to open it, you understand, but the fire inspectors always ask. I just tell them it is an unused closet with no utilities or flammable storage. They seem to accept it as such. We have never had a fire problem in this building, even during the bombing, I've been told."

"Miranda, Miranda. That is much more than I asked." Karl held up the key. "Show me the door."

"Let me lock the lobby first." Miranda secured the front door then led the way up the East stairway.

They got to the door marked 209. The lock was stiff from years of neglect, but the door opened. The room was obviously large. The light switch still worked and most of the old incandescent lights came on. The rest of the building had been converted to florescent years ago. "May I come in too?" Miranda was keeping a respectful distance outside. "Absolutely, Miranda. This is a history lesson for us all." Karl went toward an office cubical on the left side of the room. In the middle of the office was a steamer trunk. The shipping label was still attached. "For Room 209." A mahogany desk was in the office also. On it were pictures of his grandparents Stefanie and Johann and his cousins Heidi and Johann. There was a large photo of Karen when she and August first married. The cousins looked to be about four or five years old. Karl opened the file drawer in the desk and started thumbing through the folders. There were the Himmler letters that had been received by August. In the next folder were the notes August had apparently converted to microdots. In the wide drawer was a slide holder of what seemed to be microdots. He unlatched the fasteners on the steamer trunk and it opened easily. The slight odor of chemicals was his first impression. Then he noticed the SS insignia and the obvious optical and photographic nature of the equipment inside. He closed the trunk. Karl had the urge to go through every folder and every envelope but it was an overwhelming task and he also wanted witnesses. He saw some of what he needed to see, but now he would wait.

"Miranda, this room needs to be held in strict confidence for the time being, even from Johann and the other company officers. There may be important state documents or evidence from a long time ago here. If they get into the wrong hands, much harm could be done both to our company and family and even Germany herself. I am going to close the room again and, when the time is right, I will return with trusted people to inventory and preserve appropriately. Can I trust you?" She had never seen Karl this serious.

"Of course. The room has not been opened in at least 30 years that I know of and probably for a long time before that. Another few years won't matter. Minister Karl, you entertained me when I was a child and have been a friend for my whole life and comforted me when my mom died. How could I not honor your request?"

They closed the room. Karl left the factory and went to his office in Cologne and called Andy. "You won't believe what I found in an abandoned and long-locked room in the old factory. The documents you have are the tip of the iceberg as they relate to the connection between August and Himmler. I think the original of the microdot about St. Stephen's Church is there. What kind of Pandora's Box have you found, Andy?"

Andy wanted a tough PR problem but this one was becoming monumental.

Later that week, back at his office in Bonn, Karl got a copy of the Notice of Incorporation of the National Democratic Union with a Post Office address in Berlin. Bundestag members always received such notices. Life was getting a bit complicated. Sure enough there was a classified ad in *Der Spiegel* on Monday March 12. "Hansel, we are on our way. N.D."

Of course, attached to the Notice of Incorporation were dossiers on the board members of the new party that included, among others, the usual law firm, a philanthropist, and Klaus Meister. Klaus, it seems, was chairman of the "Alternative List," an organization suspected of being allied to the "Party of the Like minded New Front" or GdNF, an overtly neo-Nazi group. The West Germany's Intelligence Agency, the BND, reported that the Alternative List was suspected of being a Nazi sympathizer group. They had about 1,500 members, which was quite a large number for a group just barely on the radar. Of course, the intelligence could be wrong, but being involved with neo-Nazis and related to Hitler seemed like the ultimate career death wish to Karl on first reflection. However, Klaus had laid the foundation for the National Democratic Union. How could Karl Bergman Hittler work with the "Alternative List" Skinheads and not be crucified in the media? Karl brooded over this conundrum for several days. On March 19, the same classified ad ran again, this time in bold.

Karl wrote to Klaus.

"Klaus,

I see from your filing that the "significant organization" that you mentioned is the Alternative List, which has been tied to those who wish to bring back the Reich. That seems an unfortunate beginning for a Fraktion that hopes to attract widespread support and a particularly unfortunate association for me personally. Perhaps the Alternative List is not as radical as the BND reports.

We need to meet. There is a gazebo just northeast of the Brandenburg Gate that usually is free of visitors. I would like to meet there at 9:00 AM on Monday the 26th. I will be the suspicious looking person wearing a long gray coat, dark glasses, and a yellow beret. Please come alone for this first meeting.

Regards, Hansel"

Karl went to Berlin on Sunday night. At 8:00 the next morning, he was at the gazebo nervously leaning on the rail that surrounded the floored area. He was trying to foresee every path the coming conversation would take and plan how to move Klaus to a position he could work with.

"Hansel." The name that he had chosen so carefully did not break through his reverie immediately. He had actually never been called "Hansel" to his face before. "Hansel!" This time it got through. He turned and saw Klaus at the foot of the stairs leading up to his level.

"You must be Klaus. I did not expect someone so young. There is no one around so come on up and take a seat. We can talk here. I hope you do not mind my "disguise," as it were. I just have to be careful at this point in the plan." The men shook hands.

Klaus immediately recognized the distinctive English accent in his voice as that of Karl Schneider and smiled broadly. "I am honored that you would select me to help. Thank you for meeting me. I brought coffee. I hope you can drink it black"

The March morning was still quite cool and attention turned to the coffee for a minute. "Thanks. Black is fine for me." Karl was beginning to relax. "So tell me about the Alternative List."

Klaus was impressed that "Hansel" got right to the point. "Well, the organization is about 2,000 strong, and mainly a resistance movement against the Soviet occupation of this part of Germany for the last 40 years or so. Since the GdNF was also resisting the occupation and is so wildly visible and Nazi-oriented their reputation spills over into every other organization whose goal was to free the Eastern Sector from the Soviet yoke. We are certainly a little to the right of the Kohl government but world domination and Aryan supremacy are not part of our goals. I won't say that there are no neo-Nazis in the organization or that we have not occasionally cooperated with some of the less militant Nazi organizations to reach a common goal but the goal of putting the Fatherland above Russia in making governmental decisions does not seem to pass the test of hard-line Nazism. Hansel, your first letter hit our platform for the re-unification dead-center."

Hansel took a few moments to digest Klaus' words. "Maybe it will work. I have some public relations resources that might be brought to bear on cleaning up the Alternative List image. I will see what they think they can do. Are your members mostly in Berlin?"

"Well, yes, but our recruitment in the previously Soviet zones is going well. We have a few members in Hamburg and my brother and a small group are in Cologne." Klaus wanted to hint at what he knew about Hansel but not give it all away until the relationship was a little more solid. The hint was not lost on Karl but he let it pass. "We have considerable financial resources from a few benefactors. If you need money please let me know." Klaus knew that Karl was quite wealthy but wanted to appear still unaware of his identity.

Karl spoke carefully. "Money is always important and this venture will take a lot of it. But destiny is also at work here. I don't have a complete plan yet but the major points are starting to form.

First, we need an organizer to be the visible force behind the National Democratic Union for the first few months. He should be reasonably well known with a selfless reputation, maybe a philanthropist who gives to hospitals and such. He should be wealthy enough to not be thought as an opportunist.

Second, the Alternative List needs to be renamed into something less radical sounding, softer. The Americans have this "family values" slogan that seems to resonate yet not sound belligerent.

Third, the National Democratic Union needs offices immediately in the major industrial towns. Our most fertile base will be young people not indoctrinated by the academic elite.

Fourth, we need to start running ads with position statements of the National Democratic Union. My first letter to *Der Spiegel* is only a starting point. We need to show that our plan is complete down to the level of naming names and giving examples of the Establishment's mishandling of Affairs of State. We can't be a viable alterative without showing this kind of depth. I would like to personally oversee these ads until you and others understand and get used to nuance and courting the media and the present power brokers.

See what you can come up with on the first two. Could you come to Bonn next week? I will let you know where we can meet if you can come."

Klaus nodded. "I can be there and I have several candidates in mind for the organizer post. I will approach them and let you know next week. I am sure they will want to meet you though. At least I would in their place."

"Until next week." And Hansel was gone.

Back in Bonn, Karl was still trying to staff up for being a real elected MdB. He had requested that his second cousin, Catherine, Johann's young daughter, be hired as an intern to finally fill out his staff. There was a "not approved" memo on his desk when he arrived back in Bonn from the meeting with Klaus. Attached to the memo was a handwritten note from the party chairman. "Karl, you really need to have a more ethnically diverse staff. See if you can fill this position with a minority person." Karl was a little more than peeved. He had already told Catherine that she would be hired. His staff should be competent and compatible with each other. Where did this "ethnically diverse" policy come from?

Said "party chairman's" brother-in-law was also on Karl's staff. He wrote a terse note back, "Fine. Since I have already offered the job to Catherine I have decided to fire your brother-in-law and hire an African guy for his position."

The "not approved" memo was revoked. The attached note this time said, "We just want you to be sensitive to the issue. You do not need to hire a minority person immediately. The next time you have a vacancy in your staff please keep this policy in mind." So the "policy" was only important when the hierarchy did not suffer from its implementation. Where did these party hacks come from? It was not that there were no minority candidates who applied for the positions, only that Karl wanted his staff to be more like a family...his family.

38. A NERD THAT KEEPS ON GIVING

Peter Warren stopped by Christoph's cubical. "How is the new micro-UART simulation going? Marketing is asking if we are on schedule."

Christoph was engrossed in some scribbling on a notepad in front of him.

"Christoph! Knock, knock. It's your boss here."

Christoph looked up, startled. "Oh Herr Warren. I'm sorry, I didn't hear you come up. Did you know that there are really not many names that are anagrams for Karl Schneider? Hansel Derrick, of course, and Leda Kirschner and Earl Hendricks. Earl is an OK English name, isn't it? Aside from these I can only find nonsense. What was it you asked?"

Peter slowly shook his head, realizing that Christoph had done it again. So Hansel Derrick might be Karl Schneider. He would have to call Andy again. He turned his attention to business once more. "Is the micro-uart simulation on schedule? Marketing wants to know."

"Oh it's done. The results were even better than the breadboards predicted. I think when we get the final masks we will essentially be ready for production." Christoph turned back to his notepad.

"Christoph! Hello! Earth calling Christoph!" Peter was still there.

"Was there something else?" Christoph asked innocently.

"Have you mentioned the anagrams to anyone else?" Poor Christoph. He had no idea of the ramifications of some of his insights.

"Harald Meister, but he only said that weird things happen."

"Meister, the guy with the iron cross earring?" Peter did not know him well.

"Yes. He is always nice to me and not everyone here is." Christoph was a little hard to take at times.

"Thanks, Christoph. And good work on the simulations. I will see you later." Peter went back to his office and called Andy Becker.

"Andy. Peter Warren here. Did that information I gave you on microdots and such prove worthwhile?"

Andy was cautious. "Peter, so good to hear from you. I can't comment now but all will be out in the open soon. I hope you don't have another such momentous revelation."

"Well, I would like to drop by. It may be important."

"Can you come tonight?" Andy sensed that he probably should not put this off.

"I'll be there."

Andy was relieved when Peter arrived without a package or a briefcase. At least this time the information would be simpler. "Come in Peter. I hope this is a simpler and more pleasant call."

Peter shrugged his shoulders. "That's for you to decide. We have this guy at Philips that works for me. He is kind of a genius but also a bit of a simpleton. He is the one that Raudebusch came to see to decode the microdots. He eventually mentioned them to me and gave me the photocopies. At any rate, he has noticed that Hansel Derrick, you know, the guy that has been causing a stir in *Der Spiegel*, anyway, his name is an anagram for Karl Schneider. Now, I haven't calculated the probabilities here, but it would seem to be an amazing coincidence if that were an accident."

"Oh boy. Peter, where do you get this stuff? Does anyone else know? I'm almost afraid to ask." Andy was a bit stunned.

"He says he mentioned it to a co-worker named Harald Meister. Now Harald wears an iron cross earring but is not obviously subversive or he would not have passed the Philips vetting. That is all I know for now. Have fun." Peter was smiling.

"What is the employee's name that noticed this? Is it possible that he and Harald are both in the Nazi movement?"

"His name is Christoph Klein. I can't really conceive his being part of an organized movement, Nazi or otherwise. He is too unpredictable." Peter seemed pretty sure.

They shook hands and Peter left.

Andy made a note of the names Harald Meister and Christoph Klein. The next morning he told Helmut of the anagrammatic discovery and asked Helmut to check the two names with the BND.

Helmut agreed and also added Hansel Derrick to the list. They met later for lunch.

"So Andy, what does it mean if Hansel Derrick is really Karl Schneider. Is he just frustrated at our handling of the GDR and wants to go it tougher? Or is this a conspiracy with the neo-Nazis to take over the country again? The first Derrick letter came out in mid-January, as I remember. Karl was not told of the developments until March and he seemed genuinely surprised. I don't see how the letter could be part of a conspiracy on Karl's part, but the Nazis seem to know of the heritage." Helmut's pager went off. He excused himself and went to call his office.

Helmut returned in a few minutes. "Well, I think we have found our link to the Nazis. The new National Democratic Union that was incorporated, have you heard of it?"

Andy demurred. "No, nothing."

"Well the list of board members includes one Klaus Meister, who is the leader of the "Alternative List," a Skinhead organization. It appears that Harald Meister, the employee at Philips, is his brother. Harald is in the movement here in Cologne. He could have fed copies of the documents you started with directly to his brother in Berlin." Helmut was at least relieved to find a possible Nazi leak.

"What about Hansel Derrick?" Andy asked.

Helmut shrugged. "Unless it is the Hansel Derrick with Alzheimer's in Potsdam, the BND has no record. He doesn't seem to exist."

"We need to talk to Karl again." Andy looked worried.

39. BUSINESS AS USUAL

Karl, as a member of the Committee on Economics and Technology, organized a visit to the Trabant Auto factory by executives of Opel and Audi. The purpose was to convince one of the successful companies to take over the State-run operation. When they arrived a demonstration was in progress. It seemed that the German employees had been laid off but the foreign employees had contracts that were being honored by Bonn. The factory was closed but the foreign managers were still getting paid. Karl made his pitch to Opel and Audi and the executives made tentative commitments pending an evaluation by their engineering and production departments. Karl tried to calm the laid-off workers but was not successful. He did, however, convince the Opel and Audi people to move quickly.

When the engineering teams returned the evaluations from both companies, they were discouraging. The factory had been built in the forties and last improved in the fifties. None of the equipment was up to the task of modern automobile production. Continuation of the Trabant line was not reasonable because production of the Trabant was extremely labor-intensive. Estimates of the production costs with Western labor rates meant a sales price of over 20,000 Euros. The "cardboard car" would never command a price that high. The work force was not advanced enough for modern automated production methods and would have to be retrained even if the factory was updated. It would be much easier and cheaper to just start anew on a plant in Saxony.

Obviously the level of subsidy required to attract Opel to invest in Trabant was larger than the factory was worth.

Then word came that Olivetti, the Italian office equipment firm, had declined to reclaim a machinery factory in Leipzig that was nationalized by the Soviets when they took over East Germany. The factory still made mechanical typewriters. There was essentially no electronics production capability or test equipment. The Kohl government was hoping that the factory could be re-opened and the 12,000 workers re-employed. Olivetti estimated that the same production could be done in the West with 900 workers and modern equipment. Even a free factory was not a good deal. Perhaps the "sell the state-owned factories" was not a reasonable tactic and the state-owned assets were not assets at all. And, the 'light' industries such as software and injection molding were not converting smoothly.

Treuhandanstalt, the East German agency set up to handle acquisitions from the West was, unfortunately, staffed with GDR bureaucrats who were mainly interested in payoffs and were also inept at contractual negotiations. They had no clue as to market value of the companies or real estate. Nothing was moving.

Mercedes-Benz was interested in an East Berlin truck factory, IFA Lastkraftwagen Ludwigsfelde. They wisely did some market research and discovered that no one would buy an IFA truck even if it looked like a Mercedes and was backed by the super name. Truckers wanted Western trucks. They did invest in the factory and started building standard M-B trucks there, but it was done more as a patriotic duty then as a strictly business decision.

Cologne Wool Goods had built an Angora yarn mill in Dresden just before the end of the war. The Soviet government confiscated the mill and, soon after, closed it down. The Soviet Union's policy towards the Eastern Europe "states" was that they would do the manufacturing and Russia would provide the raw materials. Wool yarn was a raw material. The staff at the mill had all been employees of Cologne Wool Goods. They 'mothballed' the equipment properly and the buildings were sound. No one thought that the Soviet occupation would last more than a few years. Fortunately, the buildings were built well enough to weather the forty years neglect with relatively little damage.

The Kohl government approached Johann Schneider about re-opening the plant. It was the one that he had tried to save back in 1946. Unlike some of the higher tech industries, this just might be a financially viable project. Angora fabric was still in high demand and the thread and yarn were produced much the same as it had been back in 1950. Cologne Wool Goods had no other facility for producing it. All that was missing was access to a herd of Angora rabbits. The local rabbit farms had long been closed. Johann sent his VP in charge of development to the area to see if there were still farms with rabbit facilities that could be re-opened if Cologne Wool Goods provided the stock.

As negotiations progressed, it was discovered that it was illegal to import rabbits into the former GDR. The Treuhandanstalt found the regulation in an obscure part of the Soviet rules that had not specifically been nullified. It now seemed that arranging import of the rabbits would require payoffs. Insiders told Johann that it would be about four times as expensive as the rabbits themselves.

The only place with sufficient rabbit stock available to allow production to start within a year was Australia. Johann called Karl to see if he could use his influence to expedite the import of rabbits.

Karl marveled at the ineptitude of his government in all these cases. Integration of the GDR into the West German nation had enough real problems. It really didn't need these bureaucratic ones.

Karl and Klaus met for lunch on Monday April 2, in the outskirts of Bonn. Karl was in his Hansel garb, trench coat, yellow beret, and sunglasses. Klaus had not been able to entice a figurehead to lead the new party yet. Karl had not prepared any position statements. The bank account was opened, but that was about all the progress for the week. The conversation was more informal and "get to know me" this time.

Karl, or Hansel as he was known at this meeting, was a little irritated at the week's progress. "I hoped that you could find someone to lead the movement but, I guess, it is a big decision for him to make. I have been working on the detail position statements, but as I dig deeper into the morass that the GDR has created, the layers of incompetence that just keep multiplying. This Treuhandanstalt committee is astoundingly incompetent or corrupt or both. Cologne Wool Goods wants to reopen a factory they built in Dresden towards the end of the war. It was confiscated by the Commies. The factory processes rabbit wool. But this Treuhandanstalt has disallowed the importing of rabbits. Is that nuts or what?"

And it is bad enough that the Trabant factory is no good for building anything but 'cardboard' cars by hand and the old Olivetti factory can only make completely mechanical typewriters. The Treuhandanstalt has managed to keep capitalism from coming to strictly software operations and other light industry with their greed and cronyism. The more I dig, the more it seems that half of the problem is self inflicted."

Klaus was smiling slightly. "A firm hand from Bonn could straighten out much of this but, as you well know, feathers would be ruffled. If only we could deport Ex-Chancellor Honecker and his whole East German bureaucracy."

"I wish," Karl said jokingly.

They decided to meet again in a week.

Andy met Karl for lunch in Bonn on April 3 to update him on their previous discussion. They both were apprehensive about the meeting. Karl spoke first. "I hope you have some better news this time, my old friend. I am still not quite over our last meeting."

"Well, the picture is getting clearer if not yet becoming less troublesome. I think we have discovered how the Skinheads heard the story. But, it seems, that discovery has led to another discovery." Andy paused.

"What now? I hope it's good news." Karl was still apprehensive.

"Well, the same techno-nerd at Philips who had the equipment to read the microdots has noticed that the elusive Hansel Derrick has a name that is anagrammatic to yours. Do you have anything that you have been keeping from us, Karl?" Andy had a questioning look as he asked. "I need to know everything about you, Karl, and things you have done so I can have the some answers for the press when shit hits the fan."

Karl showed no emotion whatsoever except a kind of "that's curious" expression. "I am surprised that you could infer a connection from such a coincidental happenstance. My ambition is to serve our country through our party, which I seem to be achieving rather well."

Andy backed off a little but was not convinced. "It is quite a coincidence though, don't you think?"

"What was this neo-Nazi leak that you mentioned?" Karl was trying to change the subject away from Hansel Derrick.

"The Philips techno-nerd works with another Philips employee who is in the Skinhead movement and may have picked up on the story. The Skinhead at Philips in Cologne is a fellow named Harald Meister. He seems to be just a minor player, but his brother is Klaus Meister who leads a group in Berlin called the Alternative Front. While they are not particularly aggressive as such groups go, I think that they well could be the group that was watching the Petersen place in Berlin. If you don't remember, Petersen is the father of the girl whose boyfriend originally had the bottle."

Karl was still stone-faced. "It sure seems sketchy to me."

"Anyway, let's wind this up for today and I will keep you posted."

They finished lunch and parted.

It came together quickly for Karl. Klaus knew everything. He knew that Hansel was Karl and that Hitler was Karl's grandfather. And the Alternative Front was gearing up. It should have made Karl nervous but it was strangely exciting instead.

On Wednesday, the chairman of the Treuhandanstalt and his driver were killed by a car bomb. His first assistant, upon arriving at work, discovered a dead rabbit in his desk drawer. He told no one. On Thursday the ban on importing rabbits was quietly rescinded.

Karl put off his meeting with Klaus for the following week. He had to have time to make a new plan. There was no evidence yet that the Alternative Front murdered the Treuhandanstalt guy but the timing was certainly suspicious.

Johann called Karl on Monday, April 9, to thank him for his help on the rabbit-importing problem. Karl was not aware that the ban had been lifted. Johann laughingly commented that he really did not intend for Karl to kill anyone; it was just rabbits. Karl laughed politely. Was it just possible that he was obliquely involved in Nazi murders?

On Tuesday, August Schneider was taken to the hospital with pneumonia. Karl and Sonja took the corporate jet to Berlin. Karl was really stressed from being with the whole family and having to keep so many secrets. Hitler. Klaus Meister. Hansel Derrick. Room 209. August was the only one of the bunch that knew any of it and he almost certainly was dying. Karl longed to at least tell Sonja. It was too much to just keep inside. When Sonja commented that she had not seen him without a Scotch in his hand for two days, he apologized and poured it out. An hour later he poured himself another. Time just seemed to stand still as the reports on August became more discouraging. Finally it was over. August died on Friday.

The funeral was scheduled at St. Hedwig's Cathedral on Thursday, April 20. Johann and Karl would each give a Eulogy. August would then be taken to Cologne and laid to rest with those he loved, Sebastian and Sharon, Johann and Stefanie, and his brother Karl. Karen professed to wear black for the rest of her life.

40. R.I.P. AUGUST

It was raining lightly as the mourners entered the Cathedral. Old friends were somber. The curious were rubbernecking and checking out the many celebrities. The members of the Press were looking for an angle to put in their articles.

The first part of the Mass, the Mass of the Catechumens, went quickly but the Sermon was long. Finally it was time for the eulogies.

Karl spoke first. He was somber, but otherwise unemotional.

"Friends and relatives, associates and loyal employees, thank you for coming.

"As you probably know, August was like a father to me. When my father, Karl, died at only 22 years of age, August took on the responsibility of the company and his family and my mother and me, quite a load for a young man. He expanded Schneider Fabrics from just weaving into the production of yarn and thread and even the raising the sheep. He built Cologne Wool Goods from a small, successful operation into the worldwide company we have today. He also guided the company through the craziness of the War while always being there for Johann and me.

"Although we did not realize all he did at the time, he was careful to shield us from the dangers that resulted from the age of Hitler. It is likely that in the future, history will have more to say about his role in events of that time, than is now in the textbooks. Like most businessmen, he was, at times, aggressive. During the war, he had to deal with the likes of Himmler and the SS, yet he avoided the cruelty and ruthlessness of the Reich. He was an advisor to Chancellors and

215

holds 16 patents concerning the wool business. Ever conservative and thoughtful in business, ever-loving and attentive to his family, ever generous and giving to charities and even individuals, ever faithful to his commitments, and always an example of a good person, goodbye, dear Uncle. You will be missed by us all."

Johann was noticeably sadder than Karl.

"I also would like to thank you all for coming. And we would like to thank the staff here at St. Hedwig's for providing the location and services that are required for what almost amounts to a State Funeral. Selections from the Mass in B-minor are being offered by the members of the Berlin Philharmonic and the Staatsoper Chorus. It was August's favorite. For many of you, it is probably the first visit to this beautiful place that was isolated from us by the Wall for so long. As you all know, Heidi and I have tried to comfort and protect our father from the world for almost eight years now. It is with some sense of relief to us that his journey has finally come to an end. He so looked forward to the re-unification of his country and recently, at times, it seemed that he understood that it had come to pass. I pray that, in that better place where he now lives, he realizes that he lived to see it happen."

"August Schneider was the strongest personality I have ever known. Not just because he was our father and rich and politically powerful, but because he did not seem to notice these blessings. He never used his influence in a petty or greedy way. This spilled over to Karl and me so well that, at least to my mind, there was never any rivalry between us as between many siblings. I include Karl here as my brother as, for all practical purposes, he is. Sorry, Cousin." He chuckled lightly.

These thoughts are supposed to be about August, but part of August was my mother Karen. I ask all of you to pray that she can have the strength to see this season through. She has had to persevere while August was living but not alive for several years. Now, even his physical presence will disappear and, I am sure, she must give up the hope that she held out for so long.

"So, dear father, your long journey is ended. My sincerest wish is that, when I pass from this earth, I will be as loved and respected and, yes, missed as much as you."

The strains of Bach's *Credo in unum Deum* took over the space. The service continued with the second part of the Mass, the Mass of the

Faithful. Most of the press left before the Communion and Last Gospel.

Later, in the motorcade to the burial in Cologne, Johann asked Karl, "What did you mean with that comment about history?"

"August had some secrets that will probably become known eventually. I wish I could say more but let us mourn for a time first." Karl turned and gazed out the window at the countryside. Johann had never seen Karl this devious before.

On Monday, Johann met with August's attorney, Dieter Busen. Dieter had invited him to discuss the Reading of the Will. When he heard of the magnitude of the event he was astounded.

"What do you mean inviting the public and reporters to the reading of my father's Will? Have you no shame?" Johann was screaming at the man who had been the Schneider lawyer for as long as he could remember. The reading had been announced in the Berlin and Cologne newspapers for May 7 at the Compound.

"August was very specific about this in his directions to me. This is the last action in a long and colorful life and I am going to make it happen just as he wished. Don't worry. The bulk of the estate goes to you and Heidi. But August wanted to also leave a legacy that would live after him and, in some way, atone for some guilt that he felt through the years. I tried to convince him that there was nothing to feel guilty about even after he confided in me what troubled him so. But, as you said, he was a strong personality and it was his Will that we were writing. I will see you and the rest of the family at noon on the 7th. Good Day!" Dieter Busen was chuckling and remembering August as he had been in his prime as Johann walked out.

The reading was scheduled in the Great Hall at the Schneider Compound. Several dozen of the curious, the related, and the media were in attendance.

Dieter Busen took the podium, cleared his throat and adjusted the microphone.

"Ladies and gentlemen, I have never presided over or even attended a reading like the one you are about to experience, but there has never been anyone quite like August Schneider either. This was planned back in 1977 and I was instructed when August realized that he was starting a mental decline not to change it no matter what he later wanted. I am not sure that the circumstances of the last ten years would not have influenced him to change it if he had not been in failing health. But, as his friend as well as lawyer, here we are today as he planned.

"Karl, this reading will doubtless have some surprises for you, perhaps more than anyone else here today. But, since I know you well, you may handle everything better than some who are not so directly involved. Does this make any sense to you yet?"

Karl answered very distinctly, "I have recently learned of some of August' doings early on and how they concern me."

Dieter was visibly surprised. "Very well, then. Maybe this will not be as uncomfortable for me as I thought. I consider you a close friend and have long been troubled by this knowledge. But lawyer-client privilege trumps friendship as you well know."

'The Last Will and Testament of August Emmanuel Schneider, dated March 1, 1977, and witnessed by Dieter Busen and Jules Feinstein. Jules was our Miranda's grandfather." He smiled at Miranda.

"I, August Emanuel Schneider, being of sound mind and sober do make this my last Will and Testament."

"First, let me say that, though this is a bit dramatic for my taste, there are no surprises as to the benefactors of the bulk of my estate. My wife, Karen, shall receive the bulk of my estate and upon her death, my two children, Johann Sebastian and Heidi Marguerite, will share the estate equally. It is more than enough to secure their future and that of their children. I do have two special bequeaths.

"First, to Karl Schneider, my dear nephew I bequeath two million (2,000,000) DM."

"Next, I want to give back to the people of Cologne and Germany a legacy that might indicate how much the opportunities they offered me contributed to the success of Cologne Wool Goods and the Schneider family. I bequeath two million (2,000,000) DM to the University of Cologne to endow a Chair of Political Science and a museum. The subject of the museum should be "the ignored warning signs of coming dictatorships, be they Fascism, or Communism, or any new 'ism' that may be invented." The reason for this action is the nagging feeling of guilt that I, like many other businessmen, found a way to justify doing business with the scourge that was consuming our country. In hindsight, it was duplicity and treachery to our country. At the time it was just business."

"In an abandoned room in our old factory in Cologne can be found the history of that time of which I am less than proud. It is room 209. The key for this room

hangs in my study and doubtless has intrigued my family for many years. I kept the key there as a constant reminder of how the events of World War II shaped our fortune. The revelations to be found in room 209 include a description of the confession of dear Stefanie, my mother. She was gravely ill in the winter of 1932 when she called me to her side, swore me to secrecy, and confessed that my brother Karl was only my half-brother. She claimed that his paternity lay not with Johann, my father, but with none other than Adolf Hitler, himself. The story she told me still rings in my ears. The story is in the files there. I leave it to posterity to prove or disprove. To my shame, I used this story to buy production contracts for uniforms for the SS. The tale is all documented in my correspondence with Heinrich Himmler. It is ancient history now but it might shed some light and understanding on a troubled time. Also in room 209 is a microdot photography system in a trunk that we used to communicate and negotiate."

"Keeping this from Karl and my family was a continuously painful part of my life. Mother Stefanie confessed to me and swore me to secrecy as she thought she was dying. In a like manner I confess to you but the time for secrecy has gone forever. A private scrapbook that belonged to my mother, Stefanie, is also laid down in Room 209."

At this point Karl stood up. "Dieter, may I speak?" Dieter agreed that he should.

"Ladies and gentlemen and especially the reporters here, I would like to tell you what I know of this tale. It has only come to light very recently and through a bizarre and most unlikely set of coincidences. If you can stay, then Andy Becker and I will meet with you at the conclusion of the reading. Thank you, Dieter."

No one listened to the rest of the Will.

Andy and Karl got to the podium at about the same time. "Did you know this was coming?" Andy was obviously irritated. August not only betrayed Stefanie, he stole her scrapbook.

"I had no idea, Andy. I thought it strange they would select a room so large for the Will reading, but I was completely unaware." Karl was obviously a bit nervous and completely stressed.

Johann walked up. "When I heard that Dieter was inviting the public, I should have suspected something but this tops it all. Did you know any of this?"

Andy replied, "Well, Johann, we have been chasing this as a rumor for about three months. I guess that we should have told you but, if it proved to be just a rumor, the issue would be moot. We think now that the story is true, however. I will try to cast it in a reasonable light for now. You two sit down here on the dais and let me handle it as far as I can. Johann, if you are asked, just reply that you had no knowledge of any of this. Karl, I guess that we will have to own up to your knowing for a few days but were waiting for the funeral and all to be over before disclosing."

Andy walked up to the podium all the while wondering how August Schneider had been able to live with himself after betraying Stefanie and living such a lie.

"If we could have a little quiet, ladies and gentlemen."

"My name is Andrew Becker and I guess that I am as near to a press secretary to Minister Schneider as there is. I had hoped to have more time to prepare for this subject matter but, August Schneider has surprised us all with this confession in his Will."

"The most important part of this Will is the endowment of a chair and the establishment of a museum at the University of Cologne. This will reap benefits and be remembered long after the hullabaloo over Minister Schneider's heritage is forgotten. But I feel that I owe you an explanation of what we knew and when we knew it."

"I am not sure it made the news here in Berlin, but in November of last year, during the renovation of a Post Office in Cologne, a long-lost letter from August Schneider to Heinrich Himmler was discovered behind a cabinet. An alert employee at the university, while cataloging it and placing it in their collection of Himmler's works, noticed that hidden on it was a microdot, a miniature picture taken of another document. The microdot was glued to the dot over the 'i' in Himmler's name. When enlarged, the microdot described briefly the circumstances of the liaison between Stefanie Bergman Schneider and Adolf Hitler. Stefanie was August's mother and Karl Schneider II's grandmother. The liaison was before Stefanie met Johann, August's father. Are you with me so far?"

"The microdot also provided clues as to where a record of Karl, Sr.'s birth could be found. After much investigation the birth certificate, which still needs to be validated, was found about six weeks ago. Believe it or not, it was in the rubble of the torn down Wall that divided this city for so long. I am convinced that neither Minister Schneider nor his father ever knew of this heritage. And, since we, as a society, do not hold people guilty for the sins of their father or grandfather in this case, it was decided to investigate the circumstances as thoroughly as possible and when we had all the facts that could be recovered, have the meeting we are having now. Unfortunately, we could not wait."

"Karl was advised of this information only a few hours before August fell ill. Karl, could you say a few words now?"

Karl stepped up. "Wow. It is really strange to find that your history is not what it has seemed for almost threescore years. This revelation will take some getting used to, so I am announcing that I will take a sabbatical from the Bundestag until the dust settles, as it were. I am sure that a panel will be appointed to investigate the whole thing and try to see what the legal, political, and ethical implications are. I am also sure that I am innocent of any intentional wrongdoing, but I know my life will never be the same. Thank you."

Hands for questions went up all over the audience but Andy, Karl, and Johann escaped out the back door. As they hurried out, Karl noticed Klaus Meister in the audience.

The press had a field day.

Several hundred phone calls were handled that afternoon by the staff in the office wing of the Compound. Real reporters, gossip reporters, book agents, movie agents, kooks, and Klaus Meister. The note from Meister for Karl said, "It looks like the games are about over. Give me a call at 22.33.23424. Klaus Meister."

The Schneider family went into seclusion for Tuesday. Slowly and painfully, Karen, Sonja, Hannah, and Heidi began to accept the new revelations. Augie and his wife were less troubled than the older generation. Hitler was ancient history to them. But, they still felt for Karl and the impact this whole thing was having on the family. And poor Sonja. She really didn't know how to comfort her husband.

41. NO MORE SECRETS

Karl knew that he had to face Klaus Meister and deal with his "organization" and the National Democratic Union. He called Klaus directly.

"So, Klaus. A fine mess we find ourselves in. Did you enjoy the reading of the Will? How is Harald in Cologne?"

Klaus was surprised. The mention of Harald was a pretty good indicator that Karl knew what Harald knew and that Harald had told Klaus everything and that further secrecy was futile. "Minister Schneider, or should I call you Hansel or maybe Führer? Can we count on you to continue to lead the movement? You will certainly have a significant base to build from."

Karl was amazed at the bluntness of the question. "I think that you know that I am not of the cloth of Adolf. Even if he was my grandfather, I am nothing like him. The fact that I have found out that I am of his blood shocks me. Fascism has proven to be a dead end and, even if someone tries to resurrect it, it will fail miserably again. I am sorry to have recruited you and others. This revelation about my family tree has, in my opinion, made me ineligible for any leadership role on my own or as Hansel. Please understand... I do hope that you can continue to urge a more structured approach to the integration of our Eastern provinces, but my role will have to be behind the scenes and limited to those who know me and trust me and are not influenced by my infamous origins. I do not think the population at large can be convinced that I am free of this legacy."

Klaus tried one more time. "Well Minister, as they say, if you can't fix it, then feature it. I and a great many others would consider it an honor to back you as a leader to at least stem the tide of socialist legislation and internationalism that so pervades our system. I certainly do not consider myself a Fascist and only a small fraction of the movement is so inclined. For most of us, Hitler is a rallying point to remind us that Germany is the country we care most about. The savage nations and the theocracies are not about progress and education and liberty. We are! The jury is still out on Russia and her more-or-less loyal neighbors."

Karl was really touched by the offer, but still declined. "Klaus, Klaus. I think that you have known about my ancestry for much longer than I. I only learned a few days before August took ill. At this point, I am overwhelmed with the knowledge of my past and unsure of what will still be revealed. When the newness pales and the ramifications are evident, it may be possible to work with you. At this time, I cannot see it happening. If I had known back in January what I know now, I would never have written to *Der Spiegel*. Again, I want to offer my greatest apologies, and, if the situation changes, I will be in touch. I would appreciate it if you left poor Hansel as an unknown patriot. His identity will probably leak out at some time but I hope not for a few weeks. My plate is really full right now."

Klaus was resigned. "I think I understand but I am not convinced that you will not soon be influential in Germany. I remain at your service."

"Danke."

Karl poured himself a drink. Sonja walked in and he poured her one too. "What a day! Sonja, I guess you should know another secret about me, although this one is certainly not of the magnitude of yesterday's revelations. The secret is that I wrote the so-called Hansel Derrick letters to *Der Spiegel*. I actually thought that I might be able to start a new Fraktion and get out from under the heavy hand of Kohl and the Christian Democrats. They compromise everything I have ever felt about governing. Special interests and the international community and cronies from years gone by dictate most of what comes out of this government. We really need a party that will put the citizens of this great nation first. At any rate, I chose one of the groups most anxious to support me to incorporate the new party. I did not know it at the time but it turned out to be a neo-Nazi bunch. I can see the press wailing "Skinheads and Hitler's Grandson Form

New Fraktion." I just now told them to find someone else. Andy and Helmut suspect that I am Hansel, but have no real proof. I rearranged the letters in Karl Schneider to spell Hansel Derrick, in case I ever needed to sort of prove my authorship. Some guy at Philips in Cologne noticed the anagram and somehow told Andy. What are the probabilities of that happening?" Karl swirled the ice around in his glass and just stared at it, waiting for Sonja's response.

Sonja walked over behind his chair and started massaging his temples. "My poor Karl. He so wants to fix Germany but the gods are against him." She was remembering Stefanie's last words, "Keep him good…"

They were quiet for a long while.

Finally, Karl said, "Do you think Hitler was already evil back when he and Stefanie made love? Or did he become evil later? Was it some flaw in his makeup or did life push him in that direction? I could not live with myself if I thought that I was like that. Sonja, have I ever seemed inclined to evil? I am not sure Hitler realized how evil he was. Was his suicide simple cowardice or did he finally realize the world would be so much better without him?"

Sonja just shook her head. "We can never know about him but there is not an evil bone in your body. You are the most wonderful, honest person I know. You could never hurt a soul."

42. TIME OUT

There was a knock at the door. Heidi was standing there when Sonja opened it. "Sorry to bother you during this time but the Chancellor is going to be on TV in a few minutes. We are all in the den." Karl and Sonja accompanied Heidi back down the hall towards the den. Heidi spoke again to Karl. "The '209' key. I guess you still have it. Did you find the room father spoke of?"

Karl nodded. "Miranda and I opened it last week. It is pretty much like August described it. Like a time capsule from 1935. The key is in my dresser drawer." Sonja spoke, "Another secret, my love?" She was smiling broadly.

The family was gathered around the television. The Federal Seal was on the screen. After a few minutes it dissolved into a scene of Kohl behind his desk.

"My fellow citizens, by now most of you have heard of the controversy surrounding our MdB, Karl Schneider. Although our preliminary inquiries seem to indicate that the story, however incredible, is true, we really need to proceed with great care. We want to make sure that the laws of this nation have been followed and that history of that time is accurate and that there is no existing conspiracy hidden for all these years.

I have asked Herr Doktor habil, Konrad Hesse, to lead an investigation into August Schneider's confession or divulgence or whatever it was. Konrad is retired from the Federal Constitutional Court where he served honorably as judge for many years. Besides being an outstanding jurist and professor, he is an accomplished scientist and can evaluate the "microdot technology" and oversee evaluating the historical documents and items as to their authenticity and timeliness. He has agreed to start immediately.

As we speak, our security team is isolating the Schneider buildings in Cologne to both protect them from extremists and preserve the contents for Doktor Hesse's investigation. I do not believe the buildings are used for any significant production or anything else but storage of excess stock and the company's historical records.

Minister Schneider has asked for a sabbatical until this controversy is over. The sabbatical has been granted. I should also mention that Minister Schneider has, for some time, also been in consideration for other duties in this administration. Those considerations are continuing."

"Thank you for joining me tonight. God bless you all."

The Federal Seal reappeared on the screen.

Johann looked at Karl. "Other duties?"

Karl shrugged. "Its news to me. Recently, I seem to be the last to know things." Karl just hung his head and rubbed his jaw.

The butler announced that dinner was served.

The next morning Miranda called Karl. The police would not let her into the building. "What about the room?" Karl told her to go back home. "This is not exactly how I hoped the room would be reopened but it will all be OK."

The post delivery that day had the first "hate mail." Nazis who considered him a traitor. Holocaust kooks. Conspiracy freaks. Communists. Karl did not think any of them were serious but the sight of these letters made him feel unsettled. He hoped he would receive sympathy instead of disdain. How could he help whom his grandfather was and especially since no one had ever told him?

Hesse gathered his team. They included a historian, a surviving colonel from the SS, an optical engineer, and the documentation team of stenographers and photographers. He asked Johann Schneider to appoint a delegate from Cologne Wool Goods to accompany the investigation and confirm that the company's interests were not unduly violated. The team would arrive on Wednesday the 9th.

Johann asked Augie to monitor the investigation. Since Berlin Mayor Diepgen had been defeated by Momper, the Social Democrat, last year, Augie's staff position was in limbo. As Augie prepared to leave for Cologne, Karl came down and handed him the 209 key. "With this, you shouldn't have to break down the door."

"You've been in the room?" Augie was surprised. "What ever happened to openness in this bunch?"

"Miranda and I were there last month. We were careful not to disturb anything, but there may be fingerprints or some other evidence of my visit if this committee looks that closely. Augie, I hate to say it, but I think that there are secrets still. Let's see, oh yes. I wrote the Hansel Derrick letters. Please go to bat for me and try to tell them I'm not a bad guy. Hmmm, I think that might be the end of the undisclosed stuff." The men shook hands smiling and Augie drove off. Karl was extremely fond of Augie.

When the entourage arrived Wednesday morning, a very agitated Miranda was arguing with the security lieutenant. "I have been in charge of this facility for more than ten years and it will not hurt anything for me to answer the phone and take care of the company's business. You may post a guard at room 209 and shoot anyone that comes near, for all I care. But there are normal business records, which, from time to time, the management needs to reference and that is my job. I promise that nothing will be done except those things, which I have done for years and am paid to do."

Herr Doktor Hesse walked up and presented his credentials to the lieutenant. "What is the problem here officer?"

"This lady insists on violating the security line. She says she works here."

Augie interrupted the lieutenant. "Miranda has been with the company for many years. She knows more about this facility than anyone else and would probably be a great help to us. I am sure she will stay at her desk and not interfere. Could she come with us?"

"An excellent idea, Herr Schneider. Lieutenant, let her come in with us." Hesse was comfortable with the addition to the team. Miranda grinned with that "I told you so" look at the lieutenant. They all entered the lobby of the building.

"I want pictures of everything as we go, gentlemen. I know we have a single area as the target, but Lord protect us from missing something important." Hesse had a floor plan of the building and methodically started documenting the ground floor with pictures and commentary keyed to the floor plan. Then, the basement. Augie and the historian and the engineer were soon bored of the exercise. After about three hours, it was time to do the second floor. Miranda was asked to lead the way. She pointed out the door marked '209' and Hesse had the team document the rest of the second floor first. At about 2:00 PM, Hesse tried opening the door with the building passkey only to find that it did not work. Augie produced the key. "The key August mentioned. It was in his study until recently, but Karl had it. He and Miranda innocently opened this room about two weeks ago. Karl assures me that nothing was disturbed and that they were only here for about ten minutes."

Miranda added, "I can show you in the log book when Karl signed in. He locked the room afterwards and told me not to mention it to anyone. He said someone would come to catalog and preserve the contents. Only I expected him to be along."

Hesse took a few seconds to reflect on the recent visit then opened the door. "It is hard to assume that this room has been sealed and pristine for 40 years. Who knows how often August came in and muddied the water. Let us get to the task."

The room, of course, was still empty except for the office cubicle. The emptiness was duly photographed and commented on. Interest focused on the desk and the steamer trunk.

More pictures were taken.

The engineer opened the trunk. Again there was the faint smell of chemicals used in photography. He was immediately fascinated by the SS insignia and the technology from yesteryear. "I have never seen one of these, but there is an operations manual for one in the library in Berlin." The SS colonel added, "Only a very few were made, about 10, I think." The engineer continued, "This really belongs in a museum. Since the old man endowed a museum and this seems to belong to the estate, I guess that is the destination. It is in pristinely new condition and probably priceless. Will it be safe here? I would rather see it in a more secure setting."

Augie spoke. "I am sure that it can be relocated to a safer place. As long as we have a receipt and the right to claim it when the time is right."

Hesse told the engineer, "Find a place that can preserve and protect it."

Attention then turned to the desk.

In the wide drawer were the slides of microdots. The engineer had some portable microscopes and color filters in his kit. After examining the slides, he was impressed. "The microdots are apparently both the ones from Himmler and copies of the ones made by August, carefully arranged chronologically. This is an organized record of their correspondence. Amazing."

He wrapped the slides carefully for transport in his specimen case. "We need to start a confiscation receipt for what we are taking back to Bonn."

Hess directed one of the stenographers to start the receipt. "I will be happy to type it." Miranda was standing just outside the cubicle.

In the file drawer of the desk was arranged the letters from Himmler and the originals of the microdots to Himmler. All in chronological order and unharmed. In the file drawer was also the list of changes to the uniform design over the years. Make this pocket 1 cm wider or add a belt loop there and, of course, the change to the pale-gray color late in the war. This was not earth-shattering but it was interesting and part of the "big story." Then they looked in the small drawer below the file drawer. Karl had not opened this drawer. In it was a scrapbook. The scrapbook was Stefanie's. Hesse and Augie thumbed through it.

There was a coaster from the Kaffeehaus in Vienna. On it was written "that night." There was a drawing of the beautiful young Stefanie on a bed somewhat covered by a sheer sheet. There was the top from a box of morning sickness pills from 1908. There was a business card from a restaurant in Berlin. On the back was written, "Johann proposed tonight. How could I be so lucky?"

Baptisms, confirmations, school commencements, marriage photos, both of Karl and August.

Then the newspaper clipping of the airplane crash wherein Karl was killed. "KARL SCHNEIDER KILLED IN AIRPLANE CRASH. OWNER OF COLOGNE WOOL GOODS DIES." Witnesses said that the airplane "seemed to disintegrate" and crashed into the lake. The ground crew tried to get to the wreckage with small boats but the plane sank almost immediately.

Then a newspaper account of the body washing ashore two days later on the opposite side of the lake. "His wife, Emma Schneider, identified the body by the small crescent-shaped birthmark on his back. Most of his face was gone."

"Crescent-shaped birthmark on his back..." Augie suppressed a gasp as he seemed to have discovered yet another secret. Augie looked a little more like Karl than Johann, but Karl, they said, looked a lot like Stefanie. But a crescent shaped birthmark? He, too, had one.

It was adding up that Karl just might be his real father. He knew his mother Hannah had once had a thing for Karl but, dear God, what else did this family have to hide? He would keep this to himself as long possible. Few would read the newspaper account, and even fewer knew of his birthmark. Stefanie would have known. Aunt Emma must have known. No wonder she was so sweet. But neither Karl II nor Johann nor his mother seemed to know. Did August? Just how many skeletons were in the Schneider closets?

The team decided to take desk and all from Room 209. They had arranged for a truck since they knew that the steamer trunk was probably coming along. Trunk, desk, and contents, desk lamp, pictures of relatives. There were only four items on the receipt list.

The team stopped by Karl's office, then Andy's office in Cologne the next morning. There they picked up the rest of the evidence. The priest's note about the bottle, the birth certificate, and the two unused decoy bottles, and the video of Alan and Mary at the wall. They started a list of "co-conspirators" following the trail and came up with Carrie Schmidt and Wally Raudebusch, Andy and Helmut, and Werther Petersen, Alan, and Mary and Luther Glocke, and, of course, Harald and Klaus Meister. All would have to appear and give statements. The hearings would be scheduled for early June.

43. MISS SWEDEN GOES HOME

MdB Karl Schneider was on the short list of candidates for Ambassador to Sweden that was submitted to the Swedish State Department. The Swedes liked the idea of having Sonja back, but Karl was so conservative. But then, again, everyone submitted by the Kohl government was pretty conservative. Finally they asked for Karl as a first choice.

Karl was summoned to Bonn to meet with the State Department. "You should bring your wife."

"Consideration for other duties in this administration" was the phrase in Kohl's statement on TV the other night. Maybe another life-altering change is on the way. Karl was still troubled by thoughts of Hitler's evil somehow expressing in him as he and Sonja drove over to the State Department.

The Foreign Minister got right to the point.

"Minister Schneider, we took the liberty of submitting your name among others to Stockholm as a candidate for the post of Ambassador to Sweden. I am pleased to tell you that you are their choice from our list. This, of course, was previous to the present controversy in which you are unfortunately embroiled. But they have looked at the controversy and decided that it was to their advantage politically to continue to support you. It did not hurt that you are married to one of their beauty queens. We would like your answer within a week. Summer in Stockholm is very nice."

Karl looked at Sonja. They both smiled. Karl's parents were both dead. Sonja's father was still vital, but her mother was not well. Sonja was planning a trip to Sweden in the spring anyway.

Karl addressed the Foreign Minister. "Minister, I think we do not need a week. I would happily accept the assignment as Ambassador to Sweden for our government."

The press did not find this quite as juicy as the Hitler revelation but it still got large coverage.

Karl and Sonja tried to keep their departure to Sweden as low-key as possible but there were still reporters and fanfare as they left the Berlin Compound for the airport. They were scheduled to board a diplomatic flight directly to Stockholm, along with some staff that had also traveled to Berlin. Karl felt a sadness leaving, but he and Sonja had traveled a lot and really had not settled into one home for too long. This, as far as he was concerned, was just another link in the chain.

When they arrived in Stockholm, there was not much fanfare and the greeting party was small but cordial. There were about a dozen demonstrators with anti-Nazi signs and flags. Karl and Sonja chose to ignore them. A pang of fear went through Karl, but he did not let on to Sonja.

The ambassador's residence was sumptuous and well-staffed. Sonja was amazed at how quickly they settled in and became part of the diplomatic scene. Karl was still distracted by the psychological and political changes in his life. His dreams of really reforming the German government had crashed big time. He still couldn't believe how his life had changed over something he had no control over. He immersed himself in the history of the relationship between Germany and Sweden and resolved to take this piece of the international discourse and make the most of it.

There continued to be calls from the White Aryan Resistance and other neo-Nazis with inquiries as to whether Karl was interested in joining. How many times did he have to disavow Hitler?

He saw the similarity between Cologne Wool Goods and the entire country of Sweden. During the War, Sweden was able to sell goods, especially iron products and iron ore, to both Germany and the Allies. No one seemed to blame them for the duplicity. Germany never occupied or even threatened Sweden. Little Switzerland had little or no strategic value but Sweden with iron and ports and access to Denmark and Finland? How did they get off scot-free?

Trade between Sweden and Germany was the dominant diplomatic challenge but there was still time for Sonja to spend time with her parents and reconnect with her family. She seemed happy to be in her homeland. Her homeland was happy to have her back. She was still their pretty "Miss Sweden."

In June, Karl had to be back in Bonn for the Hesse hearings.

Their arrival in Germany drew many more protesters at the airport. Some were holding swastikas, others, inflammatory or lewd signs of hate. That was unnerving enough for Karl. Karl, Sonja and the driver made their way to the castle as soon as they could, but there were demonstrators already camped out at the entry gate. Police cars and police wagons lined the streets. So did camera crews. The police had set up a perimeter to keep the demonstrators at bay, but the sheer size of the crowd was unsettling. Several groups were protesting and their anger was directed as much at each other, some being pro-Nazi, some anti-Nazi, as much as against Karl Schneider. Sonja cried and hid her face against Karl's chest. Karl tried not to show fear although he felt it strongly. It was the first time he could remember being really afraid since the bombings in Britain.

The car made it through the gate and pulled up to the side entrance of the castle. The driver had radioed ahead for the staff to open the doors quickly so Karl and Sonja could run in. The police had been very vigilant in not letting any camera-crew members through the gates.

The carrying-on from the crowd could be heard inside the thick castle walls and it rattled the staff terribly. Karl and Sonja could not sleep. Karl called for some additional security to come to the castle for the night. He and Sonja turned on the late news to see what was being reported and it looked as bad on television as what they could see from one of the second story windows. They wanted tomorrow to be over with so they could make a quiet exit back to Stockholm.

The next morning were the hearings and they posed a real feeling of dread as Karl knew they would be long and drawn out. Sonja did not want to spend another night at the castle. She was too frightened. They stuffed the few clothes they had worn on the trip to Cologne back into the bags and zipped them. They grabbed their belongings and handed them to the butler for the driver to place in the trunk of the limo. Should the hearings last longer than today, they would anonymously stay in some out-of-the-way lodge where they couldn't be found. Going through this again was not what they would do.

The decision had been made for Andy and Helmut to accompany Karl and Sonja to the hearings. At least these two had Karl's best interests at heart. They came to the castle together but weren't sure if they would be riding in the limo with Karl and Sonja or driving themselves to the hearings. There was a second limo waiting for them so Andy parked his car behind the second limo and locked it. He hoped it would not sustain damage from the angry crowd who might work their way through the gates. The protesters were still at it and Andy just shook his head in disbelief.

Karl and Sonja looked weary from the all night vigil and yelling heard from the dissidents. Karl asked Andy why so many people hated them so? Nothing they had done warranted this feeling. The only thing about him that had changed was the telling of the story that some eighty years ago, two teenagers had a night of passion that had never before been disclosed. Helmut chimed in that those kind of people out by the gates just wait for controversy to happen so they can pounce on it. This was their life and what they lived for. It served no real purpose. It was just what they did.

Sonja looked beautiful in her tailored cream silk suit with a blue silk blouse and Karl looked elegant in a midnight blue suit, white shirt, and blue tie. They wanted to appear proud as they knew they would be photographed even though they seemed to be the brunt of August's cruel revelations. They were still the same people whose views had not changed.

The two limo drivers helped Karl and Sonja into the first car and two security guards climbed in behind them to shield them from the view of the crowd. Andy and Helmut got into the second limo and the two cars drove onto the road leading out the front gates. The police pushed the onlookers to either side of the large gates and motioned for the cars to come through. The unruly bystanders could not explain what happened next. The first car seemed to explode. The second limo driver slammed on the brakes and stopped short of the disintegrated car. The noise was unimaginable. Karl, Sonja, their driver and the two guards in the car with them were killed instantly. Only a few minutes later, four demonstrators and three policeman succumbed to the blast. The news crew barely escaped injury. They had been pushed behind a row of police cars lining the opposite side of the road.

The beautiful gates to the Schneider estate were destroyed. The windshield of the second limo was shattered and Andy and Helmut suffered deep cuts to their facial and chest areas from the impact of flying glass. Paramedics got them into an ambulance, placed compresses on their worst injuries, and drove off to the nearest hospital for observation. The driver had more severe cuts and lacerations and the jolt threw him against the airbag that did not properly inflate. He was rushed to a trauma hospital.

Larissa heard the bulletin on the noon news in Paris. She had never been so scared in all her life. She immediately called the Schneider Compound in Berlin and the housekeeper said the rest of the family that had not been called to testify, were on their way to Cologne. Larissa called Miranda at the Cologne factory, but Miranda did not know which hospital Andy and Helmut had been taken to. Miranda was so shaken she could hardly speak. She said there was only one major hospital and that was Cologne University Hospital. Larissa should try there first.

A hospital receptionist put Larissa right through to the Emergency Room where all accident victims were taken. She actually spoke to a knowledgeable person who confirmed that Andrew Becker had been brought in at 9:30 AM that morning and was admitted. She could not, however, give her a condition report, but said he was resting comfortably and that he was in room 302 in the Staats wing of the hospital. Larissa asked if she could ring that room. The staff person said "no," that he was still being observed, and only the next of kin could speak to his doctor.

Larissa said, "Thank you," hung up the phone and in helter-skelter fashion, threw a few things into an overnight bag, tossed the milk out of the fridge, and locked up the apartment. She didn't know when she would be back. She stuffed her things into the trunk of the car and headed the 482 kilometers to Cologne. It was a five-hour drive, but she would still get to the hospital before visiting hours were over. She stopped for gas and coffee and decided not to stop again unless she just became exhausted.

When Larissa entered Andy's room, the lights were dim and he seemed to be sedated. She saw large patches over his left eye and the left side of his face. There was also a large patch on his shoulder that she could see as she gently pulled away the loose fitting hospital gown from his neck area. She started to sob.

A nurse came in to give him a shot. Larissa asked how he was. The nurse said he would be fine, that he was suffering from a few very deep lacerations above his eye and mainly shock. She said he was fortunate that the glass did not take out his eye. Larissa asked the nurse if it would be okay for her to stay in Andy's hospital room for most of the night. The nurse said it usually wasn't allowed, but she would quietly make an exception. Larissa thanked her and told her how much that meant to her. The nurse gave Andy his shot and left the room, smiling at Larissa.

Larissa took Andy's hand and bent over to kiss his forehead. Andy's eyes opened slightly. He didn't say anything. He opened his eyes wider and said "Larissa?" And she said, "What, love?" He was groggy from the sedation but recognized that she was there. He said, "What are you doing here?"

"I can't let you go through this by yourself, love. I heard what happened on the news and I am stunned and so worried about you. How are you?"

Andy said he had just "a few little cuts." Larissa knew he had more than little cuts. "It was awful, Larissa." Andy rolled on his back and seemed to be more coherent. Larissa propped a pillow under his head and helped him get comfortable. He touched Larissa's face with his hand that didn't have the IV attached to it. "Karl and Sonja are dead, Larissa. I can't believe it yet. I really can't believe it..."

Larissa was glad she was there. She just realized how greatly it affected Andy. Karl, after all, had been his lifelong friend, not only his employer. She wondered about Helmut. "Was he admitted to the hospital too and if so, what room was he in?" She went to the nurse's station to inquire. Apparently, Helmut's wounds were not as bad as Andy's and he was released earlier this evening. The doctors were more concerned with Andy's state of mind than his wounds, and wanted to keep him under their watchful eye for another day or two. Larissa agreed that it was a good idea.

Larissa returned to Andy's room and told him she was staying in his room for the night and they were going to put her a cot beside his bed. Andy smiled. "I'm so glad you are here." He motioned for her to come to the bed.

"Larissa, sweet baby, I can't take this kind of life anymore. The rat race just about got me this morning and that was too, too close a call. And this is not the sedative talking. I want to settle down to being a regular guy with a regular gal and a regular family. Would you consider settling down with an unemployed regular guy if he promised to get another job?"

Larissa squeezed Andy's hand and said, "Is this just another living arrangement?"

Andy looked at her through glazed eyes with as much sincerity as he could muster and sweetly said "Larissa, would you marry me even if I'm left with a couple of war wounds?"

Larissa squealed and a nurse came running. "Is something wrong in here?" The nurse was concerned. Larissa said, "You are the first to know that I am saying 'yes' to this mess of a guy laying in this bed, but you have to be my witness that he just asked me to marry him. Now tomorrow, if he doesn't remember it and it was just the drugs talking, I want witnesses."

The nurse giggled and ran out to tell the others on duty. They all came to Andy's door and started clapping. The head nurse in a stern voice said "Mr. Becker, that shot should start taking affect and you need some sleep. Your lady fair will be by your side." She flipped off the light. Larissa kissed Andy and he drifted off. She went to the vending machine to see if there was anything worth eating.

44. THE END OF THE LINE

The investigation found that the limo was destroyed by an anti-tank weapon of Soviet design. These were among the many black-market weapons from the old East German Army. No group claimed responsibility and no perpetrators were ever caught. Joanie heard later that it was a Jewish extremist group that launched the rocket. She also heard from "trusted sources" that the BND, the West German intelligence agency, was responsible and the command came from Kohl, himself. There is no end to the theories that spring up after an assassination.

A modest number of condolences were received at the Compound, including one from President Reagan. Karen and the rest of the family agreed that a small, private funeral was best. They were not equipped at this time to deal with the press or the curious. Every member of the Schneiders felt the pain and the grief and each was trying to justify it in their own way. Stunned described them best. There were no answers. Augie asked to say a few words and Heidi would sing at the service. It would be held in the little chapel on the grounds in Cologne.

Sonja's father came but her mother was too frail to make the trip. All in all there were only about 30 mourners. Andy and Larissa, Helmut and his lady friend, the staff at Cologne Wool Goods, the family, and the Petersens were there. After the opening prayers, Augie stepped up to the pulpit.

"How will we all remember Karl? The complicated one? The troubled and frustrated one? Or, the Schneider who seemed to be able to live life to the fullest? I cannot think of Karl and Sonja without marveling at their enthusiasm for life and optimism and great expectations. Karl's dreams and ambitions led him to occasionally hide his actions, but not out of some desire to cheat or subvert the system. He only saw these shortcuts as a means to the end he thought best for us all."

"How will we remember Sonja? That is easy. The beautiful and bright and sensitive one who brought the best out in Karl. They say that grandfather August matched these two up. If that is true then it is another example of August's excellent vision and leadership. They were meant to be together and now they always will."

Augie stepped down and Heidi approached the center of the Sacristy.

"Sonja hummed this melody often. I asked her about it and she said that it was sort of a Christmas Carol. Saint Lucia was almost the Patron of Sweden since Lucia was about light and it was dark much of the year in her hometown of Malmö. I will sing it in memory of her and my cousin Karl."

She sang *a capella*,

Hark! through the darksome night
Sounds come a winging:
Lo! 'tis the Queen of Light
Joyfully singing.
Clad in her garment white,
Wearing her crown of light,
Santa Lucia, Santa Lucia!

Deep in the northern sky
Bright stars are beaming;
Christmas is drawing nigh
Candles are gleaming.
Welcome thou vision rare,
Lights glowing in thy hair.
Santa Lucia, Santa Lucia!

After the service, Larissa sought out Heidi. They had met several times in the last year but Heidi's voice was never discussed.

"Why did no one tell me that you sang? Your voice is glorious. Why are you not singing professionally?" Larissa had always wanted to try classical singing.

"I studied a while at the Paris Conservatory, but it just wasn't in me to be on stage. I've heard you with your father's group. I wish I could do what you do in jazz." Heidi was flattered that the younger singer was impressed.

Andy walked up and Heidi hugged him. "Andy was Karl's rock through all of this. It is a shame that this tragedy cut it all short. How are you feeling, Andy? We didn't even expect you at the funeral considering what you went through." There were still patches covering the left side of his forehead.

"The loss of these two has certainly left a huge crater in my life. For the last three months I don't think I have had time for anything else, especially Larissa here. But being that Larissa will be my wife in the very near future, I will make it up to her."

Heidi congratulated them and said she wanted to be invited to the wedding if outsiders were being asked to attend.

Karl and Sonja's remains were buried near his parents, Emma and Karl Schneider, Sr. Cologne Wool Goods became less political and less controversial.

The Hesse committee investigations went on as scheduled without much fanfare since the Hitler line was assumed ended. There was nothing of any particular consequence in the rest of the microdots. Himmler gave August some information that helped him in the competitive bids. August mainly communicated his appreciation. Stephanie's scrapbook was not made public but delivered to Karen. Karen never opened it, but had it, the diaries, and August' pocket watch put in August's lock box in the family vault at the Compound.

Alan and Mary had been summoned back to Berlin for the hearings and the engagement ring on Mary's finger was hard to miss. Alan and Luther Glocke hit it off immediately and Luther offered him an internship with his firm, Glocke and Glocke. Luther hoped Alan would consider finishing his studies in Berlin. Werther and Elsie prayed that Alan would finish in Berlin.

The two students marveled that they had unknowingly walked around Berlin with the birth record of Adolf Hitler's son in a bottle and had so innocently played a part in such a tragic episode in history.

The involvement of Wollweber and his associates never came up. The meddling of Rudolph Klimpt was mentioned, but, since no German laws were broken, the postal tampering in the US was kept confidential.

Back at the Compound after the hearings, things were quiet and there really wasn't much anyone could say or add. Exhaustion had set in. Augie poured his mother and himself a snifter of brandy after Polly and the rest of the family had gone up to bed. They kicked off their shoes, flopped on the sofa, and tapped their glasses together toasting that "tomorrow just had to be better." After a few minutes, Augie casually asked his mother about Karl and his birthmark.

Hannah just smiled and answered, "Does it matter?"

The phone rang although it was already past 10:00 PM and late for calls. It was Eberhard Diepgen. He was gearing up to run again for Mayor of the united Berlin against Momper, the Social Democrat. Would Augie join the fight? And what about this Andy Becker?

ABOUT THE AUTHORS

With a keen interest in the history of scientific inquiry and a professional engineering background that has taken him into the covert world of Cold War secrecy, James Henson has spent much of his career on classified projects for the U.S. Defense Department. He has authored and co-authored refereed papers on state-of-the-art technologies and their applications.

As an interior designer with a long list of Manhattan clients, Annita Henson has indulged her passion for Old World craft in art and architecture and the intellectual movements behind great works that continue to inspire us today.

They live in Manhattan. *Room 209* is their first novel.

12009529R00147

Made in the USA
Charleston, SC
05 April 2012